She suffered a peculiar lapse of memory

"You said there was a message for me," Gabe said, his hands gently stroking her arms through the thin fabric of her sweater. "What is it?"

At that moment Dana couldn't remember who had called, much less what the caller had wanted. Her mind was filled with Gabe, his body between her jeans-clad knees, her feet hooked on the rung of the stool. He was so close she could feel his body heat, his breath against her cheek. Unable to help herself, she put both hands on his chest and ran them lightly up to his shoulders. His muscles felt like armor plate under the flannel shirt. She moved her fingers to his neck, looking for warmth and pliability.

I'm falling in love, she realized in panic. *I can't stop it. I love his face, his mind, his body, his talent. I'm losing control.*

ABOUT THE AUTHOR

A resident of Oregon, Muriel Jensen is a
full-time bookstore manager, as well as a
part-time author. She is also a cat collector—
of both live animals and porcelain ones. She
began writing stories in the sixth grade and
hasn't stopped since. Personal experience
provided the inspiration for this novel—for
two years she and her husband owned and
edited a weekly paper in Astoria, Oregon.

Books by Muriel Jensen

HARLEQUIN AMERICAN ROMANCE
  73—WINTER'S BOUNTY
119—LOVERS NEVER LOSE

These books may be available at your local bookseller.

Don't miss any of our special offers. Write to us at the
following address for information on our newest releases.

Harlequin Reader Service
P.O. Box 52040, Phoenix, AZ 85072-2040
Canadian address: P.O. Box 2800, Postal Station A,
5170 Yonge St., Willowdale, Ont. M2N 6J3

Lovers
Never Lose

MURIEL JENSEN

Harlequin Books

TORONTO • NEW YORK • LONDON
AMSTERDAM • PARIS • SYDNEY • HAMBURG
STOCKHOLM • ATHENS • TOKYO • MILAN

Published September 1985

First printing July 1985

ISBN 0-373-16119-0

Chapter One

Dana MacKenzie yanked the sun visor down against the late-afternoon glare. Her hands clenched the steering wheel; her small, fine-featured face frowned in concentration although the coast highway traffic was light.

Tall evergreens bordered both sides of the road, then broke ranks on her left to reveal the plush, rolling green velvet of a freshly manicured golf course. But Dana failed to notice. On her right, ducks frolicked in a small pond strewn with water lilies. They also escaped her attention.

She was busy pondering the question that had plagued her since the previous morning, when she had thrown one large bag into the back of her little white Cimarron and left San Francisco in search of Warrenton, Oregon, and her brother, Jack. How could a reasonably attractive, fairly intelligent woman reach the age of twenty-eight without ever having been loved by anyone?

To her mother, Dana had always been a stumbling block in the path of parties and the social whirl that were the foundation of Helene Freeman's life-style. Housekeepers and "companions" had tried to keep the inquisitive little girl out of the way, but the child needed to get acquainted with the woman who seemed always to be running past her on her way to a place where Dana could never go. And the need was not reciprocal, and so, in her late teens, Dana had finally given up.

Barton Freeman, her father, publisher of three major metropolitan newspapers, had been home so seldom she often wondered if they would recognize each other if they were to meet accidentally.

Glancing in the rearview mirror, she saw reflected glimmering brown eyes in a china-doll face. Scott MacKenzie had claimed to love that face; and Dana, bursting with love no one seemed to want, had believed him and married him. It hadn't taken long to realize that money and power had attracted the young executive to Dana rather than any of her personal qualities.

Dana had tried to keep up appearances, but Scott hadn't bothered. His lack of discretion was embarrassing, but for over a year she managed to ignore his unfaithfulness because that meant she wouldn't have to face it.

It was finally his blatant arrival at a staff function with a tall brunette, whom Dana recognized from the marketing department, that pushed her into filing for divorce.

This move to Warrenton had been Jack's suggestion. He claimed to have a friend who published a small weekly newspaper that needed another reporter. It had been an open-ended invitation issued during the messy court proceedings.

At first, it had been such a relief to be out from under her relationship with Scott that she hadn't felt the need to get away. She had sold the big house Scott had insisted they buy and settled into a small apartment, anxious to forget. Her job on the San Francisco *Daily News* had kept her busy, but just lately a restlessness had begun to gnaw at her.

With the divorce behind her, Dana awakened one morning as though from a coma and felt an urge to make an important change in her life and to be with Jack.

For the first time since she had begun this trip, a slight smile began to alter her frown. It would be so good to see her brother again. Inseparable as children, Jack and Dana had been in constant trouble with a long line of household help, usually at Jack's instigation. But Dana had cooperated willingly in his pranks because her brother had been someone to love—and the only person in the world who loved her back.

After graduation and a bitter argument with their father, Jack enlisted in the navy, a move that had finally taken her brother from Dana. Since then, her marriage and his career as a photographer for a national news magazine had kept them apart. She had tried to get in touch with him several times in the past week, but the line had either been busy or no one answered. Finally deciding that she had to make a move whether or not the job was still available, Dana had put everything she owned in storage and set out for the northern Oregon coast where Jack lived between assignments.

This move would not be a panacea, she knew that, but it would be something new and, right now, that was important for her sanity.

Aware suddenly of the absence of the glare that had so annoyed her earlier, Dana saw that large clouds were crowding overhead. Glancing down at the map a helpful gas station attendant had marked for her earlier that

day, she realized that she was just about to enter Warrenton, population 2,490.

To a girl who had grown up in San Francisco, this
really was the far reaches of beyond. The ferns and
evergreens and the wild, bright yellow bushes that
seemed to be everywhere painted such an alien environment that for a moment she wondered what she was
doing there. But only for a moment. She knew why she
had come. She came to find Jack and to take charge of
her life.

Several more blocks took her into a small commercial area. She noted a bank, a restaurant, a hardware
store, a tavern, a beauty shop and a church. Then, on a
lot by itself, in a converted storefront, was the Warrenton *Register*. She smiled for the second time. It was a
far cry from the full-block, multistoried San Francisco
Daily News.

Fumbling under the map for the return address on
Jack's letter, Dana was surprised to find herself on the
right street and within several blocks of the right house
number. She scanned with interest the New England
saltbox houses and the more decorative Victorians living side by side on this little downtown thoroughfare.

Slowing down almost to a stop, she checked the
number on the envelope against the numbers on a
slate-blue Victorian trimmed in gray and black, and felt
a flutter in the pit of her stomach. She had found Jack.

Parking the car, she didn't even stop to freshen her
makeup or comb her hair. She leapt out of the car and
hurried through the gate of the white picket fence that
enclosed a small front lawn. She ran lightly up six steps
to the front porch and rang the doorbell.

Within seconds she heard footsteps and her heart
somersaulted. The door opened; through her tears she

caught a quick glance of the dearly familiar blue base-ball cap that Jack wore even in the bathtub and launched herself at him.

"Oh, Jack!" she cried, laughter and tears confused in her voice. "Oh, it's so good to see you!"

And it was only then that her mind, preoccupied with this reunion, registered the little incongruities of the situation. Jack's hair was baby-fine and inclined to curl, but the hair under her fingers was coarse and thick. Smallness of frame was something they had both inherited from their mother, yet the neck and shoulders she held were brawny, and clinging to them had brought her feet several inches off the ground.

The breath caught in her throat, Dana leaned back against the arms that held her, and looked into eyes that were blue, not brown. She closed her own and a little gasp of embarrassment escaped her.

"Who are you?" she asked feebly.

"Someone who's very sorry he *isn't* Jack," a deep voice replied.

She opened her eyes; under the bill of the baseball cap, a pair of blue eyes were laughing. She lowered her lashes again and swallowed as she felt a tide of red advance from her neck to her hairline.

"Does Jack Freeman live here?" she asked, her voice suddenly hoarse.

"Yes," the strange man still holding her replied.

"May I see him, please?"

"Of course." The man leaned down to set her on her feet, and with great reluctance she opened her eyes again. She found herself looking at the points of a white collar emerging from the neck of a gray sweatshirt. Emblazoned in red across the chest of the shirt was the word *Stanford*.

Struggling to regain the dignity Scott had always teased her about, Dana flipped a stream of dark hair over her shoulder and tugged at the hem of her beige wool blazer. She cleared her throat.

"I'm...I'm Jack's sister."

For some reason, her pulse refused to settle down.

The man swept a hand toward a long, airy room decorated in brown and white. "Come in," he said. He snatched a jacket from a deep leather chair, but before she could respond to his gesture to sit there was a noisy commotion on the stairs.

They both turned toward the sound as Jack barreled into the room. He wore three cameras around his neck, carried a suitcase in one hand and a paperback novel in the other. Unaware of Dana, he swung the suitcase onto the sofa and then carefully shed the cameras.

"What time is it?" he demanded of "Stanford." "If I make that plane, it's going to be a miracle! I left my rent on the dresser and—" he glanced up from putting his cameras into a padded box, the frantic quality in his voice softening. "—and a letter for Sheila. Would you see that she gets it?"

Standing behind the wall that was "Stanford's" body, Dana knew she was still invisible to her brother.

"For the fourth time," "Stanford" said patiently, "I will see that she gets it."

"Oh, you found my hat! Thanks!" And as Jack came forward to snatch it, he saw Dana over the other man's shoulder.

"Dana?" he asked softly, blinking his dark eyes, refocusing.

"Hi, Jack!" She forced a bright tone into her voice while inside her chest her heart plummeted to the pit of her stomach. This looked and sounded very much as though he was leaving on assignment.

As "Stanford" stepped aside, Jack swept Dana into a bear hug that spun her off her feet.

"How are you, babe?" he asked, finally putting her down. Inspecting her at arm's length, he frowned. "You're skinny!"

"You're not exactly Arnold Schwarzenegger," she laughed, shrugging off his reference to what she knew was an unbecoming slenderness and pallor brought on by the heightened loneliness of the past year. She gestured toward the sofa strewn with his things and asked casually, "Where are you off to?"

"Afghanistan," he replied. "But what are you doing here?"

She shrugged uncomfortably. "I . . . you . . . once mentioned a job."

He looked confused and she added hastily, "I tried to call you all last week, after I decided to take you up on it, but I couldn't get through. You said you had a friend who had a newspaper—"

"Oh, yeah!" Jack said, waving a hand toward "Stanford." "Meet the friend. Also my landlord. Gabe Cameron, my sister, Dana MacKenzie."

Gabe nodded and grinned. "We've met. What's this about a job?"

"Well, you're always grumbling that you'd sell your soul for another reporter. Here she is! Fresh from the San Francisco *Daily News*."

The amusement was gone now, and her brother's friend was studying her analytically. She felt herself square her shoulders.

"Fashion or gardening?" he asked.

Dana felt a stirring of temper, something she hadn't known in a year. Remembering that she was a guest in this man's home, she swallowed and replied politely, "Neither. Police beat."

He arched an eyebrow and inclined his head. "I stand corrected. Can you type?"

She responded quietly. "Can't most writers?"

"I mean, can you type well?" he explained. "In a two-man office, you'd be typing a lot more than just your own work."

Remembering the *News'* slick word processor setup that made corrections a simple matter, she nodded. "I can type well."

"Any pasteup or darkroom experience?"

"No."

"Ever sell advertising?"

"No."

"But she's not a bad photographer," Jack put in. "Taught her myself and she learns fast." Then with a glance at his watch, he groaned and looked pleadingly at his landlord. "Gabe, I've got to go. I can't leave it like this. Has she got a job?"

Dana pulled on her brother's arm. "Jack, go! I'll be fine. I've been taking care of myself for a long time now."

Ignoring her, Jack continued talking to his friend. "She can move into my room and keep up my end of the bills till I get back."

"Jack..." Cameron began doubtfully, his wary glance bouncing off Dana.

"Jack, that's crazy!" Dana interposed. "Get going and we'll work out the job. I'll find an apartment—"

"In Warrenton? There are no apartments."

"A hotel, then."

"Dana, this isn't San Francisco and I'm not leaving until—"

"All right! All right!" the other man said loudly, both hands raised to quiet the argument. "She's hired and she can have your room."

"I don't want..." Dana began, but no one was listening to her.

"Thanks, buddy!" Jack clapped him on the shoulder, then hugged his sputtering sister. "Look, I'll be home in a couple of weeks and Gabe will take good care of you until then—or when I come home, I'll kill him."

A smile at his friend accompanied the threat and Cameron smiled back. Of course he'd taken the threat lightly, Dana noted. He was half a head taller than Jack and probably outweighed him by forty pounds.

"Jack, look—" she began frantically.

"It's all taken care of," Jack said. Apparently pleased with his handling of the situation, he was hefting suitcase, camera bag and jacket.

"My hat!" he remembered.

Cameron swept it off his own head and placed it on Jack's. "Here. Keep in touch."

Dana noted in surprise that Cameron had a thick thatch of gray hair, parted on the side but falling forward without the confinement of the hat. He sensed her attention and turned. Noting her eyes on his hair, he smiled.

"Living with your brother has done it to me." Turning back to Jack, he took the suitcase from him and followed him out the door.

Dana trailed along behind them, feeling exactly as she had when she was nineteen and had waved Jack off as he left to join the navy, as though the only point of light in her life was going out. Feeling her courage of only thirty minutes ago swamped by Jack's departure, she swallowed a growing lump in her throat.

Jack's things were stowed in the backseat of a Jeep that didn't look as though it would make it to the main highway, much less the nearest airport.

"How far do you have to go in that thing?" Dana asked.

"Portland," Jack replied. "A hundred miles. That thing belongs to your landlord, so be careful how you talk about it."

She glanced up at Gabe. "Sorry," she said.

"Too late," he replied, straight-faced. "Your rent's been raised already."

"Then I hope my employer pays well," she sallied, hugging Jack one final time.

Gabe shook Jack's hand. "Are you sure you wouldn't rather take her along with you? The Russians might run in self-defense."

Jack laughed, sliding into the driver's seat. "Nothin' doin'. She's your responsibility for a couple of weeks." Then the light in his eyes steadied, and he said soberly, "Take care of her, will you?"

Gabe glanced down at the woman beside him, the smile in his eyes asking who would take care of him. But he replied gravely, "I will. Drive carefully. There's always another plane."

"Right. 'Bye, sis." Jack smiled regretfully. "I'm sorry about having to leave—"

"It's all right," she assured him, her throat hurting. "We'll talk when you get home. 'Bye. And please be careful."

"'Bye, babe." Jack was off, the Jeep sounding more like a cranky percolator than an automobile.

As the quaint rumble faded away, an early-evening breeze sighed through the tall cedar tree under which Dana had parked her car. Tears brimmed in her eyes, and she went to remove her bag from the car so Gabe wouldn't see them. Angry at herself for her loss of composure after a year of feeling nothing and repressing all emotion, and the awkward situation in which she now found herself, Dana yanked on the case, succeeding in lodging it between the dashboard and the front seat. Muttering to herself, she pulled on it, only making matters worse. She had lost the key to the case years ago, and as she yanked one final time the latch gave and a shower of lavender lingerie drifted down to the curb. She made an unladylike exclamation and the tears fell despite her efforts to hold them back.

Only half aware of what was happening, she allowed herself to be led back to the house by a firm hand that pushed at the small of her back. Gabe Cameron put her in the leather chair she hadn't had a chance to sit in earlier, then disappeared. Almost immediately he was back with her case and carried it upstairs.

Several moments later he was offering her a steaming mug of coffee. She accepted it gratefully and gave him an apologetic glance through spiky lashes.

"I'm sorry," she said, composed once again. "I ... don't know what happened."

Gabe gave her a sympathetic smile. "I felt the tension in you when you flew into my arms, thinking I was Jack. You really needed to talk to him today, didn't you?"

She nodded, putting the mug to her lips. "I should have written, I guess, but ... well, it was sort of a spur-of-the-moment thing." She frowned. "Last I heard, Jack was assigned to Washington. What's he going to do in Afghanistan?"

Gabe grinned dryly. "He volunteered. Jack, for reasons of his own, also had to get away."

"Really?" Dana's eyebrows disappeared under thick, dark bangs. Then she remembered something her brother had said to Gabe. "Has it to do with... Sheila?"

"You do have a nose for news." Gabe sat opposite her on the stone hearth bench. "Yes, it has. Sheila is my sister."

She smiled hopefully. "You mean he's interested in someone? I never thought the day would come."

The man sat back, resting the ankle of one foot on his other knee. Dana couldn't help but marvel at the length of the Nike on that foot. "The day came, but it's not exactly cloud-free. They've both got a few hang-ups they've been arguing about for weeks. Jack seemed to think the better part of valor at the moment was to run. The magazine's doing a story on the Afghan guerrillas still harassing Russian troops. Jack will be reporting and taking pictures."

Dana's eyes widened with fear. "But that's... that's dangerous!"

When Gabe's quick smile came and went she realized that hadn't been a bright remark. She asked grimly, "Are things so bad between them that he has a death wish?"

"No." He laughed. "Jack knows what he has to do. He just can't face it. He's a survivor. He'll be home."

"But... that's a combat situation. How do you know he'll be all right?"

"Because we served in the Mekong Delta together. He'll be all right. He's very cool in a crunch."

Somehow, it was hard to imagine lighthearted Jack "cool in a crunch." "Then why is he running away from your sister?" she challenged.

He shrugged. "Because he can't shoot at her. An enemy you have to live with rather than destroy can be hell. Especially an enemy you love."

Dana nodded. She could vouch for that. Living with Scott had been hell, though she hadn't loved him. At least not for long.

"What's Sheila like?" she asked, sipping her coffee.

Gabe leaned his shaggy head back to think about that. "She's on the classic guilt trip," he said finally. "She was married to a coast guardsman and his being away so much was really getting to her. She was going to give him an ultimatum—either he left the coast guard or she was leaving him—only he never came home to hear it. He was on an icebreaker in the Bering Strait and it went down."

"And she blames herself for that?" Dana queried.

Gabe nodded. "She feels she wasn't a good wife the last few months of their marriage, and I suppose it makes her feel better to beat herself with it. The problem with Jack is that he refuses to give up his work, and Sheila can't stand the thought of being married again to a man who'll be gone at the drop of a hat for long periods of time."

There was nothing like a bad marriage, Dana thought wistfully, to make a woman realize that she'd put up with any inconvenience for a man who would love and understand her and be kind to her.

"I think if Jack and Sheila would just do it, they could make a marriage work," Gabe went on. "But they're both afraid."

Dana nodded thoughtfully. "It's not a world for cowards, is it?"

The silence that met her comment brought her eyes up to Gabe's and found them studying her. They were a soft blue, like the sky clouding over, and for a moment she felt trapped in their gaze. But she looked away and stood up.

"About this job. I know Jack never mentioned it to you and I don't expect—"

Gabe stood up also, his formidable height dwarfing her. "You've got to stay," he said simply. "I promised Jack I'd look after you."

"Thank you, but I'm not your responsibility, just as I wasn't Jack's. I simply came because..."

And then, as she tried to explain why, she couldn't, at least not to someone who had no reason to care.

"Why don't you explain it to me over dinner?" he suggested.

"Because I'm not staying. But thank you." She picked up her small clutch bag and started toward the door.

"Dana!" He sounded exasperated as he reached out and caught hold of her arm, stopping her in her tracks. She looked down at the large warm fingers that held her arm in a shackling but gentle grip, then up into those quiet eyes, surprise filling her dark ones.

She could hardly recall either parent ever touching her. And it hadn't taken long before Scott's deception made the very thought of his touch revolting. Only Jack had ever touched her in kindness.

She felt warm from her shoulder to her wrist, a curious sort of awareness in that area of her skin under his fingers, as though a message was being transmitted and received.

At her expression, Gabe dropped his hand. "Sorry. But I promised Jack," he said, moving around her to stand with his back to the door. "And I owe him."

A little disturbed about her reaction to his touch, she said with a trace of cynicism, "Don't tell me. He saved your life in the Mekong Delta."

"A nose for news and psychic, too," he observed with a grin. "You're going to be an invaluable employee. Come on. I'll show you up to Jack's room and you can freshen up before dinner."

And that was that. End of discussion—until he chose to open it again at dinner. They were seated by a window in the small Buccaneer Restaurant overlooking the Warrenton Mooring Basin. The setting sun was glinting off fiberglass and chrome, tall masts on sleek sailboats rising like minarets among the flying bridges of the charter fishing boats. The clouds that had been gathering overhead when she arrived in Warrenton had now dispersed and it was a golden evening.

"Does one of those boats belong to you?" Dana asked, poking at a mushroom in her crisp green salad.

"No, I'm not much of a fisherman." He smiled at her across the table, his hair still damp from the shower. Shampooed and combed away from his face, his hair was a darker gray with streaks of silver, the wayward sweep across his forehead still slipping forward. His eyes, slitted against the glare from the window, sparkled with humor. "And, after the navy, well, I've seen enough boats to last me a lifetime."

"Then what are you doing on the Oregon coast?" she asked. "Were you born here?"

"No. Seattle, Washington. I grew up and worked there before and after the navy, but a couple of years ago I decided I needed a change. I came here because the *Register* was for sale. Sheila came to be near me after Bill died. What about you?" he asked gently. "What made you decide to move?"

So many things had come to a head for her that morning, yet she doubted that she could explain to anyone her specific reasons for throwing caution to the wind and packing the car.

She shrugged. "I needed a change of scenery."

"Were you in love with your husband?" he asked. At her look of surprise, he explained, "Jack told me about your divorce."

She nodded and admitted candidly, "I loved him for six weeks before we were married and about ten minutes after. Our marriage was over long before we made the break legal."

"Then why so grim?" he asked. "You're free of him. You can start all over."

Dana wondered how to explain how sobering it was to have never been loved and yet finally take a chance on someone only to find yourself dead wrong. She finally chose not to try.

"That's why I'm here, I guess," she said. "To start over."

They leaned back as the waitress placed large platters of scallops Delmonico before them. Dana closed her eyes, inhaling the herby aroma. She dug in with gusto, realizing she had skipped lunch and was starving.

"You're going to have to be more cheerful if you're going to be coming in contact with my sister," Gabe warned with a grin, opening his linen napkin and placing it across his lap. "With Jack gone she'll be suicidal."

"Does she know he's gone?"

"They spent most of the night fighting in my living room about his leaving. He thinks she's crowding him, and she thinks he's running out on her."

Dana studied him surreptitiously behind a forkful of baked potato. He was attractive, apparently sensitive and caring. There was strength in his face, along the sturdy set of his jaw, the broad forehead and in the quiet depths of his eyes. The hands working over his dinner were large and well-made and unadorned except for the calloused top knuckle of the middle finger, a badge worn by everyone who made his living with a pencil.

"How long have you been a publisher?" she asked.

"Since I bought the *Register* a couple of years ago."

"And before that?"

He shrugged. "I did a little writing. This and that."

He was obviously avoiding a straight answer and Dana wondered if she had offended him, asking him about his past.

"I didn't mean to pry," she said apologetically.

"I know," he assured her with a smile. "I wasn't offended. I just don't talk about myself much. I'm usually the one who does the interviewing."

Dana studied his winning grin and thought that it already seemed familiar, that already she found herself watching for it.

She frowned. "Say I take this job. When would I start?"

"We go to press at noon Wednesday—tomorrow. You can have the morning to settle in at home; it wouldn't be fair to throw you in on deadline morning. But it would help if you could be there about four in the afternoon for the mailing."

"Mailing?" she asked, puzzled.

"Addressing the papers to be sent out in the mail."

"*You* do that?"

He grinned at her surprise. "The pixies don't do it."

"I'm sorry," she said, a laugh in her voice. "I'm used to reporting and writing, and then everything else happens by magic."

"You'll catch on. You can do some typing Thursday to get used to the equipment, then Friday your first assignment will be to cover the grade school's Spring Week activities. The kids compete at sports and all kinds of playground games. It should be good for a full page of pictures. That always sells papers. Got your own camera?"

"Yes," she said after the briefest pause, acknowledging defeat and an elusive sense of apprehension. In the face of his insistence that she had the job, she would not risk her dignity and act panicky, even if the job did include a room in his house. "A Minolta."

"Good. Well..." He glanced down at her empty plate. "Keep eating like that and Jack won't accuse you of being skinny anymore."

She smiled sheepishly. "It's been so long since I've had seafood. That was delicious."

"Got room for dessert?"

"That would be pushing it. I'd be up all night with a stomachache." As she said that, the awkwardness of the situation made her more uncomfortable. "About my taking over Jack's room...."

"That's settled," Gabe said firmly.

"But you were reluctant when he first mentioned it. Please don't feel obligated."

"I do," he insisted. "I explained that. And you don't have to worry about your virtue. I'm at the paper most of the time, and when I am home, I'm too dog tired to be a threat to anyone."

She stared at her plate. "That's not what I meant."

"What did you mean?"

She looked at him with a level gaze. "I meant that Jack put you on the spot, and it wasn't fair. Certainly there's a room for rent somewhere in this town. Anyway, you were probably looking forward to a little privacy with Jack gone."

"I don't require privacy," he said, his eyes steady on hers. "Sheila is always coming and going, and friends often drop in unannounced. When the world closes in on me, I head for the beach. But that doesn't happen too often. I'm a very social individual."

"But what will your sister and your friends think when they discover that I'm living with you?"

"Nothing," he said, as though he firmly believed it. Then he leaned forward on his elbows and smiled. "Or we can put a banner headline on tomorrow's edition: 'Cameron and MacKenzie Not Lovers.'"

Dana had to laugh. "That's silly."

He nodded, picking up the bill and reaching into his hip pocket. "Yes, it is. And so is the idea that anyone would have anything to say about it. Ready?"

"I PROBABLY WON'T BE HOME tonight," Gabe explained, pulling up in front of his house. The van shuddered to a stop and Gabe reached to close the glove compartment as the vehicle's palsied condition jarred it open. "Rig's a little quirky," he explained good-naturedly. "I'll see you inside, but I've got to get back to the office. Thanks to your brother and his last-minute plans, I didn't get much done today."

"I hope you won't mind if I rummage around for towels or a bedtime cup of tea," she said as he unlocked the front door.

"Help yourself. Go ahead and lock the doors. I'll have a key made for you in the morning. Did you see the *Register* office when you came into town?" At her nod he said, "That's about three blocks straight ahead of us. Just be there by four tomorrow afternoon so you can see how a weekly gets mailed out, and we can lay in some groceries. All right?''

''All right,'' she agreed.

''Then good night. I'll see you tomorrow afternoon. If you have any problems, the phone book is on the counter right under the kitchen phone. I'll be at the office.''

She nodded and wished him good-night, but instead of shutting the door she watched him drive away. Dana experienced a curious sense of deprivation. He was such a nice person, and he was putting himself out for her, or for Jack, really, because he had promised. Well, whatever the reason, it was nice to have someone concerned for her welfare and considerate of the little details that smoothed the path ahead of her.

In the tidy, well-organized kitchen she found a mug and a box of tea. She filled the kettle that sat on the stove, then ran upstairs to fill the bathtub. The old ball-and-claw tub, painted brown to match the brown-and-blue decor, made her smile. This house, though neat as a pin considering it was lived in by two bachelors, was furnished in comfortable old chairs and sofas and was a far cry from the home she had sold in San Francisco.

She had hated her house, but it presented the image Scott had thought so important, so she had agreed to it. But already, after a mere hour, she felt more at home here than she had ever felt in the sprawling split-level. She found towels in a hall closet and, pulling her nightie out of her suitcase, threw it atop the closed commode. She had just stepped out of her slacks when she heard the shrill whistle of the kettle.

Barefooted, she raced downstairs in lacy lavender briefs and the red cotton shirt she hadn't had time to remove. Standing with one foot atop the other on the bare linoleum, she made the tea quickly while a chilling draft ran along her bare legs. Thinking longingly of the hot bath, she held the full mug carefully and started back to the bathroom. She had gotten as far as the doorway to the living room when the sound of a key in the lock halted her, frozen; Gabe materialized as the door opened.

For a long moment they stared at each other, she mortified, he surprised, almost as though he had forgotten someone else now shared his home. He recovered first with a smile.

"Sorry," he said, snatching a steno pad off a small table right by the door. "I was working on notes for my editorial while helping Jack pack, and I forgot them. Night." He turned to leave, then looked back at Dana and stopped.

The sigh of relief she had been about to breathe caught in her throat and settled there like something sharp as he came slowly toward her. He stopped with barely an inch between them, and her heart beat like a trip-hammer, the mug of tea trembling in her hand.

More excited than afraid, she watched his long arm reach out toward her, then past her shoulder and somewhere behind her. There was a soft click, then a rumbling beneath them as an oil furnace went on.

"If you're going to run around like that," he said softly, his eyes slipping down her slim legs, "put the heat on. There's a control upstairs, too. You can turn it off when you go to bed. Good night."

When the door closed behind him, Dana leaned against the molding and closed her eyes, trying to catch her breath. It came, but rapidly, and she felt as though she'd just run the New York Marathon.

A sip of tea revived her long enough to get her upstairs and into the bathtub. Settling into the hot water, she felt herself relax and tried not to think about her landlord and employer.

She had come to Warrenton to take a positive step toward her future, and she had the feeling that if she thought about Gabe Cameron, she would realize that he could be a dangerous complication.

Chapter Two

The following day dawned sunny and bright. Dressed in blue cotton slacks with a blue-and-white-striped drawstring top, Dana made room for her things in Jack's closet.

The picture of a young woman on his nightstand caught her attention, and she sat on the edge of the bed to pick it up and study it more closely. The girl was tall and blond and, though it was hard to clearly discern her features in the full-length photo of her leaning against a garden fence, there was something uncertain in her posture. Dana found herself smiling at the photo. This must be Sheila.

She replaced the picture and went about putting her things away, unable to push the photo from her mind. She, of all people, could identify with the uncertainty, the lost feeling the young woman emanated.

As Dana placed a cologne bottle and a jar of hand cream on the dresser, she found the check Jack had left made out to Gabe and a white envelope with "Sheila" written across it in Jack's scrawl.

Picking up both items, Dana took them downstairs with her and placed them on the small table by the door so that Gabe would notice them. She went toward the

kitchen in search of breakfast and rounded the corner
as another figure flew out of the room. They collided,
and two startled screams rent the air. As Dana backed
away instinctively, her heart rocketing, the other woman was trying desperately to save a blue-and-white casserole dish in her hands from spilling its contents on
the floor.

"I'm sorry!" Dana cried out in a shout of laughter,
reaching out to help the woman steady her burden.

Gray eyes looked at Dana in confusion and then
closed as the other woman tried to collect herself.

"I'm Dana MacKenzie, Jack's sister," Dana said. As
the gray eyes flew open again, she smiled. "You're
Sheila, aren't you?"

Sheila opened her mouth to answer, then her still-
wary eyes went from the stranger to the pot in her
hands. "Maybe I'd better put this down before Gabe
has chili all over his beige carpet."

Dana followed Sheila into the kitchen and turned on
the coffeepot while the other woman placed her casserole in the refrigerator.

"Now." Sheila turned to face Dana, pulling off a
blue nylon jacket. Dana jealously admired her height
and the honey-blond hair wound into a casual knot at
the back of her head. Sheila had a dancer's slender
neck and slipped gracefully into a kitchen chair. It was
easy to see why Jack, who had a sensitivity to beauty
and loved to capture it on film, would love this woman.
"You're Dana. But I thought Jack's only sister lived in
San Francisco?"

"I did live in San Francisco," she offered, sitting opposite Sheila. "until I decided that I needed a change.
Of course, had I known Jack was leaving, I wouldn't
have come...."

Pain crossed the girl's eyes and Dana cursed herself for her insensitivity. "I'm sorry. Gabe told me about your...problems with Jack. I wish I could help."

Sheila shook her head, her smile wry. "I keep trying to tèll myself that if it's meant to work out, he'll come back to me. But this morning I don't feel very philosophical."

"He left you a note," Dana said, hoping to cheer her. She ran to get it, and Sheila took it from her as though afraid to touch it. Anxious gray eyes looked into Dana's sympathetic brown ones.

"Jack is often immature and sometimes irresponsible," Dana said, giving the girl's hand a friendly pat. "But if he wasn't planning to come back, he wouldn't break it to you in a letter. I know he wouldn't. Open it. Would you like some breakfast?"

Dana took the girl's silence for assent and put bacon and eggs in a frying pan, carefully keeping her back to the table until Sheila spoke.

"Well." The girl finally drew a ragged breath. "I suppose all I can do is wait. Trouble is, I've never been very patient."

Dana put bread in the toaster and went to the refrigerator in search of jam and butter.

"Are you living here?" Sheila asked, watching her move around the kitchen.

A jar of strawberry jam balanced on top of a tub of margarine in her hand, Dana emerged from the refrigerator ready to assume the defensive—until she noticed that Sheila seemed pleased rather than disapproving.

"Yes," she replied. "Jack and Gabe both insisted that there was not a room to rent in this town. Jack felt so badly because he had to leave ten minutes after I got here that he made your brother promise he'd give me a job and a place to stay."

With the spatula poised over the eggs, Dana looked over her shoulder at her landlord's sister. "Sunny-side up or over easy?"

"Over," Sheila answered, walking to the counter when the toast popped up. She buttered the golden bread and poured coffee. "Do you start work today?"

"Gabe gave me today to settle in. I don't have to report in until late this afternoon for the mailing out."

Sheila rolled her eyes. "Good luck! Wear something you hate, or something you'll never have to wear again. I helped him with that once when Darlene, his office girl, was on vacation. I had ink from my nose to my toes!" She looked critically at Dana's white pants. "Be sure you change those slacks!"

In packing for this adventure, grubbies were something she hadn't considered, Dana realized. All her whites and pretty pastels would have to hang in the closet for leisure-time wear. Weekly newspaper production was going to be considerably different from big-city reporting.

"Can you suggest a good place to buy jeans?" Dana asked Sheila, peppering her egg.

"Not only that," Sheila said cheerfully, "I could show you. If you wouldn't mind the company."

Dana shook her head. "Of course I wouldn't mind."

"Frankly," Sheila admitted, leaning across the table, "with my brother and your brother as my closest companions, I'm starved for female company."

"Well, if we're being honest—" Dana leaned forward, too, "I'm a big-city girl, and though I think I'll be happy here, it's a strange environment to me; it would be nice to have a friend."

"Gabe says I'm hopelessly hung-up," Sheila warned.

Dana nodded, her mouth full. Then she swallowed. "That makes two of us. I think we were made for each other, Sheila."

With breakfast dishes done and the kitchen tidied, Dana and Sheila climbed into the Cimarron.

"I'm impressed!" Sheila exclaimed, sinking into the oatmeal-colored leather upholstery and settling long, graceful feet in the thick carpeting. Her fingers touched the elegant dash and then the thickly padded door panels. "I didn't realize reporters did this well!"

Dana laughed, pleased with her new friend's straightforward approach. "My father is quite wealthy," she explained casually. "Didn't Jack tell you that?"

Sheila shrugged. "I keep forgetting. Jack acts just like the rest of us, like somebody just struggling along, so I forget he's got all that money. I suppose you do, too."

"Actually, my taste runs to little sports cars; my husband wanted this."

"You're married?" Sheila's delicate pale eyebrows went up.

"Was," Dana corrected. "I'm divorced."

"That's right. Jack mentioned it." Sheila made a production of getting comfortable and said with what Dana knew was forced lightness, "I lost my husband last year."

"Gabe told me," Dana said gently, putting the key in the ignition. But before turning the key and flooding the small space with sound, she turned to Sheila, her expression sympathetic. "You're foolish to blame yourself."

Sheila's reluctant smile was wry. "That's what Gabe says."

"Then you should listen to him." Dana turned the key and the car roared to life.

Under Sheila's direction they found a small shopping mall.

"Betty's is one of my favorite places," Sheila enthused. "You'll be able to find your jeans there and probably anything else you're looking for."

An hour later the two women emerged from the shop, laughing over Dana's tottering stack of boxes as they made their way to the car.

"If you live only on what you earn," Sheila said, holding the rear door open as Dana tossed her bundles into the back, "like Jack does, I hope my brother's paying you a big salary!"

"So do I." Dana closed and locked the door. "Of course, there's nothing like a credit card at times like this."

AT FIVE MINUTES OF FOUR Dana walked through the door of the Warrenton *Register* in a new pair of jeans and a gray sweatshirt.

Her nostrils were immediately assailed by the elemental smells of ink and paper. The office was small, hopelessly cluttered and in absolute chaos at the moment. She felt instantly at home.

Whether it was the San Francisco *Daily News* with a circulation approaching 800,000 or the Warrenton *Register* with a payroll of three people, the excitement in the air was the same. The mystery and power of the printed word had kept her alive this past year, and as she advanced into the office, she knew she was taking the vital step she had come a thousand miles to find.

"Hi!" A teenage girl with wild red hair and freckles emerged from a door at the back of the small office.

She wore large glasses and a pencil behind her ear. "Can I help you?"

"I've come to help you," Dana explained, dropping her purse and jacket on the counter. "I'm Dana Mac-Kenzie and I'll be working here for a while. Mr. Cameron told me to be here at four."

"Great!" The girl smiled. "Gabe's unloading now. I'm Darlene West, by the way. I work after school, and sometimes I type on weekends if I don't have a date." She sighed dramatically. "Which is usually the case. Go on in back while I lock up the front."

Dana wandered into a cavernous room where back issues were neatly stacked against one wall. On the opposite wall were supplies and several pieces of equipment that she guessed were antiques. At least she had never seen the likes of them before. Off to the side was a small kitchen table and several chairs, and a bar next to it held instant coffee, tea bags, sugar, cream and straws and several coffee cups.

Suddenly the side door rolled up and Dana spun around, startled. A tall stack of newspapers sailed out of the open door of the old blue van. With a little yelp, she jumped aside just in time, and the stack landed harmlessly, raising a cloud of dust on the concrete floor.

"Sorry," Gabe called from the van with a wave. After eight or nine more stacks landed beside the first, Gabe leapt out of the van and slammed the sliding door closed.

Striding into the room, he grinned at Dana and turned to pull the freight door down. Her heart somersaulted, and she placed a hand over it, annoyed.

"Get settled in?" he asked, picking up two stacks of papers and carrying them across the room to where one of the pieces of ancient equipment stood. He came back for two more bundles, and Dana hefted another and half-carried, half-dragged it to where he had placed the others. By the time she arrived with it he had made the necessary trip back for the last two.

"Yes, thank you," she said, her voice breathless from the exertion—or was it from something else? "And I met your sister."

"What do you think?" he asked. He leaned over the machine to flip on the small light over the worktable part of it, then turned another switch that made a motor come to life. The machine sounded worse than the old Jeep in which Jack had left for Portland.

"I like her. We spent the morning shopping, had lunch and would have done some more shopping only I wasn't sure when payday is."

He grinned into her teasing glance. "Sounds like I'll have to give you a raise already so you can pay your rent."

"Oh," she said. "I put Jack's check on the table near the door where you left—" color flooded her face as she remembered his unexpected return home last night "—your notes."

Amusement flickered in his eyes. While she expected a chiding remark, he simply put a fraternal arm around her shoulders and pulled her closer to the machine.

"This is an Addressograph," he said. Placing his large hand on a metal box with small file drawers, he continued, "This is our subscription list filed alphabetically and by zip code. We run and bundle the papers that way to make delivery easy for the post office. That way they don't revoke our permit if I'm late paying my postage bill."

"That machine works?" Dana asked, surprised.

"Usually," Gabe qualified. "Darlene has a way with it. What you'll do tonight is simply set the papers up for her while I bundle. Then we'll all make the run to the post office; after that we're free for dinner until the whole routine starts all over again tomorrow morning. Sit here." He pulled up an old wooden chair for her and stacked the bundles of papers at her feet, using a pocketknife to cut the string that bound them.

Then Darlene appeared, and Gabe placed a stack of papers about a foot high on the side of the machine, left side of the headline uppermost.

"Keep the stack about that high," Gabe instructed. He crossed to the other side of the room to cut lengths of string.

Darlene sat at the machine, flexed her fingers as though she were about to play Chopin, and pulled the stack of papers a little closer. Then she reached behind her back for a file drawer, tucked it into a little niche under the machine, and placed her foot on a pedal. Dana watched, fascinated.

As Darlene worked the pedal, the metal plates containing subscriber addresses advanced along a track until they lay in a neat row across the machine to the spot under the light where a strip of inked ribbon would imprint them. The plates now in place, Darlene began imprinting, her hands almost faster than the eye. Intrigued, Dana forgot the purpose of her presence until Gabe shouted, "Papers, Dana!" and she hurriedly reached for another stack and placed it on the machine as she had been shown. It seemed that no sooner had she placed it than Darlene was ready for another stack, then another, until the first drawer was finished.

"Think you can take over when she goes on vacation?" Gabe asked from the floor on the other side of the machine, where he bundled the last stack of papers ready to be mailed.

Dana shook her head. "I was just wondering how many times I would have addressed my hand."

It was after six o'clock when the final drawer was completed and Dana and Darlene helped Gabe haul the stacks of papers back to the van. Then they drove the short distance to the post office and deposited the papers on the loading dock around back.

"Want to join us for dinner, Darlene?" Gabe asked, climbing back into the van.

The young girl grimaced. "Thanks, but I've got homework. And don't forget, I won't be in tomorrow. I'm going to that youth convention in Eugene."

Gabe groaned. "I did forget. I suppose you'll even have a good time and not even think about Dana and me here slaving away."

Darlene's grin was wide. "That's right."

"How'd you like a pay cut?" Gabe demanded, pulling out of the parking lot.

"How'd you like to be short one slave?" Darlene shot back.

Stifling a grin, Gabe looked over at Dana. "This is a very heartless generation."

"Oh, did I tell you Mr. Sorensen called?" Darlene's bantering tone had changed and she sounded grave.

Gabe glanced at his office assistant in the rearview mirror, a slight smile on his lips. "No. What did he say?"

"The usual. Stop the editorials about the Work Corps or he'll pull out his advertising. Gabe, what'll we do if he does that?"

"We'll survive," he replied easily.

"How? We're barely making ends meet now. If you lose that full page every week and the double truck once a month, we'll be down the tubes."

Gabe smiled broadly into the mirror. "Who's the publisher of this rag? You or me?"

"Who's the bookkeeper?"

"Trust me, Dee."

"That's what you said when you did my algebra homework. Who has to look forward to algebra in summer school instead of sitting on the beach?"

Gabe uttered an indignant sound, his smile broadening further. "That's a low blow. I thought I remembered how to do it."

"You probably never learned. I don't think they had algebra that long ago." Gabe had pulled the van to a stop on a well-lit residential street, and Darlene slid the door open, laughing. "Thanks for the lift. See you Friday."

Gabe waited until Darlene ran up the walk and a man with a newspaper in hand appeared in the open doorway. The man waved and Gabe pulled away.

"Good grief, what a wit!" Dana exclaimed. "Is she always like that?"

Gabe laughed. "She comes by it naturally. Her father is my attorney and her mother is my accountant. The kid's a genius. She's never late for work and she always does her job well—those are rare qualities even in an adult. I don't know what I'll do when she graduates next year."

Next June, Dana thought to herself. *I wonder where I'll be in fourteen months.*

"So, you and Sheila got on all right?" Gabe asked, pulling back onto the main highway and bringing Dana out of her thoughts.

"Very well, and she left a bowl of chili in the refrigerator."

"Great!" Gabe said enthusiastically, then glanced at his watch. "Do you have a sensitive constitution?"

"No."

"Then if we've got chili for tonight, let's skip the shopping till tomorrow. I'm beat."

"Sounds good to me."

Dana volunteered to put the chili in the oven and fix a salad while Gabe ran upstairs to shower. With everything prepared and waiting for her host, Dana took one of the newspapers from the stack Gabe brought into the house and spread it on the kitchen table to look it over.

Her eyes glanced over the neat, open layout; the good, sharp photographs and a fair amount of advertising. Though ads had not been a concern of hers on a daily paper, she knew the hoped-for ratio of news to ads was fifty-fifty. This edition looked pretty healthy to her and, flipping to the back, she found a full page of classified ads, a sure sign of reader interest.

Turning back to the editorial page, she poured herself a cup of coffee and settled down to read. By the time she had finished, she heard Gabe come down the stairs and stop at the doorway into the kitchen. Dana refused to look up, knowing there would be adoration in her eyes.

Gabe Cameron possessed two of the qualities she admired in a writer. First, he had a crisp, neat style that was tidily journalistic yet rhythmically flawless. And second, this editorial proved that he was noble in what he believed, and forthright and intrepid in stating those beliefs.

"Don't tell me," he said, advancing into the room. "You found a typo in the headline."

She laughed, going to the stove without looking at him. "Nope. No errors that I could see. I was reading your editorial."

Gabe folded the paper and tossed it on the counter while Dana carried the chili to the table. "And?"

"I like your style," she said, trying to sound casual. "And I admire your crusading spirit."

"Thank you. But I think you're in the minority."

She shrugged, reaching into the refrigerator for the salad. "Crusaders are never popular. They upset the status quo. Nothing threatens the ordinary man like the unfamiliar. How do your readers feel about it? Do you think they'll let the government build a Work Corps Center here where underprivileged kids can learn a trade? Where would they put it anyway?"

"There's an old private school owned by the city of Hammond right next door to us. With a little renovation it would be perfect. Of course, the people don't really have a choice; the city council will make the decision. But you can bet they won't do anything they know our influential citizens won't like."

"Like Sorensen."

"Exactly."

"I gathered from your editorial that one of the principal fears is that criminally inclined young people will be bumping up against and corrupting the local kids."

Gabe nodded. "What isn't getting through, no matter how hard we try to get it across, is that it's not just for kids who've been in trouble; some are just poor kids who wouldn't have a chance to rise above their poverty without the special skills this program can give them. Others are kids from unsettled environments referred to the Work Corps by the courts. I'm sure a percentage of them are toughs, but then so are a percentage of the local kids. Someone, somewhere has to make room for these young people so they'll have a chance."

"And how does it look at this stage?"

"I suppose it has a fifty-fifty chance. Some well-respected citizens are supporting it, like Darlene's parents. But then there are others, like Sorensen, who are waging a strong battle against it."

"Does Sorensen buy that grocery ad?" she asked, nodding toward the paper on the counter.

Gabe nodded, sprinkling onions and grated cheese on the steaming chili. "I suspect he's got another reason for wanting the sale of the property shot down, something more personal."

"Maybe we can prove it!" Her chili forgotten, Dana leaned across the table toward him, her eyes bright with interest. "I'll help you check it out. What do you think it is?"

Gabe pointed his spoon at her, his jaw firming. "Look, Brenda Starr, you do what I assign you and leave Sorensen to me. His connections are suspect in a few cases, and I promised Jack..."

"Oh, come on!" she shouted, her temper sparking like a downed power line, her mellow thoughts about him taking flight. "I'm not Darlene. You and my brother can make whatever pacts you want between you, but don't you dare try to come down on me! I covered San Francisco, remember? And I'll be damned if I'll let you relegate me to school events and store openings!"

"Well, if you find those dull, Miss Starr," he replied

evenly, "you've come to the wrong place. That's usually all that happens here. Some weeks, a sneeze at the city council meeting is worthy of a headline."

She drew a steadying breath. "I'll do whatever you want me to do," she explained in frustration, making an effort to lower her voice, "but please don't become protective. I've never been treated like that and I don't like it!"

"All right, objection noted," he said, giving her an underbrowed look that made her lower her eyes. "But if I find you snooping where you don't belong, you're fired. I'm in no financial shape to handle a lawsuit. And Sorensen wouldn't be above taking me to court."

"You can't fire me," she reminded him with a sarcastic smile. "You promised Jack."

"I promised Jack I'd take care of you," he said, spoon poised over his chili while he glared at her. "And if you mess with me, young lady, I will take care of you, believe me."

The phrase took on a different meaning the way he said it. She narrowed her eyes at him and snatched up her spoon, stabbing it into her bowl.

They ate in silence for a few moments; then he asked, his manner easy, as though they hadn't just shouted at each other, "Wasn't your husband protective?"

She began to snicker, but stopped herself immediately. That was an indication of bitterness, and she was trying not to be bitter.

"No," she replied. "The only thing he was interested in protecting was himself."

His chili finished, Gabe put down his spoon and crossed his forearms on the table. "Why did he marry you?"

She shrugged and poked at her salad. "A few years ago I was still young and pretty...and rich."

He looked heavenward and shook his head lazily. "And you've become such a matron. I can see why he lost interest. Why'd you marry him?"

"Because he loved me," she said simply. "Or so I thought. It was a new experience for me; I didn't realize that I'd been mistaken about it until it was too late."

"Being loved was a new experience? I can't believe that."

"It's true."

"So you've given up on it?"

She looked at him, surprised by the question. "No. I just don't want to have to deal with it now," she lied. The truth was, she was afraid to take another chance and be wrong again. Money was a stronger attraction to many men than a small young woman with dark hair and eyes.

There was quiet for a few moments while Dana helped Gabe clear the dishes. He rinsed them off, put them in the sink, then brought the pot of coffee to the table.

"Wasn't your father protective?" he asked, as though unable to believe there had been no one in her life to look after her.

"If he'd been there, he might have been. But I saw very little of him. Doesn't the fact that I'm still here confirm that I don't need anyone's protection?"

"It just makes one wonder about the young men in the area where you grew up." He smiled at her, his blue eyes roving over her small features. "You make me feel like donning my armor and shielding you with my body. You're so small."

"Next to you, chief—" she grinned wryly "—King

Kong is small. What time do I have to be at work tomorrow?"

"Ten will be early enough."

"Okay." She nodded and stood up quickly, her pulse rippling erratically under his gaze. "I . . . I think I'll take a bath and go right to bed."

"All right," he said evenly, his eyes still on her. "Good night, Dana."

She took the stairs two at a time, and closing her bedroom door behind her, she leaned against it while her heart raced. She didn't like the way things were falling into place. This had all the earmarks of . . . infatuation?

Maybe she was upsetting herself unnecessarily, she reasoned as she went to the dresser where she had placed a pair of tailored silk pajamas purchased that morning at Betty's. She'd been wrong about love before. This was just simple attraction. Gabe Cameron was a formidable and caring man, and that was a new element in her life. This pulse fluttering and heart stopping were just overemotional reactions to something she'd never encountered before. Marching into the bathroom and turning on the taps full force, she stepped into the tub and pulled the antique shower curtains around.

There. With a little shield about herself maybe she would be able to think straight. Slipping into the hot water, she remembered something he'd said. "You make me feel like donning my armor and shielding you with my body." Following on that thought was an image in her mind of his body shielding her, without armor or anything else between them. With an audible groan, she submerged her head in the hope of clearing it.

IT WAS AFTER MIDNIGHT when she decided that the chili was not going to digest and that it had other plans altogether. Nausea had been rising steadily for the past hour and she had been pacing for the last fifteen minutes, hoping to stave off the inevitable.

Deciding that she couldn't wait a moment longer, Dana tore open her door and ran for the bathroom, colliding with a large, solid object.

"What is it?" Gabe demanded.

She tore away from him just in time to land in a graceless heap at the foot of the commode. She was noisily, humiliatingly sick.

Finally slumping to her heels, exhausted, she was not surprised to find the light flipped on and Gabe beside her. He flushed the commode, closed the lid and sat her on it. Then a blessedly cool washcloth was applied to her face.

"You and your armor!" she whimpered peevishly, feeling as limp as a dead flower.

"To get your badge in knighthood," he said dryly, wetting the cloth again and reapplying it, "you have to help one damsel who's lost her dinner. How lucky for me that you came along."

"You're being smart!" she accused.

"And you're being rude," he corrected mildly. "When someone offers a helping hand, it's customary to accept it gratefully and graciously, not to snarl at the Samaritan."

Chastened brown eyes looked at him over the washcloth. He pulled the cloth away and she drew a deep breath. "I'm sorry," she said. "But it's embarrassing to have someone there when you're sick."

"That's absurd," he countered, throwing the cloth into the sink. "Especially since I'm the one who made you sick. I should never have let you have chili at that hour."

"There you go again!" she shouted at him, a touch of color returning to her cheeks. "I ate the chili because I wanted it! I'm also partial to french-fried onion rings and hot dogs on a stick and two crust pies and all sorts of indigestible things!" Looking up into his calm reaction to her tirade, she stopped and sighed weakly. "I just shouldn't have them when I'm excited, that's all."

"What's got you excited?" he asked quietly. "Certainly not me?"

She gave him a murderous look. "Not that kind of excited. It's just what with traveling all day yesterday—"

"I know what you mean." He cut her off with a smile in his voice. "It's just so gratifying to tease you and watch you react."

She stood up to leave him alone with his perverted sense of humor but the room spun and he caught her as she crumpled.

"I can walk," she protested in a hoarse whisper at the same time that her head fell against his warm chest and one hand reached around his neck and clung. "You're not wearing anything," she observed in a fog, the fingers of her other hand toying with his wiry chest hair.

"No," he said, placing her on her bed. "At least not where you're touching. Get under the covers. That's it."

A silky sheet drifted over her, then a blanket. "I thought . . . all tough men slept naked," she said drowsily.

"How many tough men have you known?" he asked, tucking the blanket in under her feet.

"None," she said with a yawn. "Except for Jack, they've all been wimps."

"Then it's unsupported rumor," he pointed out, coming to the head of the bed to lean over her, pushing her bangs back and touching her forehead. "Are you okay?"

"I'd better be." She settled deeper into her pillow and tucked the blanket under her chin, feeling herself slipping away. "Or...Jack...will kill...you."

She fell asleep to the sound of Gabe's laughter.

Chapter Three

Dana awoke headachy and grumpy. She had vague memories of having been sick while Gabe looked on, of having been carried back to her bed and of saying nonsensical things. And lying as a disconcerting undercurrent to that humiliating occurrence were the thoughts she had entertained last night in the bathtub. Was she falling into a trap again? Was she a little bit in love with her landlord?

She went down to the kitchen, one hand to her throbbing head, a frown line between her eyes. She felt so out of sorts, she half expected to see garlic growing where she had stepped. She confronted Gabe's smiling good morning with a stiff response.

He turned from a pan of sizzling bacon, his eyebrow arched. "Are you crabby, Miss Starr?"

Her glower deepened. "I didn't sleep well."

"Scrambled eggs and toast will perk you right up," he said, filling a plate. "But considering last night, you'd better pass on the bacon."

"I'm not hungry," she said, pushing the plate away.

He pushed it back. "Darlene's off today, remember? You might be stuck in the office all day without lunch."

She sighed wearily. "Isn't abuse of an employee illegal around here?"

"Probably," he agreed blandly, "but I know you won't complain because pride will insist that you earn your keep."

Eating was easier than fighting, and she speared a small bite of egg. It was light and fluffy and slipped right down without effort.

Dana glanced up to see the top of Gabe's shaggy gray head, combed into order this morning, bent over his own plate. Confident that she would do as he asked, he was busily devouring his breakfast. She stuck her tongue out at the lock of hair that always fell forward. Only the target had moved and she was looking into his eyes. He grinned in amusement but said nothing.

Their dishes in the sink, Gabe pulled his jacket from the back of his chair. "Ready?" he asked.

She nodded, picking up her clutch bag.

He looked doubtfully at the light, rainbow-striped sweater she wore over her jeans. "Got a jacket? It's chilly this morning and we're walking."

Would he never stop hovering? "I'll be fine," she insisted coolly.

He shook his head at her and started for the door. "Then, let's go."

It was chilly and she could have used a jacket, but she'd rather contract double pneumonia than tell him that. Thankfully, it was a brief three blocks to the office.

Once inside she wandered around while he went into the back, put on a pot of coffee, then came out front again to clear off a spare desk hidden under back issues and the debris of yesterday's pasteup.

Dana, meanwhile, was staring at a complex piece of

equipment that was placed in front of a window, apparently so that the operator could look out; and a nagging uneasiness made her forget her headache. This was not the sleek, efficient word processor she had become proficient on at the *Daily News*. This was some monster from another age. There was an On and Off switch, and when she flipped it, a sound like that of a locomotive contained in a small closet filled the room. She turned it off instantly.

"Ever use a Just-o-Writer before?" Gabe asked, coming up behind her and pulling out the chair.

"No," she said grimly. "I didn't know they still existed outside of the Smithsonian."

"Actually, it's a very efficient piece of machinery," he said, angling her a challenging glance. "As long as the operator is on her toes."

I'd like to be on my toes, she thought archly, *in flight to somewhere far away from here.* She was beginning to think this brave step into her future was a grave mistake.

He sat her in the chair and pulled a large spool out from under the machine, showed her where it was connected, then replaced it. Then he took the end of the reel of paper tape on the spool and placed it in a series of teeth atop the machine where it was clamped into place. He pushed a key that ran out a length of tape that he then attached to an empty spool.

"Okay, pay attention." Gabe leaned over her to reach around and put his long fingers on the keyboard. She felt her heart accelerate but tried hard not to react. "You use this like an ordinary keyboard, the only difference being that you have to help the machine justify the right side of your columns. You do that by backspacing between letters until the lines are flush to the left and right margins. When you become used to it, your eye will almost tell you when you begin the line and you'll make the right amount of spaces before you get to the last word. Of course, it looks more professional that way."

Thinking longingly of her word processor that justified at the touch of a button, she frowned at the monstrosity in front of her. But she had to pay attention because Gabe was still talking.

"Your typing will create this tape—" he indicated the strip of punch tape he had just connected to the empty reel. "—which will roll onto the empty spool as long as you've fed it properly. When you've finished with it, we'll transfer it to the machine beside you, which reads the tape and types it onto galleys for us. This was quite an innovation in its day."

"That must have been in the last century," she said under her breath.

"Pardon me?"

"How do I make corrections?" she asked, instead of repeating her remark.

"You just retype the line or word after you've finished with everything else and we cut it out and wax it right on top of the error."

She groaned. The word processor would have deleted the error right on the screen and turned out a perfect copy.

"Are you sure I can do this?" she asked feebly.

Instead of the confident assurance she had hoped for, he taunted her with, "Darlene can do it, and she never even covered San Francisco."

She glared up at him. "Darlene's a genius."

"So are you, cupcake," he said, patting her shoulder as he moved toward the door. "Type that story beside you while I run to the post office for the mail. I'll help you put it on the reader when I get back, and we can see if you'll have any problems with it."

After the door closed behind Gabe, Dana spent the next five minutes staring at the keyboard, trying to recover from that "cupcake" endearment. It infuriated her and warmed her at the same time. What did that mean? Finally deciding that analyzing her behavior and operating this medieval instrument could not be done at the same time, she placed her fingers on the keys.

She discovered instantly that it required pounding, much like a manual typewriter, rather than the gentle touch one used on an electric machine or the touch-sensitive word processor keyboard. Reaching the end of the line of copy, she found to her surprise that the last word fit perfectly and there was no need to justify. Feeling triumphant, she advanced to the second line. No such luck this time, of course, and she backtracked several times until she was able to make the word fit. At that rate, she had only typed one very small story by the time Gabe returned from the post office.

"How's it going?" he asked, smiling at her from the counter where he dropped the mail.

"If we were a monthly instead of a weekly," she joked grimly, "I might make it."

"You'll catch on," he insisted, coming to stand over her again. The breath left her lungs in a rush when he leaned over her to see what she had typed. "Not bad. Let's take it off the reel and read it."

Replacing the reel on the machine next to hers, he then took long strips of white paper from a box under the machine. He placed one in the rollers like an ordinary piece of typing paper.

Feeding the end of the punch tape into sprockets, he

turned the machine on and Dana came to stand by him and watch, fascinated, while what she had typed was transferred line by line onto the galley. It made a terrible racket but it did work.

"The danger with this half of the operation is that you can get the tape going and leave it, so try not to get too involved in something else because you'll run out of galley paper before you run out of tape, and you'll be imprinting your carefully written story on nothing but the typewriter roller. So be sure to keep an eye on it."

The telephone rang and Gabe looked at her over his shoulder as he went to answer it. "Try the next couple of stories."

Sitting down at the machine, feeling a little more confident now that she saw that it did work, Dana started typing. It was more than an hour later when the office door opened and a handsome older man stepped inside. He wore jeans, a flannel shirt and red suspenders. His dress was curiously at odds with his carefully combed white hair and beautifully groomed mustache. Dana smiled.

"May I help you?" she asked.

"Gabe in?" the man questioned.

"He's in the darkroom," she explained, getting out of her chair. "I'll see if he can get free."

"Tell him I'd like to take him to lunch and discuss my advertising."

"Sit down, please," Dana said, indicating the vinyl chair by the door. "I'll run back and check with him."

"Gabe?" she called through the black curtain that substituted for a door to the small cubicle in the back room.

"Yeah?"

"There's a gentleman in the office who wants to take you to lunch to discuss advertising."

"Who is it?"

"I don't know. He's wearing jeans, a flannel shirt and red suspenders."

She heard his throaty chuckle. "Well, that narrows it down to sixty percent of this population of loggers and fishermen."

Cursing herself for not having the sense to ask the man his name, she added, "Gray hair and a mustache."

"Ah!" he said, as though that clarified it. "I'll be out in a minute."

When Gabe did emerge, he shook the man's hand and introduced him to Dana as Ben Wagner, owner of a sporting goods store up the street.

"Thanks for the invitation," Gabe said as Dana went back to her machine. "But I've got a new employee today—"

Dana stopped him midsentence, a smile on her lips but a look in her eye that clearly told him to stop hovering. "I can handle it, Gabe. Please go to lunch with Mr. Wagner."

"But—"

"Gabe," she interrupted charmingly, warningly, "I can certainly answer the phone and take messages."

He studied her consideringly for a moment, then nodded to Ben Wagner. "Give me a minute to get the chemicals off my hands and I'll be right with you. Shall I bring you back a sandwich, Dana?"

"Yes, please. Something light."

"You got it."

An hour had passed in relative quiet. Apart from a few unladylike exclamations when Dana tried to trans-

fer her completed spool of punch tape to the reader and
had to crawl under the machine in order to do it, the
lunch hour was uneventful. It was after one o'clock,
and the machine next to her was efficiently banging
away, filling the blank galley with her copy, when the
office door opened again, but with a crash this time.

Dana jumped and sprang out of her chair as a large,
fair-featured man slammed the door behind him. He
had a florid complexion and appeared to be on the
verge of apoplexy.

"Where's Cameron?" he demanded, advancing on
Dana.

She had no idea who he was or what he wanted, but
something about him made her stand her ground. He
wore a three-piece suit that was obviously expensive
though a poor color choice. It was a plummy pink, and
the Western cut accentuated rather than concealed a
very portly form. His shoes and his belt were white,
and Dana barely held back a grimace of disgust.

"He's out to lunch," she explained politely. "May I
help you?"

He waved a newspaper clutched in his right hand,
then slapped it against the counter with a resounding
thwack. Dana forced herself not to flinch.

"You tell him Sorensen says he'll be out to lunch
permanently if this garbage doesn't stop!"

Dana studied him with contempt. She had known a
lot of people like him when she had lived at home.
Many of her mother's friends felt that their money
made them invincible.

"Come now, Mr. Sorensen," she heard herself say.
"I couldn't repeat a ludicrous statement like that. Perhaps if you stated your objections to the Work Corps
more clearly..."

The man's light-blue eyes bulged, and he looked as though he would burst out of his pink suit at any moment.

"Who are you?" he asked, his voice low in his throat.

"I'm Dana MacKenzie," she said cheerfully and extended her hand.

Ignoring her gesture, he looked down at her as though he would derive great satisfaction from slapping her. She almost hoped he'd try it.

"You tell him," Sorensen enunciated carefully, obviously taking great pains to hold himself in check, "that I'm pulling my advertising."

She had a lot to learn about how a small newspaper operated, but she guessed that the rules governing advertising were probably universal.

"Aren't you under contract?" she asked innocently.

"I'm breaking it!"

She said calmly, "Then the *Register* will have to take you to court."

As he towered over Dana, the veins at his temples stood out and she wondered idly if she'd remember how to administer CPR. Then he seemed to make an effort to recover his composure. "Tell Cameron what I said," he ordered heavily, "or I'll..."

Dana snatched Gabe's notepad off the counter. "Are you about to make a threat, Mr. Sorensen?" she asked, pretending to take notes. "Can we quote you on that?"

"I don't want those criminals in this town!" he shouted.

"Why is that precisely?" she asked calmly. "We'd be happy to report your side if you relate it reasonably."

He snickered. "Just tell Cameron what I said."

Sorensen tore the door open and it smashed back against the wall, the window in it rattling dangerously. He drove away with a screech of tires as Gabe walked back into the office. Looking over his shoulder as the truck sped away, he then turned back to Dana, placing a paper sack on the counter. "Rattled his cage, did you? What happened?"

She recounted their conversation and watched Gabe's expression change from incredulity to open laughter.

"You told him we'd take him to court?"

"Yes. Will you?"

Gabe shook his head. "Maybe one day, but not over his advertising contract. When an advertiser pulls out because of an editorial stand I take, I figure he has as much right to his opinion as I do to mine. I wouldn't refuse his advertising simply because I disagree with his politics, so I don't think I have the right to penalize him because he disagrees with mine."

She opened her mouth to question the usefulness of having contracts at all. But Gabe's reply was so nobly logical that she thought better of it. What a man. She changed the subject.

"Did you remember my sandwich?"

He handed her the bag. "Did he upset you?"

"Sorensen?" She pulled out two foil-wrapped triangles and opened them out on the counter. "Of course not. I've met his type before."

He grinned in amusement. "In San Francisco?"

"People who throw their weight and their money around are the same all over the world." The foil dispensed with, she looked down at the sandwich, then up at Gabe. "Chicken, ham, two kinds of cheese, lettuce and three slices of bread is your idea of a light sandwich?"

"I thought after fighting the Just-o-Writer all morning, you might need something substantial."

She was about to agree with him when she suddenly remembered the galley she had been in the process of printing when Sorensen burst into the office.

"Oh, no!" she shrieked, running back to the machine. It ticked away inconsequentially, both the galley and the punch tape long since finished. She was willing to bet her sandwich that they hadn't finished together.

Gabe laughed and, taking her by the shoulders, pushed her toward the back room. "Go sit down and eat your lunch. I'll figure out where we lost the story and get it running again."

"How do you do that?" she asked woefully, looking at that mass of tangled tape and feeling sure it was impossible.

"It's not too difficult. I'll show you another time. Right now I want you to eat your lunch. Go on."

She started toward the back room, her lunch clutched to her, then she turned back. "Gabe?"

"Yeah?" he asked absently, running the tape through his long fingers.

"I'm sorry if my making him mad is going to make things hard for you. Had I been a little more... tactful... he might not have pulled his advertising."

"He's been threatening to do it since the issue arose. And if I had been here I'd have told him the same thing." He paused to smile. "Well, almost. We'll get along just fine without his advertising. Go eat your lunch."

THE FOLLOWING DAY Dana made every effort to be efficient and unobtrusive. Though Gabe insisted he would have handled the encounter with Sorensen in the same way she had, she felt sure her deliberate antagonism of the man had precipitated the scene.

That night, before falling asleep, she had tried to analyze just why she had reacted to Sorensen that way. The man's attitude had sparked her temper, to be sure, but it had been more than that. Somehow, the thought of that man threatening Gabe and all he was trying to accomplish with an obviously meager budget and outdated equipment had whipped up her fury. She had known that nothing would deflate Sorensen's ego as much as having his intelligence challenged by a five-foot, one-inch woman.

However, in satisfying her need to puncture the big man's pride, she had lost Gabe a valuable advertising account.

Thinking about that had made her quiet all morning and strengthened her determination to gain proficiency on the confounded Just-o-Writer, thus relieving her employer of at least a few of his headaches.

It was midmorning when Gabe's long arm reached around her to turn off the machine.

"What are you doing?" she demanded.

He raised an eyebrow at her tone of voice and pointed to the sprockets that should have held punch tape and didn't. "You're out of tape," he said patiently.

Dana groaned; visions of the last hour's work wasted dampened her spirits even further.

Changing the reel, Gabe looked into her crestfallen face and poked her playfully. "Hey, cupcake, it's okay. You just have to keep your eye on it. You'll get used to it."

"Don't call me that!" she snapped as an alternative to bursting into tears of frustration. His particularly charming brand of chauvinism was not what she needed right now. Glancing at her watch, she scraped her chair back and grabbed her jacket off the coat tree by the door.

"I'm going to the school for the story. I'll finish typing when I get back."

She was aware of Gabe watching her leave and flung her dark hair over her jacket collar in what she thought was a controlled and dignified gesture. Tucking purse and notebook under her arm and shouldering her camera, she started down the street—then realized she had no idea where the school was. Reluctantly retracing her steps, she pushed the office door open, the snap in her eyes daring him to make light of her predicament.

"Follow the main highway," he said, without being asked. "Turn right on Ninth Street. You can't miss it."

"Thank you," she replied stiffly and saw him bite back a smile as she closed the door behind her.

Dana found the school, a surprisingly modern structure in this town full of turn-of-the-century homes. The playground was pandemonium—exactly what she needed to clear her mind and force her to concentrate on the matter at hand.

It wasn't a drug bust or a crime of passion or any one of a number of important events or significant tragedies that had sent her rushing from her office and into the San Francisco streets, but it was important to Gabe and to the Warrenton *Register* and that made it important to her.

By the time the events Gabe wanted her to cover were over, she had laughed with the children over their antics; swallowed a lump in her throat at their exuberance, their drive to be best and their philosophical acceptance of defeat; and taken three rolls of pictures.

When Dana returned to the office Darlene was hard

at work at the Just-o-Writer and she looked over the girl's shoulder admiringly as the slender fingers flew. Then she looked up to see the stories she thought she had lost that morning hanging on the hook that held completed galleys.

"Did you retype my work?" Dana asked.

Darlene grinned over her shoulder, hardly slackening her pace. "No. Gabe said you'd had a problem this morning and thought you might appreciate the help. He did it."

"Where is he?"

"In the darkroom. He said to bring your film in as soon as you got back."

"Gabe, it's Dana!" she called through the darkroom's lightproof fabric door. "Do you want my film?"

"Come on in!" Gabe called back.

Dana inched the black fabric aside and stepped into the room. It was in darkness as she expected, a red haze covering the area, but she was so completely disoriented for a moment that she stood silent, waiting for guiding impressions to register.

"Your eyes will adjust in a few minutes. Relax. You're in a narrow corridor about ten feet long." Gabe's voice came out of the dark. "Put your left hand out and walk forward until you no longer feel the wall. Then turn left and double back."

Doing as he directed, Dana suddenly felt his warm grip through the sleeve of her sweater. The sudden contact made her gasp, and she heard his soft laugh.

"Only me," he reassured her. "Or is that what frightened you?"

"No," she said, her voice small and shaky. "I don't like the dark."

She could hear the smile in his voice. "There's something incongruous about a young woman who would take on Sorensen and yet be afraid of the dark."

"Yes, well, I never claimed to be consistent." She was nervous suddenly, and it had nothing to do with the dark. She could feel Gabe's arm against hers but she was afraid to move, knowing there were trays with chemical solutions all around them. "Here's my camera."

She reached a hand out, hoping to connect with his hand and place the camera in it, but she encountered instead the warmth of cotton covering his flat stomach just above his belt buckle. She pulled her hand away as though the buckle had bitten her.

Then Gabe reached out in search of her hand. She felt his fingers brush her breast and she leapt back, an electric current running through her. She struck something cold and metallic and heard it crash to the floor. Something liquid ran down the leg of her jeans.

"Dana!" Gabe growled impatiently, stopping her nervous movements by shackling her waist with a brawny arm.

"I'm sorry," she said on the brink of tears. "I... maybe I'd better find another job."

With a disgruntled exclamation, he led her along the wall, turned down the narrow corridor, then brushed the black curtain aside. They stood in the dimly lit back room and he held her away from him, his eyes going to the bleached-out streaks on her new jeans.

"You'd better go right home and take a bath," he said, looking at her with an expression bordering on pity. "You've got developer all over you. You might be sensitive to it. Leave your Cadillac and take the van. You don't want to get it on your upholstery."

"I'm sorry!" she said again, her voice tight. "Now you've got a mess in the darkroom. Can't I help you clean up?"

"No, I'll take care of it. Go on home."

"I'll start dinner," she volunteered, hoping desperately to make amends for the trouble she had caused him.

"The larder's low," he replied, pushing open the freight door beyond which the van was parked. Delving into his pocket, he handed her his keys. "But if you can find something to fix, please do. I'll be home about six."

Dana soaked in a hot tub for half an hour, forcing her mind to blank out all the evidence of her sudden but complete loss of poise whenever Gabe came near her.

After shampooing her hair, she secured it in a loose knot on top of her head and slipped into a red velour robe. The robe had seen better days, but she was sentimentally attached to it because Jack had sent it to her from New York one Christmas.

An inventory of the kitchen cupboard revealed a can of vegetable soup and a loaf of grainy bread. There was a block of cheddar cheese in the refrigerator and, after a lengthy but finally fruitful search for a cheese slicer, she began warming the grill to toast sandwiches to accompany the soup.

The table was set and the coffeepot perking when Dana heard the front door open.

"You did find something." Gabe sounded surprised, walking up behind her to look over her shoulder.

"Just soup and grilled cheese," she said, trying to hold down the blush his proximity was causing. She was too old to behave this way.

"Sounds good." Shedding his jacket, he sniffed the air approvingly. "Anything I can do?"

"You can pour the coffee," she suggested. Then she asked as he opened a cupboard door for the cups, "Was the darkroom a horrible mess?"

"The developer left a stain on the flooring, but in there it doesn't matter." He smiled at her warmly as they crossed each other, performing their duties. "How about you? Any harm done besides your jeans?"

"No, I'm fine." Then she said with a grin, "Your van had an attack of palsy again when I pulled up in front of the house, and the glove compartment fell open. I think I got everything back in."

"I hope so," he said, grinning. "Other people have a safety deposit box for important papers. I have my glove compartment."

"If that's a ploy to get me to donate from my salary to help you afford one, forget it. Get the twelve dollars somewhere else. I owe Betty's Fashions my next two paychecks."

They sat across from each other at the two mugs of soup placed on the table, the plate of golden-brown sandwiches and the pot of coffee between them. Dana frowned, suddenly serious.

"I'm sorry about all the trouble I've been," she said sincerely. "I think Warrenton has done something to me. I've always been so controlled."

Gabe looked up from stirring his soup. "Are you sure? Maybe you've been deluding yourself. I think you feel too much to be as controlled as you claim. It could be that this... butterfly... is the real you."

"Butterfly," she repeated doubtfully. "Nothing so romantic, surely?"

"Oh, yes." His eyes glowed with a soft smile.

"There's something very soft and touching about an attractive woman in a dither."

She closed her eyes against the picture of herself that that remark created in her mind. Thinking back, she remembered herself as a lively child, a volatile teenager. The closing down of her emotions had been a gradual thing, beginning shortly after she married Scott. Then it had hurt too much to feel, and she discovered that she could turn the feelings off if she tried. In fact, she became an expert at it.

"I imagine there are a few graceless flutters when a cocoon is shed," Gabe said quietly, as though she had spoken her thoughts aloud.

Dana frowned at him, wondering how he could seem not to notice her, and then read her like the proverbial book.

"Incidentally, it's Sheila's birthday tomorrow," he announced unexpectedly. "Want to help me take her to dinner?"

"Yes...." She looked at him uncertainly. "But you don't need to feel that you have to entertain me."

He laughed. "I don't mind. And I promised Jack, remember?"

She looked at him, a growl in her eyes, and he grinned back. "I knew that would end the argument. I don't feel as though I have to entertain you. I don't mind having you around."

A little disappointed at that casually spoken "I don't mind having you around," Dana nodded and dropped the subject.

Gabe had finished his second sandwich when he poured another round of coffee and wandered to the kitchen window with his cup. "If I don't mow that lawn soon I'll have to use a machete," he said lightly.

"Maybe I'll get to it Sunday. I'm sure not in the mood tonight."

"Is the office open tomorrow?"

"Yes, but you can have the day off. Saturdays I usually stay in just long enough to get an editorial roughed out."

"You just don't want me to come in to work and set us back again," she joked.

He wandered back to the table, laughing. "Don't take it so hard. By the end of next week you'll be able to put out the paper single-handed. Do you have any plans for tonight?"

Her heart fluttered like the butterfly he had called her. "No," she said.

"Good. Let's go get some ice cream."

Preceding him out the door, Dana smiled to herself. That was not the romantic suggestion she had been afraid of. Her smile turned to a frown of puzzlement: Why was she disappointed?

Chapter Four

Gabe had already left for the office by the time Dana yawned her way downstairs for a cup of coffee. Thoughts of her landlord/employer had kept her awake most of the night, and she grumbled at herself disgustedly while fixing a slice of toast. If she was going to be here until Jack returned from Afghanistan, this had to stop!

She had never experienced such breathless sensations with Scott, such trembling inside every time he came near. Last night she had even imagined Gabe beside her in bed.

Deciding that activity was the only antidote for too much time to think, she tidied the kitchen, then went back upstairs. Gathering a load of laundry from her room, she crept stealthily into Gabe's room expecting to find clothes lying on the floor or at least across the foot of the bed. But the room was picked up and, though not spotless, considerably neater than any room Jack or Scott had ever kept.

The hamper in the bathroom was full, however, and she carried the clothes downstairs to the basement where the washer and dryer were kept.

The washer churning loudly, Dana went back to the main floor and straightened up and dusted. She found a vacuum cleaner to apply to the carpets and a cleaning solution for the kitchen floor. She transferred the clothes in the washer to the dryer, then put in another load.

It was midafternoon when she finished upstairs and placed a fragrant stack of folded clothes on Gabe's bed. Then she went to the garage in search of a lawn mower.

Gabe seemed to have the same preference for antiquated gardening machinery that he had for office equipment. She looked from the push-driven lawn mower to the high grass in the wide backyard and decided that it couldn't be any more difficult than operating the Just-o-Writer.

She was going over it for the second time, perspiration beading on her forehead, when Gabe emerged from the kitchen door. He paused on the step, watching her, then shook his head in exasperation and came across to her.

"What are you doing?" he asked, reaching out to stop the mower.

"You typed my work; I'm mowing your lawn." She smiled up at him. "Seemed fair." Her voice had an almost Marilyn Monroe quality of breathlessness that she hoped he would attribute to her exertion while mowing the lawn. Actually, his presence was having the effect on her that it always had, but it was a little more intense this time.

In jeans and a red-and-white rugby shirt he looked casually sexy. The afternoon sun turned the gray in his hair to silver and burnished the blue eyes that were studying her so intently. His expression had sobered from the smile that greeted her as he had walked across the lawn. He was now looking at her as though she confused him.

Her breath was trapped in her throat, and she looked away from him in hopes of breaking the spell. But he took the point of her chin between his thumb and forefinger and turned her face up to his. For an interminable moment, he looked at her. Her heart rocketed out of control and she was unable to swallow. Then he lowered his head, his shoulders blotting out the sun, and his lips touched hers. The kiss was like a stroke of warm velvet. Then he lifted his head and pinched her chin teasingly.

"Go get cleaned up for dinner and I'll finish this."

Dana obeyed because she had no voice with which to disagree. Bells clanged in her ears; rockets exploded behind her eyes; a warm longing invaded her body from her hairline to the tips of her toes.

SHEILA LOOKED DELICATE and a little flushed in pink sweater and slacks as she sat across from Gabe and Dana in a back booth at the Marketplace Restaurant in Astoria, a short drive from Warrenton.

She grimaced at Dana. "Once you pass thirty, men start hiding you in dark corners."

Dana looked around her at the terrazzo flooring, the lush plants in bright pots and rough baskets hanging and standing everywhere.

"You're being sensitive," she teased back. "This is hardly a dark corner, and you're looking positively devastating for thirty-three."

"Thirty-two!" Sheila corrected, distressed.

Dana elbowed Gabe. "You told me she was thirty-three."

"My mistake," he acknowledged, tossing a small wrapped package on the tabletop. "I just know she's been a problem to me for a major part of my life.

Happy birthday, Sheila!" he added with a smile that negated his remark.

"Oh!" She scooped up the package delightedly, tearing it open. Her long fingers emerged from the crinkly tissue with a fine gold chain, one single opal the very color of her eyes woven in it. "Oh, Gabe!" her eyes softened and she reached across the table to hug him. "Thank you! This makes today just perfect. I got flowers from Jack delivered at work this morning."

"Was there a note? What did he say?" Dana asked, sitting up at the prospect of news from her brother.

"Nothing. I suppose he ordered the flowers before he left." Sheila drew a breath, her voice quiet and unsteady. "The card was very Jack. Not 'Love, Jack,' or even 'See you, Jack.' Just...just 'Jack.'"

"Be fair, Sheila," Gabe scolded gently, pouring wine from a frosty carafe. "He remembered. He even planned ahead, knowing he'd be gone. Give him *some* credit."

"It's just that this is the sort of thing we've been fighting about," Sheila pointed out with a frown. "It's my birthday and I'd like him here with me."

"Well, if we're not good enough to celebrate with, we'll leave right now," Gabe threatened, and Dana found herself hard put to decide whether or not he was serious, "and you can eat three portions of prime rib by yourself and handle the bill."

"Don't be a bully, Gabe," Dana interceded. She met his censuring eyes with a smile, holding her wineglass out for more of the fine rosé. "Sheila can't help how she feels. Denying her resentment won't make it go away."

Gabe glanced up from pouring, a slight smile on his face. "It isn't polite to contradict your host."

"I'm just supposed to let you be wrong?" Dana asked blandly.

He put the carafe down and looked at her with a trace of impatience. "Is Jack wrong to do his job? You love someone for what they are, not for how conveniently they fit into your scheme of things."

"Is that why you're still a bachelor? No one fit and you didn't want to have to trim her into place?" The question was a little saucy, a little flip, and Dana spoke it with a teasing grin.

He shrugged and smiled. "When I was a foreign correspondent I spent a lot of time in seamy places and dangerous situations. It didn't seem the kind of life to ask a woman to share."

"What about now?" she asked, her eyes a little dreamy as she imagined him in a trench coat on a foggy foreign dock or in fatigues covering some South American civil war.

"Now," he said softly, looking directly into her eyes, "is different."

She snapped out of her dreamy mood as that remark, heavy with suggestion, penetrated. Convinced she'd misunderstood, she tried to ignore the quickening of her pulse.

"You need to marry a good seventy-year-old typist," she said, leaning back as the waiter brought their food, grateful for the distraction.

Sheila frowned. "Why seventy years old?"

Picking up her fork, ready to attack the juicy prime rib and beautiful asparagus, Dana slanted a teasing grin at their host.

"It'd take somebody that old to know how to deal with his equipment—and that lawn mower."

"You made her mow the lawn?" Sheila accused Gabe in horror.

"No, she volunteered," he replied calmly. "In order to make up for all the lost business she's cost me this week." He returned Dana's taunting glance, turning the bowl of his wineglass in long fingers. "And I doubt that a seventy-year-old could keep up."

"Come now." Dana made a dismissing gesture with a wave of her fork. "The work isn't that hard."

"It's not the work I'm talking about," he assured her with a look that stopped her from sampling her dinner. Was it possible she hadn't misunderstood after all?

Though she didn't dare ask him what he meant, he chose to clarify the statement anyway. "There's a lot more to me than work," he offered by way of explanation. "I have personal plans that require a young..." he paused, then added, his eyes dancing, "agile... woman of about your height and proportions."

Gabe and Dana stared at each other, he letting her absorb the challenge while she looked back at him in startled silence, her cheeks reddening, the deep, ruffled collar of her dress fluttering with her shallow, nervous breaths.

"Shall I leave the table?" Sheila asked, looking uncertainly from her brother to her new friend.

"Of course not," Gabe replied, giving Dana one long, lingering look before turning to his sister. "You've got to catch me up on what's happening at the college. I missed the last board meeting."

Completely off balance from Gabe's suddenly playful attitude, Dana concentrated on her dinner, paying minimal attention to Sheila's sharing of news about the community college in Astoria where she worked as a secretary.

Dana's pulse was beginning to stabilize when she was startled again by the raucous arrival at their table of the restaurant staff with a large, candlelit birthday cake.

"Oh, Gabe!" Sheila groaned as the staff began to sing the birthday song and the rest of the diners joined in. Her cheeks were pink, her eyes misty as she blew out the candles.

A small, wiry man with lively eyes and dark gray hair and mustache handed Sheila a knife and several dessert plates. As she sliced the cake, the man leaned over to Gabe.

"Can you come into the kitchen for a few minutes before you leave? I've got a promotion idea for our new menu I'd like to talk over with you."

"You bet. Soon as I eat my share of this cake."

"Good enough. Happy birthday, Sheila."

"Thanks, Darrell." Beaming, Sheila passed cake to Gabe and Dana. "I'll never forgive you for making such a fuss over the fact that I'm getting older," she threatened her brother, her expression anything but angry. "But I'll never forget how nice it was, either. You've made it very special. Thank you."

"You're welcome. Many happy returns." Gabe touched the rim of his glass to Sheila's, then to Dana's.

Still slightly uncomfortable, Dana shared the toast, then looked quickly away, pretending interest in her cake.

After finishing, Gabe signaled for more coffee for Dana and Sheila, then excused himself to keep his appointment in the kitchen. As soon as he was out of earshot, Sheila reached across the table and patted Dana's hand.

"Thanks for coming to my defense about Jack." She frowned, her eyes darkening. "I did say some awful things to him Tuesday night."

Dana could imagine the woman's frustration, with

Jack deliberately taking that assignment to escape a situation he couldn't handle.

"Maybe he deserved them," she suggested.

"I don't know." Sheila put her cup down and rested her chin wearily on the heel of her hand. "I know I haven't the right to ask him to give up his work, but...I couldn't live that way again. It seemed every time I had a problem, Bill was away. And then it got to where I resented him so much while he was away that the resentment carried over when he came home. Our last year together was a disaster."

"Was he in the coast guard when you got married?"

"Yes. And I know that means I have no right to complain."

Dana frowned, studying the girl's gentle face closely. "Are you sure his absences were the problem?" she asked. "Could it have been something else, a little harder to face, maybe? Were the separations just easy to blame?"

Sheila straightened, her expression startled for a moment, then she looked embarrassed. She picked up her coffee cup again.

"Maybe. I married Bill because he was settled and steady. Isn't that what you're supposed to do? Marry a man with his feet on the ground who'll keep security uppermost in his mind for you and your family?"

Dana's smile was wry. "Don't ask me, Sheila. I looked for someone who was fun and who would love me, and I blew it, too."

"Bill did not have a breath of fun in him," the other woman said, unhappy memories in her eyes. "He was steady, and in his way I think he loved me. But we never laughed." She drew a deep breath and sipped her coffee. Then she smiled. "Jack, on the other hand, has me hysterical with laughter ninety percent of the time. The other ten I could kill him."

"Maybe the life you shared with Bill wasn't...fulfilling enough to sustain you while he was gone. Maybe it would be different with Jack."

Sheila stared thoughtfully at her coffee cup. "Maybe. In any case, you just might be right, Dana. The problem is probably with me instead of with Jack."

Dana smiled philosophically. "The separation will give you both time to think. That can't be bad."

"You and Gabe seem to be getting along well," Sheila observed, leaning back in the corner of the booth.

"Mostly. He gets a bit overprotective at times, but I just have to stand up for myself."

"That's Gabe. He got me out of more scrapes when we were kids and saved me from more mashers when I was a headstrong, adventuresome teenager." She shook her head. "He even tried to make me think twice about marrying Bill, but I was so sure...."

Sheila took a sip of cold coffee and grimaced. "Our parents were doctors, and though they loved us, our lives were constantly disrupted. I think a normal, steady life was what I was looking for when I married Bill. Unfortunately, I was wrong."

"In your choice of a partner, maybe," Dana offered. "But not in what you wanted. I've been looking for security all my life—not in money or possessions, because I've always had those, but in protective arms to run to, a sympathetic shoulder to cry on."

Sheila frowned. "Then why does Gabe's protectiveness upset you?"

That stopped Dana for a moment and she grinned.

"Because I've found it a lot harder to make sense of what I want since I've come to Warrenton."

Sheila laughed. "How's the job going?"

"Fine, so far. I haven't had a chance to do much but a story at the school. I'd like to get into some investigative work eventually. I minored in geology in school. I'd love to check out Mount Saint Helens, too, and find out what's happening there."

"The husband of one of the girls I work with—" Sheila's voice halted as she reached under the table for her purse "—has a flying service and takes passengers over the mountain. I'll give you his card. It's in here someplace." She rummaged through a long gray envelope clutch for her wallet. "There!" She produced the card and handed it to Dana.

"Great! I'll call him Monday."

"Who?" Gabe asked, appearing at Sheila's shoulder.

"Ben Brewster," Sheila supplied before Dana could stop her. She would have broken the news a little differently. "Dana wants to fly over Mount Saint Helens for a story."

Gabe's eyes went to Dana and, though he said nothing, she saw his disapproval. She looked back at him steadily, refusing to be intimidated.

"Ready, ladies?" Sidestepping the issue of the story, Gabe handed Sheila a cardboard box. "Pack up your calories, birthday girl. Your coach is about to turn into a pumpkin."

Dana studied Gabe as she stood up and shrugged into her light jacket. He helped Sheila into her coat, saying something quietly to her. The young woman turned, laughing, to give him a hug. Unembarrassed, he hugged her back.

Despite the protectiveness she had complained about to Sheila, and the argument Dana knew was coming over her proposed flight with Ben Brewster, she couldn't dispel a certain excitement at the knowledge that she was going home with Gabe.

IT WAS AFTER MIDNIGHT when Gabe and Dana pulled into the driveway of the old blue Victorian. It had been a silent drive, and Dana felt tension rising between them as Gabe helped her out of the car and pushed the house door open, allowing her to precede him inside.

The light over the kitchen table had been left on, and Dana walked through the darkened living room toward the stairs.

"Thanks for dinner," she said casually, pulling off her jacket as she walked. "Good night, Gabe."

"Not yet."

Her progress halted by Gabe's hand on the empty sleeve of her jacket, Dana turned to him.

"We have to talk," he said.

A little reluctant, she allowed him to pull her jacket the rest of the way off and lead her to the sofa. He crossed the room to turn on the light, and Dana blinked against it, her heart picking up an unsteady beat.

"About your flight over the mountain," Gabe said quietly as he walked back to join her on the sofa. "Don't call Brewster."

Relieved yet disappointed that the pilot was what he wanted to discuss, she bristled with anger.

"Why not?" she demanded.

He looked calmly into her stormy face. "Brewster is notorious for his casual approach to flying, and there's too much practical work to do during the next few weeks to take time out for joy flying."

Dana sat a little straighter, her color rising.

"I intended," she said evenly, "to get a story out of it, not a joy ride."

"At the moment, what's happening on the mountain would be of little value to our readers," he insisted firmly.

Dana sprang to her feet, looking down at him with her fists clenched at her sides. "When I left California the news was full of rumblings coming from the mountain. A volcano is getting ready to erupt again on our doorstep and that isn't of value to our readers?"

"It rumbles all the time. It isn't getting ready to erupt. I've checked." Gabe stood up also, a small smile forming that she took instant exception to.

"Then where's the danger?" she asked.

"Where's the value?" he countered.

"Are you afraid I'll write a better story than you could?" Even as the words tumbled out of her mouth she knew she was making an absurd suggestion, but it was also absurd that this man could make her so confused and so angry!

"I'm afraid you'll get hurt," he explained quietly, taking her arm as she turned away from him in disgust.

She shook free of him, her eyes sparking danger. "Do you have any idea what goes on in San Francisco?" she shouted, then turning her hand to point at herself, she added furiously, "I covered a lot of it! And nobody worried about my getting hurt!"

"Well, you weren't working for me at the time," he replied mildly.

"No!" she gasped. "Now all I'll ever do is school news so that I'll be safe! Perhaps you should bring the typing home to me Monday. Who knows what could happen when I set foot out of the house!"

"Now you're being infantile." He turned away from her and went to the kitchen.

She stomped after him. "I suppose your attitude is reasonable? It's about as Victorian as your typesetting equipment and your lawn mower!"

He filled the teakettle and put it on the stove. Then he turned to look at her, his eyes quiet and unmoved by her temper.

"If it's Victorian to avoid having you dropped into the crater of a volcano—" he waved a "so be it" gesture "—then I'm flattered to be considered Victorian. And someday, when this paper begins to pay its way, I'll get some new equipment."

"Gabe," she tried to plead reasonably, "you can't tie my hands like that!"

"Look, Dana," he said, his eyes darkening as a threat formed in them, "you do what I assign you to do, do you understand me? I don't care how qualified a professional you are, or how bold and fearless. Risking your life for a story I don't want will get you nothing but trouble. Is that clear?"

Gabe was doing his best to look fearsome; she had to admit that with the light over the kitchen table casting shadows across the hollows of his face and leaving only craggy angles in burnished relief, he succeeded. He was standing tall, hands loosely on his hips—that, too, was an attempt to intimidate her.

She arched an unimpressed eyebrow. "Maybe," she said casually and turned away from him.

He yanked her back so fast the room spun.

"If you take that attitude," he warned in a voice just louder than a whisper, his fingers biting into her arms, "you're fired."

Her heart lurched because she knew he meant it. But

she managed to stay calm. "And if you're going to persist in your attitude, Gabe, I quit." Then to her utter and complete chagrin, she felt her composure slip and her bottom lip began to quiver as she challenged, "Though how you can fire me when you promised Jack—"

"Jack," he ground through clenched teeth, "has nothing the hell to do with this."

A tear fell, followed by a steady stream, and Dana knew it had nothing to do with Jack. It had to do with the two of them. But this was not going to happen, she told herself determinedly. She was not going to allow her attraction for this man to develop into anything. She was still recovering from the sting of the way Scott had used her, and she needed no further complications to her recovery.

Attempting to wriggle free of his hold, Dana felt his hands on her waist; then she was lifted and set on the countertop. She kicked against Gabe, but his large hands clamped down on her thighs, stopping her as effectively as though he had strapped her down. Dana's breath escaped in a rush.

"Now, stop it!" he said sharply. In her sitting position on the counter, she found herself at his eye level, but the glare she aimed at him bounced back at her. He took a handkerchief out of his hip pocket and handed it to her.

"All right, if you like the job so much," he said with just a hint of a smile, "you can have it back. But if you're the professional you say you are, you'll listen to your editor."

Since he put it that way, she had no argument to offer. It seemed suddenly to have lost its importance anyway. She dabbed at her eyes with the large square of linen.

"All right," she agreed on a broken breath.

"Do you mean that?" he asked seriously.

Her eyes were level, her tears dried. "I mean it. But I resent you for it."

"Management is never popular with the labor force." He grinned wryly. "Do you want a brandy before bed?"

Now that she no longer struggled, his hands had relaxed, one resting lightly on each of her hips. She was conscious of every fingertip in contact with her body, and he knew it.

"No, I'm all right," she whispered.

"Then, it's late." His hands slid along her thighs to tuck behind her knees to pull her toward him. She reached instinctively for his shoulders as he moved his hands to her waist and lifted her. Her body slid along his as he set her down, the points of her sweater-clad breasts touching his chest and still in contact until just below his rib cage. As her feet touched the floor she stepped away from him, her eyes betraying an inner struggle against sudden, urgent reaction.

"Good night," Gabe said softly, amusement in his clear blue eyes.

Without bothering to reply Dana ran upstairs to her room. As she undressed for bed, the photo of Sheila accused her of the same tactic of which she had suggested Gabe's sister had been guilty. It wasn't Gabe's constant protective attitude that annoyed her so much. It was that sensual antenna with which women were equipped that told her Gabe was attracted to her, even wanted her.

She felt frustrated by her own insistent resistance. But tonight there'd been no need for antennae. She'd have had to be deaf, blind and wearing armor herself to have missed all the signals he'd been sending.

The problem was that her own body was reacting

contrary to her firm assertion that she wanted no part of a relationship with Gabe. Her pulse was still drumming, her legs still tingling where he had touched her.

It was the wine and the evening's festive atmosphere, she told herself. It had been so long since she'd relaxed and had fun. Tomorrow, she felt sure, she'd have things in perspective again.

CONSIDERING THE STATE she'd been in when she'd gone to bed the night before, Dana felt positive and in control when church bells and bright sunshine woke her the following morning.

After a hot shower, she slipped into her white pants and a ruffled prairie blouse. She brushed her hair and caught it back in a demure bun.

The house was so quiet, as she made her way downstairs, that she wondered if Gabe had gone to the office already. But he was sitting at the kitchen table in jeans and a blue sweatshirt, a cup of coffee in his hand, reading the *Sunday Oregonian.*

"Your breakfast is in the oven." He looked up at her with a smile.

"Thank you," she replied, crossing to the stove. She glanced back over her shoulder to find him involved in the paper once again, his manner relaxed, nothing more than simply friendly.

Relieved, Dana went to the table with her plate. Gabe folded the paper and tossed it on a chair.

"Don't stop reading on my account," she said, topping off his coffee before pouring her own.

"How about a day at the beach?" he suggested, surprising her.

She looked out the window at the still gusty April morning, her expression doubtful. "Isn't it too cold?"

"You sound like a Californian," he criticized gently. "You go to the beach to soak up the sun. Oregonians go to the beach for drama and excitement. We'll just walk and beachcomb."

She looked up from her breakfast, her dark eyes bright. "Sounds like fun."

"You'll have to change."

She eyed him warily. "Me personally, or my clothes?"

He laughed, a deep, rich sound that set her world on the right course again. "Your clothes. I wouldn't have you any other way."

She made a doubtful sound and speared a piece of sausage.

"Wear the jeans you ruined in the darkroom. And bring a hooded sweatshirt if you've got one, or a jacket and a scarf." Waiting for her to protest as she had when he suggested she bring a jacket along when they walked to work, he noted her silence with a raised eyebrow. "No argument?"

"No," she said truthfully. "They're beginning to wear me out."

"Hmm." His expression was thoughtful. "You aren't going to get sweet and obedient on me, are you?"

She sat back to enjoy a piece of toast and asked pertly, "Isn't that what you want?"

"No. And you know it isn't. I just want to keep you from harm."

"For Jack?" she challenged before she could stop herself.

He looked back at her evenly. "I thought we already settled that." He scraped back his chair. "Unplug the coffeepot when you're finished, will you?"

IN GABE'S OLD VAN Dana watched the blossoming countryside speed by as they passed.

"What is that yellow bush?" she asked, pointing to the bright banks of mustard gold on both sides of the highway.

"Scotch broom," Gabe informed her with a laugh. "It is beautiful, but it's the bane of every allergy sufferer from April to July."

"Oh." She grinned sheepishly. "I was going to ask why no one has it planted in gardens."

Gabe turned into the heavily forested right side of the road at a large wooden sign marked "Fort Stevens."

"During the summer you can hardly get in here," he explained. "With the beach and a beautiful lake, it's a favorite campsite for tourists. And on weekends, lots of the locals pull their trailers or vans in, too; it's such a different atmosphere just a few miles out of town."

Driving down the sun-dappled road was like driving through an old-fashioned moving picture show, Dana noted, where light flickered with lightning speed. Side by side with the tall evergreens and interspersed with the glowing Scotch broom were dozens of different varieties of trees and bushes in more shades of green than she had known existed.

As they drove on, passing a curved overhead bridge, the green canopy disappeared and they passed through a lower, less dense growth of green, still brightened by Scotch broom. Then, gradually, that disappeared, too, and the terrain flattened out to sand dunes, and they could hear the roar of the ocean.

Gabe turned off into a large parking lot where only one other car was parked and turned off the ignition. The van shuddered and Gabe absently reached across Dana to hold the glove compartment closed. He turned to Dana, the blue of his eyes intensified by the blue of his sweatshirt. She tried not to betray the melting sensation she felt inside when he looked at her.

"Ready? Sure you're warm enough?"

"I'm sure."

The distance from the parking lot to the top of a high slope that blotted the ocean from view, about two hundred feet, was dotted by thin vegetation. They started toward the hill, Dana trailing behind Gabe, inhaling the intoxicating air. Closing her eyes to take a deep breath, she stumbled over a rock and flailed the air to maintain her balance. She looked up, embarrassed to find Gabe grinning exasperatedly at her, his hand extended toward her.

"You'd better hold on to me, cupcake. I'd hate to have to explain to Jack that I let you injure yourself on the beach before we even reached the water."

"Funny," she said dryly, accepting his hand, feeling her small one engulfed in it. The warmth of it touched her deep inside.

Dana and Gabe reached a trail where they had to walk single file. He stayed behind her until they topped the steep slope, then he went ahead and towed her up behind him. They stopped at the crest to catch their breath, Gabe sheltering her in the curve of his shoulder as a strong wind whipped around them, stirring the sea grass and the delicate wild strawberries that nestled in it.

She filled her lungs again with the perfumed air. "I'd like to bottle that," she said, "and splash it on every morning."

"No, you always smell like a rose garden. That's more you."

She looked up at him, surprised he had noticed. A self-deprecating grimace wrinkled her nose. "Roses are long-stemmed and elegant."

He shook his head. "You're like a tea rose, small and dainty. When you're not falling over things," he added wickedly, "or being a pill."

She narrowed her eyes at him, but the laughter was still visible in them. "Roses have thorns, remember. Even tea roses."

"Yes," he agreed with a broad smile. "But they're still my favorite flower. I guess the fragrance makes them worth it." Then he nuzzled her hair and planted a kiss lightly on her forehead.

As they went carefully down the other side of the slope to the sand, Dana felt very much as though she could have flown.

For several hours they walked along the beach, Dana tucked into Gabe's shoulder, her arm around his waist, her thumb hooked in a belt loop of his jeans. She felt in tune with God and nature for the first time in her life, and all the precautions she'd repeated to herself most of the night flew to the winds. *It can't hurt to indulge a simple infatuation,* she thought, and allowed her mind to follow all sorts of fanciful roads of speculation.

"Did you go to Stanford?" she asked, blinking up at him against the brightness of the sky.

He looked down at her in surprise. "How'd you know that?"

"The sweatshirt you were wearing the day I arrived."

"Oh. Yes, I did. How about you?"

"UCLA."

"Is that where you met your husband?"

The question surprised Dana, and she looked up at Gabe, wondering if she could read the intent of that question in his eyes. But he was looking out over the frothy, blue-gray ocean, his eyes reflecting its color.

"No," she replied. "He worked for my father. I met him at a staff dinner during the holidays three years ago."

Waiting for him to ask another question or comment on her reply, she shuffled along beside him, noting that the sky was clouding over. When he was silent, still looking out to sea, she said softly, "I've often wondered if another woman might have made him happier."

"If he fooled around on you during such a brief marriage, I think that's doubtful," Gabe said. "He was probably out for what he could get rather than what he could give. Nobody can make that kind of a person happy. Why did you stay with him?"

She drew a deep sigh, trying to remember. It all seemed so long ago. "It was easier than taking action, I guess," she finally admitted with a weak smile. "I was a wimp in those days."

He laughed aloud at that, the sound carried off to sea by the wind. "You certainly got over it," he teased, squeezing her shoulder.

She smiled ruefully. "I was very hurt and bitter after the divorce. I knew developing those traits would be self-destructive. So I gave everything to my job. I got over the hurt simply because I discovered that you can't work and feel sorry for yourself at the same time. And I got over the bitterness because I saw so many lives in worse messes and under worse strains than I had ever imagined. So I had an unfaithful husband. I wouldn't die of it."

They had reached an enormous, fire-scarred log washed up on the beach and Gabe led her to it, sitting astride it after helping her settle into a comfortable corner formed by a broken limb. While they'd been walking, clouds had massed overhead and the wind along the shoreline blew bitterly cold.

Dana's nose was frozen, her hands stuffed into the pockets of her sweatshirt, but she'd never felt warmer in her life. It had been a beautiful afternoon. The wind now whipping around them seemed to enclose her in a comfortable dome with Gabe.

Short wisps of gray hair fluttered in attractive disarray as he studied her face, framed by the hood of her bright-red sweatshirt.

"Your nose is red," he noted.

"Matches my shirt," she quipped. "A true sense of style demands that *everything* be coordinated."

He laughed. "Never at a loss for words, are you?" Then after a brief but heavy pause, he added, "Unless I look as though I want you." He was no longer laughing, but looking at her with eyes that reflected the turbulence of sea and sky. "Then you seem to suffer attacks of speechless paralysis. Do I frighten you?"

Her instinctive reaction to the conversation's sudden turn was alarm that he had broached the subject of their relationship. Then she forced herself to relax, finally deciding that perhaps discussing it was best.

"Yes," she admitted candidly, "you do."

"Why?"

She looked at him levelly, offering a smile as apology for her honesty. "Because you're coming on to me and I'm not ready for that."

A wild gust of wind blew Dana's hood off and Gabe reached out to replace it, smiling gently into her eyes as he tied the cord under her chin.

"Even widows aren't expected to grieve longer than a year," he said.

"It's not grief," she assured him quickly, looking

out at the water as she searched for a way to explain her feelings. "It's fear. Not . . . fear of you, but fear of getting involved again, of—" She glanced at him quickly, then dropped her eyes "—of being used again."

"Used," he repeated, as though her meaning wasn't clear. Then he added, "You mean for your money?"

She shrugged. "It happened before." Chancing a look at him she found the anger she'd been afraid would result. But as he caught her wary glance, his expression softened and he swatted her knee playfully.

"Well, you've misjudged me," he said. "I had designs on your body, not your bank account."

She laughed despite herself. "Now I *know* you're not to be trusted."

"Seriously." Gabe caught her hands in his. They were cold and rough, as cold as hers, but she felt the energy in them and felt herself absorb it. "Do you really think I would use you for your money?"

She squeezed his hands, enjoying the contact. "It isn't that you would, exactly, but that I'd always be afraid you would."

When the anger flashed back in his eyes she hurried on. "I'm sorry, but I can't help it. I knew as a child that a lot of my friends were friends because I had the greatest toys, a tree house, a four-acre front lawn. Then, as a teenager, I had a Ferrari, and we summered at Lahaina. I had to beat my friends off with a stick!"

She didn't realize that she was grinding his hands in hers as she went on. "When boys and then men started coming around, I was determined it was going to be me and not my money that figured in the commitment. To that point, no one had ever loved me except Jack, and I believed I was worthy of being loved."

The pain was suddenly fresh, and she fought tears with

a deep breath. Dropping Gabe's hands, she wrapped her arms around herself.

"Scott was such a good actor," she said with a touch of the bitterness she'd fought so hard against. "He was so subtle, so..." She gulped and gave Gabe a look so full of pain that he shook his head helplessly, not knowing what to do for her.

"Forgive me, Gabe, but he was so much like you; seeming to need me, to be delighted by me—aroused by me."

She closed her eyes as tears fell onto the knees of her jeans. "I'm afraid. Please understand that. It isn't you; it's me."

"All right," he said gently, pulling her closer to put both arms around her. "Don't cry. I understand. But I'm not going to stand back, either. I care for you and I'm going to make you care for me."

"You've already done that," she admitted grudgingly.

"Then I'm going to make you trust me. Be warned. Caring and trust make love." He grinned. "When that's established, *we'll* make love and you'll never be afraid of anything again."

Feeling as though a burden had been lifted from her, Dana smiled teasingly. "Are you claiming to be Superman?"

"No," he said, laughing. "But we *will* fly."

A large raindrop plopped on Dana's nose, and when she looked up at the sky her reddened cheeks were washed by a sudden downpour. She made an instinctive movement to rise and run, but Gabe held her back.

"We'll never outrun it. May as well take it slow. We're going to get drenched anyway."

Dana was grateful for the slow, cleansing walk back to the car, her hand in his. Gabe took a blanket out of the trunk and wrapped it around her, then helped her inside, lifting her mummified legs into the van. He turned the heater on the moment they were under way, and Dana, shivering, looked at his drenched figure in concern.

"Aren't you cold?" she asked, her teeth chattering.

"When you live on the northwest coast you get as accustomed to being wet as you Californians are to being warm. You okay?"

"I will be as soon as I get into a hot tub." She wrapped the blanket more tightly around herself. "I hope you're fixing dinner," she teased. "I'm helpless when I'm cold."

He glanced away from the road, his eyes dark in the dim interior of the van. He grinned. "Helpless? Really? Don't tempt me."

He was joking, but she looked back at him gravely, wishing she had the self-confidence to do that very thing.

Chapter Five

Holding the blanket snug around her, Dana ran from the driveway to the front porch while Gabe locked the van and followed her at a slower pace. He smiled at the picture she made, huddled against the door waiting for him to unlock it.

She smiled up at him, curiously happy to be back home. She'd only lived in the old blue Victorian five days but it already felt more like home than her parents' estate or the sprawling home she had shared with Scott. Despite the antagonism that sprang up between her and Gabe, she felt sheltered here, secure.

Before inserting the key in the lock, Gabe looked at her deeply for a moment, and she wondered if he read her thoughts. Then he yanked at the bow tied under her chin and pulled her hood down, his fingers working gently in her hair, untangling the wet strands.

Gooseflesh rose on her scalp and she fought to remain still, wondering what it would be like to warm her chilled body against his.

With an abrupt movement he turned the key and pushed the door open. "You're soaked to the skin. I'll build a fire while you're bathing," he said, giving her a light shove toward the stairs.

She frowned in mock protest. "That means I'll end up cooking while you're bathing."

Squatting down before the fireplace, parting the protective screen, he paused to grin at her. "You could build the fire, but then you're helpless when you're cold, remember? You've probably never built a fire anyway—except in me."

She stopped on the third step, only her pale face visible above the blanket clutched around her shoulders.

"Gabe..." she scolded, her eyes enormous.

"I told you I wasn't giving up," he replied impenitently. "Hurry up; you're dripping on the stairs."

DESPITE GABE'S INSISTENCE that he wasn't cold, Dana hurried through her bath and shampoo, wanting to leave the warm, steamy bathroom free for his use.

"I'm out!" she called, scurrying from the bathroom to her bedroom clad in a skimpy towel, her wet clothes bunched in her arms.

"I see that," Gabe said with a low chuckle as he topped the stairs and advanced slowly down the hall, his eyes skimming her trim legs.

"I...I left you plenty of hot water," she said, wondering where her breath had fled as she hurried into her room.

He stopped at the bathroom doorway, leaning his forearm against the old pine molding as he studied her wet head, peeking out from her bedroom. "And that's right where you've got me, isn't it?"

She looked confused. "Where?"

"In hot water." With that he stepped into the bathroom and closed the door behind him.

Dressed in jeans and a pink sweatshirt, her hair

wrapped in a towel, Dana knocked on the bathroom door. There was a moment of silence.

"Yeah?" Gabe asked.

"If you'll throw out your stuff," she shouted through the door, "I'll put it in the washer with my things."

"Okay. Just a minute."

The door opened and he contributed jeans, a sweatshirt and a pair of yard-long socks to the soggy pile in her arms. Half of his face was covered by white lather.

She laughed. "Have you got rabies, or are you shaving?"

He shook a razor at her threateningly. "You're going to find out in a minute if you don't get cracking on dinner."

"Boy!" she complained. "Do this! Do that! Wait till I tell Jack."

"Having lived with you himself, he'll be sympathetic, I'm sure, to my position."

"Having lived with you," she sassed, "he probably has clouded judgment." With a victorious grin she turned down the hall. But before she had taken three steps a sharp sting on her bottom stopped her with a yelp. She spun around just as the bathroom door closed on laughter and she realized that she'd been snapped by the towel Gabe had been wearing around his waist. Her face flushed and her pulse accelerated. It was interesting, she thought, how panic and excitement could live side by side in someone.

AT THE FOOT of the basement stairs, Dana groped for the light pull she vaguely recalled seeing when she'd done laundry the previous morning. Finally connecting with it, she yanked. Nothing. She drew a deep breath, telling herself that this was no different from learning to negotiate the darkroom at the office. She walked cautiously forward in the direction of the appliances.

The silence was loud in her ears. Never having gotten over a childhood fear of the dark, she forced herself to keep moving, groping ahead of her for the cold, metallic feel of the washer.

"Ah!" Jamming her fingers into the front of the machine she felt relief as well as pain. Shaking her fingers, she flipped open the lid and strained through the dark trying to read the numbers on the dial. But her efforts were short-circuited by the sudden, clear memory of every horror film she'd ever seen. She had hated them herself, but Jack loved them, and being so often right behind him as a child, she had sat through many, her hands over her ears, her eyes tightly closed.

"You are being stupid!" she told herself severely. "Get the clothes in there, pour the soap, turn the thing on...." The swift rush of water startled her and she jumped back. The lid of the washer fell with a crash. She stumbled back into something that clattered to the concrete floor; then there was a demoniacal shriek followed by the contact on her shoulder of something with sharp talons and two elliptical gold eyes.

Her scream reminded her of all those horror movies in its shrill pitch of absolute terror. She screamed again and again, flailing her arms wildly, knocking the demon off her.

Running headlong in the dark, she collided with a stack of boxes, sending them toppling and herself sprawling, hard angles and corners stabbing the soft skin of her arms and legs.

"Dana!" Gabe's voice was a swift, loud shout.

"Here!" she sobbed, throwing an arm up and miraculously connecting with his jeans-clad leg. He hauled her to her feet in the darkness and she fell against him, her arms tight about his waist, screams still renting the dank stillness.

"What is it?" he demanded.

Totally incoherent, she was unable to form a reply.

He tried to pull her away; but terror gave her the strength to resist and she clung to him madly, her face buried in his shoulder, screaming.

Tearing the towel off her hair, Gabe wound his fingers in the wet mass and pulled firmly while she cried in protest, clamping his other hand over her mouth.

"Dana," he said calmly but loudly, "stop it!"

She tried to pull at the hand over her mouth but he held firm. "Stop it!" he said again, a tone louder. "Now!"

Something about his voice finally reached her and she stopped screaming long enough to blurt, "There's something...something...evil down here!"

He was silent a moment and she could hear the amusement in his voice as he asked, "You or me?"

His tone annoyed her and helped her pull herself together. "It jumped on me!"

"Where?"

"By the washer!"

"What did it look like?"

"How do I know?" she shouted. "It's so dark!"

He rephrased the question. "Then what made you think it was evil?"

"It was furry and it had talons and awful yellow eyes!" She shuddered and he pulled her back against him. She realized for the first time that he wore no shirt.

"That sounds evil to me, all right," he said, a smile in his voice. "Come on, I'll turn on the shop light."

"I want to go upstairs," she said raspily.

"All right." He moved toward the other side of the basement, where he kept his tools. "Go ahead."

She groped in the dark and caught his warm, strong arm. "I want you to come with me!"

"In a minute." He tried to disengage his arm but she held fast. "Dana, I don't want some furry, taloned thing with yellow eyes in my basement. As a pillar of the community I have an image to maintain."

"You're laughing at me!" she accused.

A light kiss landed on her forehead. "Just a little. If you don't want to know what it was, go on upstairs. Otherwise, stay by me and we'll find the light."

She didn't want to know what it was, but she didn't want to leave him, either. "All right," she said defeatedly. "I'll stay."

Holding her close beside him, Gabe moved unerringly toward the long shop bench. He reached overhead and suddenly there was a strong yellowish light illuminating the messy shop corner of the basement.

The screech Dana had heard earlier rose again, and she shrank against Gabe. "See?" she said. "I told you!"

He began to laugh, a deep, easy sound that both annoyed and comforted her. Leaving her standing under the light, he crossed the basement into the shadows, calling softly, "Where are you, Sidney? Come on, Sid. I hear you. Here, kitty."

Kitty? Dana froze to the spot in mortification. Fur, not talons but claws, and yellow eyes. Of course.

Gabe emerged from the darkness with a fat black bundle in his arms. He was scratching under its chin and the evil gold eyes were slit in pleasure, a strong purr issuing from the arched throat.

"Sidney came with the house, but he roams a lot. He always comes home when he can't chisel a meal out of somebody else."

Sidney swatted at Gabe's chin and the man settled the cat on his shoulder, a position he must have been accustomed to, for the purr grew even louder and his tail swished wide behind his master's head.

Dana let out a deep sigh as Gabe studied her, his eyes dancing in amusement. "He is fat and demanding and promiscuous," her landlord said. "But he isn't evil."

Dana rolled her eyes heavenward, then covered them with both hands. "I'm so embarrassed!" she groaned.

His laughter rang out again and Sidney jumped from his shoulder to the stairs as Gabe took Dana into his arms. "I'm not laughing at you," he assured her, stroking her wet hair back. "It just strikes me funny that you're willing, even eager, to dip your toes in a volcano but you're afraid of a cat in the dark."

Dana glanced up at him ruefully. "It's all those horror movies Jack dragged me to."

Gabe turned her to the stairs and pushed her up ahead of him. "Well, I'll fix him for that when he gets home."

Now she didn't want to go upstairs. She wanted to stay in Gabe's arms, her cheek resting against his rock-hard chest, hearing the strong, steady heartbeat against her ear as though it were the pace of her own body. But he hurried her uncertain pace with a slap on the seat of her jeans.

"Move it!" he ordered. "It'll be time to fix breakfast before we ever get dinner."

They topped the stairs into the light and sanity of the

kitchen, and Dana tried hard to get her emotions back
in balance.

"Why don't you go dry your hair," Gabe said,
pulling open the refrigerator. "I'll fix dinner. I knew
you'd figure a way to get out of it."

She grimaced at him. "That episode may have been
fun for you but it scared me out of my socks."

He looked over the refrigerator door down at her
bare feet. "And put some slippers on."

Counting to ten, she made her way back upstairs to
dry her hair and obediently don her slippers. The man
was going to drive her crazy!

By the time Dana ran downstairs, a sharp, spicy smell
was coming from the kitchen and there was a pot of
coffee and two mugs on the stone hearth in the living
room. The fire burned merrily and Dana succumbed to
a smile of pure happiness.

At that moment, Gabe, who had donned a plaid flannel shirt in shades of blue, emerged from the kitchen
with a platter of sandwiches and noted her expression.
"Pleased with yourself that you got out of it, aren't
you?" he teased.

She sank down to the carpet as he placed the sandwiches beside the coffeepot. "Sandwiches are hardly
duck à l'orange, you know," she said, raising an eyebrow. "No need to act so superior."

He slid her a dark glance. "You're going to pay for
your ingratitude." Then he offered her the sandwich
plate. "Taste before you judge."

The sandwich, almost too wide to fit into her mouth,
contained a fat, succulent German sausage with Swiss
cheese, sprouts and pickle. It was delicious.

"Well?" he asked.

She made a so-so gesture with her hand. "It's all right."

"What?" he demanded indignantly, and she burst into peals of laughter. "You little brat." He grinned at her as he handed her a steaming mug of coffee. "If you didn't look so delicious yourself, I'd paddle you for that."

She put a self-conscious hand to the wild hair framing her pink, freckled skin. "Without makeup and with electricity in my hair?" she asked. She wasn't fishing for a compliment, but was genuinely surprised.

He shrugged, leaning back against the sofa and stretching his long legs out. He put the sandwiches and the coffeepot between them. "We've all got our preferences. For the first time since you came, you look more Warrenton than San Francisco."

"What have you got against San Francisco?"

"Nothing. I'm just ready to be in Warrenton."

"Ready?"

"Yes, ready. When I came here two years ago it was as though at this point in my life I was destined to fix my position at this place in the universe. I felt at home instantly." He bent a knee up and rested his elbow on it, his cup balanced comfortably in that hand. "The way you look right now is the way I felt that day, as though you've marched out with purpose, headed for whatever it is you've always wanted."

Dana put her cup down, studying the dark liquid in it. She gave him a frail smile. "I guess I feel...comfortable...for the first time in a long while."

"As though you've come home?" he suggested quietly.

Afraid to admit it, she said instead, "As though I've found a haven."

He gave her a smile that was both gentle and threatening. "You realize that your haven has a wolf?" he asked.

She admitted gravely, "I do sometimes sense danger."

"Good," he said easily. "As long as you're aware." And he bit into his sandwich.

They were talking over the following week's work schedule when the telephone rang.

"It's your turn to answer the phone," Gabe said, refilling his coffee cup.

Dana shook her head. "It's my turn to clear the table."

"What table?" he demanded. "We're eating on the floor."

She smiled sweetly. "I know. Better get the phone."

With a threatening grin over his shoulder, Gabe loped into the kitchen. Then he was back in an instant.

"Phone for you."

"For me?" She stood in surprise and was conscious of him turning to watch her as she crossed to the phone. "Hello?" she said into the receiver.

"Dana? It's your father." Barton Freeman announced himself as only he would have to, she thought, trying to cope with the shock of hearing his voice. She recognized it instantly, but it said something for their relationship that he had thought she might not know it was he. "What in the hell are you doing in Oregon?" he demanded.

The predictably quarrelsome quality in his voice brought her out of her openmouthed silence. On the few occasions when she had seen him, they'd fought like the born enemies they seemed to be.

"I'm working," she replied shortly. "What do you want?"

The clear phone connection was absolutely still for several seconds, then Freeman's voice scolded, "Is that any way to talk to your father?"

"Forgive me," she said sarcastically. "Guess I'm out of practice."

After another brief silence he said condemningly, "Haven't changed, have you? You're just like your mother."

No vitriolic string of profanity could have hurt her more. She swallowed pain and said swiftly, "Look, if you've called to insult me—"

"I called you," he interrupted loudly, "to tell you that I'm speaking at the Oregon Newspaper Publishers' Association convention in Portland. I'd like to see you."

That statement brought a myriad of emotions to a painful point in her throat. She felt shock, fear, dread and, uppermost, outright panic.

"Warrenton's a hundred miles from Portland," she said in an attempt to discourage him.

"I'm renting a car."

"I told you I'm working."

Ignoring that, Freeman asked, "Who answered the phone?"

"My boss."

"At your home?"

Startled, confused, she replied, "He lives with me. I mean, I live with him," she corrected, then realized that did nothing to change the conclusion she could hear him jumping to in the silence. "I'm renting Jack's room," she said after a heavy sigh. Red-faced, she looked up to see Gabe unabashedly listening, amusement in his eyes. She turned her back to him.

"Is Jack there?" Freeman asked.

"He's in Afghanistan," she replied wearily. "Barton—"

Her father muttered a pithy expletive. "What the hell are you two running away from anyway?"

"Our happy childhood memories!" she snapped. "Look, Barton! Jack's on assignment, and I'm trying to start over without having to run into Scott every day. Why the parental concern all of a sudden?"

Silence again. "I'll be there Thursday morning," he said.

"I'm working Thursday morning," she repeated.

Gabe came around in front of her as her father insisted that he could arrive later and see her after work.

"I'll be busy after work," she said, turning away from Gabe as he tried to speak to her. He reached around her and took the phone from her. "Hold on a minute, Mr. Freeman," he said, then covered the mouthpiece with the palm of his hand. "Does he want to see you?" he asked Dana quietly.

"I don't want to see him!" she whispered harshly.

"I'll give you Thursday off."

"I don't *want* Thursday off!"

"What does he want?"

"I don't care."

"That isn't fair," he said. "Maybe he's trying to build a bridge."

"I'd rather get my feet wet!" She glared at Gabe, reaching for the phone. He held it out of reach.

"Tell him you'll see him," he said.

"I won't!"

He studied her flushed face evenly. "Afraid?"

"Sure!" she admitted angrily. "All he's ever done is hurt me, and I'm not going to set myself up for it again."

Gabe looked back at her for a long moment, and she saw pity and a curious tenderness in his eyes. She put her hand out for the phone, and he brought it down but put it to his mouth instead of in her hand.

"What time Thursday, Mr. Freeman?" he asked.

Dana ran from the kitchen, through the living room and up the stairs to the sanctuary of her room. She closed the door and threw herself on the bed, consumed by a terror as stark as what she had experienced in the dark basement earlier. And besides that terror was an anger so hot she saw red. How dare Gabe do that to her! How dare he take something as personal from her as the choice of whether or not to see her father again!

Once she had been old enough to understand, Dana had expected nothing from her mother because she saw that she had nothing to give. She was beautiful, delicately built and completely without substance. She loved no one but herself and was interested in nothing but that which gave her pleasure. It was an ugly truth, but Dana accepted it. When she died of cancer less than a year ago, the only emotion Dana felt was surprise that anything, even killer cells, had been able to grow in her.

But her father had been a different matter. On the few occasions when he'd spent any length of time at home—at birthdays, during Christmas, at graduations—he had seemed so alive, so dynamic, that Dana resented his absence and his negligence. Hatred grew rapidly and powerfully. During Dana's teenage years she had enjoyed baiting him when he came home because she sensed that it hurt him, and that pleased her.

The only time she ever allowed him to do anything for her was when she accepted his offer of a job on the staff of the *Daily News* after college. Though she hated Barton Freeman, she had respect for his publishing empire, for his insistence on the truth and the responsibility with which he wanted it reported. But she had wanted no other link with him than that, not then and not now. She did not want to see him Thursday.

The door opened and Gabe came through with a snifter filled with an amber liquid. She rolled to a sitting position in the middle of the bed, turning her back to him.

She felt the bed take his weight, then the touch of his hand on her shoulder. She shook it off.

"Go away," she said coldly.

"I've brought you a brandy."

"I don't want it."

"It's been a rough day. You need it."

She snickered. "You'd better get out before I forget you've got seventy pounds on me."

She heard the glass connect with the top of the night-stand before she was taken roughly by the arm and turned around. She looked into his impatient expression with wide, wounded eyes.

"How old are you anyway?" he asked, his eyes snapping. "Dana MacKenzie, star reporter, four years old. Is that the byline you're looking for?"

She leapt at him, her free hand curled to scratch, and landed on top of him on the old, bouncy mattress. She fell flat against him, fighting the movement of the springs that made her awkward, while trying to evade his shackling hands.

"You rat!" she screamed at him. "What difference does it make to you whether or not I make peace with my father?'' Then a dark thought occurred to her, and she said spitefully, ''Of course, you don't want me out of his will, you being so interested in me and all!''

For an instant he was still. The dark fan of his lashes lay against angular cheekbones for a quiet moment, and the look he gave her was dark with anger. Then he rolled over suddenly, pinning her to the cool bed-spread, her dark hair splayed across the colorful fabric.

''Money has nothing to do with it,'' he said breathless-ly, as though biting back his anger was costing him. ''There's always a second chance to find someone to share your life, but with parents you only get one shot.''

She pushed at his chest, writhing under him to free herself. ''He had his chance and he blew it!''

''Don't be so unforgiving,'' he chided. He pinned her troublesome hands over her head and glared down at her. ''He lived with your mother, too, remember? Imagine what life was like for him.''

Dana frowned at him suspiciously, her struggles stilled. ''How do you know about her?''

''Jack and I spent a lot of empty hours in Nam talk-ing. All kinds of things come out of you that you never talk about under normal circumstances.''

Thinking back, Dana realized that all her memories of her mother related to what she withheld rather than what she gave: the total lack of emotion in her eyes; her cold, impersonal touch; her notable absence when either of her children was sick or hurt. What must it have been like to share a bed with a woman like that?

Then, instantly following that thought, was the same question applied to the man who now lay atop her, his body pressed to hers from breastbone to knee. And as the thought formed, her body came alive with heat and tension, every nerve ending vibrating with awareness.

Impaled by Gabe's shadowy blue eyes, in which she saw the same realization dawn, she lay absolutely still, breath trapped in her lungs.

He watched the play of emotion in her turbulent eyes, then his gaze roamed her face, taking in her sudden rush of color, the delicate flare of her nostrils, halting finally in fascination on her mouth.

A frown line appeared between his eyes as his mouth came down with slow deliberation. He kissed her sweetly, gently, as though afraid she would break or disappear. Pulling back, he looked into her face, and his eyes ignited at what he saw there.

No sensuous taking of her lips could have touched her as deeply as that tender kiss. Scott's every touch had been for his own gratification, without regard for her pleasure or her pain. Gabe's kiss held such kindness, and the experience was so new, that the longing for more was bright in her eyes.

He swooped on her this time with an ardor that delighted her. His tongue filled her mouth with sensuous pleasure, and she drew on it, stroking it with her own. She arched her torso against his confining body, feeling the tough breastplate of his chest muscles against her cupped softness. The mattress bounced and she groaned inarticulately against his mouth as he turned to lay beside her.

Sensations hinted at but never quite known before began to pulse along her limbs. The shifting of his body denied her the closeness she sought, and she wriggled closer to him, launching her own assault on his mouth.

Finally, Gabe's strong arms held her away, and he rolled off her, still pinning her wrists.

"I'd like an apology," he said raggedly, "for that crack about your money."

Angry at him and at herself, Dana replied coolly, "Don't hang by your toes."

"An apology," he repeated, leaning down to kiss her again until she was senseless, "or we take this...communication...to its conclusion."

She'd be lost, she knew, entangled with Gabe in the throes of lovemaking. She'd commit herself to loving him and leave herself open to pain all over again.

She glared at him. "I'm sorry."

"And you're meeting your father Thursday."

Though he didn't repeat it, she knew the same threat applied. "Why not?" she said stiffly. "It is my life. The least I can do is fall in with your plans for it."

"Your plan was a dead end, cupcake."

"That's been my address lately."

"Oh, spare me!" he said sharply, getting to his feet to look down on her, hands on his hips. "I'm not going to let you write yourself into some soap-opera role of the much-abused heroine. You had a tough childhood and a bad marriage but that doesn't give you the right to hide when other people need you."

With a scream of rage, Dana leapt to her feet to confront him nose to nose—or nose to collarbone. "Get out of my room! If I'm paying the rent I don't have to listen to my character being dissected...."

With a firm push of Gabe's finger on her shoulder she bounced to a sitting position on the bed.

"You haven't paid any rent yet," he reminded her darkly. "I'm your landlord, and your employer, and by God one day I'm going to be your lover, so you'd better give a thought to what I have to say. So far, since your divorce, it sounds as if you've had a holding action. That's okay...."

"Why, thank you."

"But now," he spoke over her, "you have to move ahead and reach out or end up a pitiful recluse caught in a Victorian decline."

"Ah!" she said, as though all was suddenly clear. "This is where you tell me that a fling with you is just what I need to straighten me out. Good line, Cameron. Good line."

"I've never taken a frightened virgin to bed," he corrected brutally.

For some reason she couldn't understand, her face flamed. "I was married, remember? I'll admit I've never 'flown'—" She repeated his word caustically. "—as you promised we would, but I am no longer a virgin."

"Hard to tell," he noted with an arched eyebrow. "You protect your feelings by putting up bars."

"They've been hurt," she told him with a quiver in her now pale lips.

"I'm sorry," he said gravely. "But they're going to hurt forever if you never let anybody else in—me or your father—to let you know you're loved."

"He *never* loved me!" she screamed at him, tears falling. "And you haven't known me long enough to love me."

"See?" he replied quietly. "Bars. You hide behind them, and you never know what miracles can happen in the space of a few days. Good night, Dana."

Gabe closed the door as she pithily described his forebears.

Chapter Six

Monday and most of Tuesday passed in a blur of fever-
ish activity. With deadline coming up Wednesday
noon, Dana learned to sell subscriptions to the Warrenton *Register* over the counter and to handle complaints
over the phone. She learned to speed up her typesetting
and to tune out the banging racket of the printing half
of the process while writing her own stories. She laid
out ads and put them together.

A new skill that provided a lot of entertainment was
editing five pages of country news—typed single-
spaced by a seventy-three-year-old correspondent in
neighboring Hammond—into a half column of chum-
my news.

"Have you ever heard so many adjectives?" she
asked Gabe Tuesday afternoon. He sat across the office
at his desk, typing what must have been sixty words a
minute with his two index fingers. He paused to look at
her, a pencil between his teeth.

She had remained silent all of Monday after their
weekend argument, but in the face of his continued
good humor, she had given up.

"'Young Priscilla Olson, daughter of Lydia and Carl
Olson, granddaughter of Mabel and Olaf Olson and

Trygve and Vesla Knutinen, visited Hammond Friday night and Saturday morning. She arrived in a persimmon wool suit with an ivory scarf and persimmon-and-ivory spectator pumps. Isn't it good to see those coming back?'" Dana paused to throw him an amused grin and to speculate, "I presume she means the shoes." Then she read on. "'She is studying arithmetic in Portland—'" Dana looked up again with a frown of confusion.

Gabe was grinning. "She's an accounting major."

"Ah." Dana scribbled a note in the margin, then continued reading. "'... but tells me it always feels so good to come home to little Hammond. She would have stayed through Sunday but hinted that a young man was anxiously awaiting her return. I suspect it's Harold Pederakis, son of our own bookmaker, Julia Pederakis, who also attends Portland State.'" Dana's head came up again, laughter in her eyes. "We have a grandmother in this town who's a bookie?"

Gabe was laughing now. "She earns extra money by handcrafting cloth-covered books and repairing old bindings. Sift it down to something usable."

"Won't she be angry if we cut it down?"

"Of course. She always calls me to complain. But I pay her for every inch of copy she sends, and that keeps her happy. Believe it or not, those words are pure gold to some of our little old subscribers."

IT WAS SIX O'CLOCK when Gabe looked up from his typewriter again.

"Ready for a break?" he asked, seeing Dana kneading the muscles in her neck.

"If you are." She rotated her shoulders and threw her head back, stretching from side to side. "How long do we have to stay," she asked, her voice strangled by her gyrations, "in order to be ready for tomorrow?"

He leaned back in his chair, pointing to the pasteup boards against the far wall holding ten blank page formats ready to be filled with type. "Until at least six or seven of those ten pages are pasted up. I'm usually here until two or three in the morning and back again a few hours later."

She grimaced. "Honest?"

"Honest." He smiled and stood up, giving a long stretch. She had to look away from his long, fit body to keep her mind on business. "But you can go home whenever you're ready. Dee will be back to help me after dinner."

Since their argument Sunday she'd been working even harder than before, unconsciously hoping to dispel the vague image in her mind of a frightened virgin wearing her face.

"I'd like to see how you put it together," she said.

"Then you're welcome to stay. But it will take both of us at full efficiency tomorrow."

"You aren't the only one who can stay up all night and function the following day, you know."

"I just thought you'd appreciate the choice," he said mildly.

"Well, I don't want it, thanks," she responded testily.

He came to sit on the edge of her desk. "You sound like you need a nap already."

She slammed both hands noisily on the desk top and sprang to her feet. Standing, she had a fractional height advantage over his sitting position. But he didn't look the least bit intimidated by her stance.

She sighed irritably. "Shall we go to Pop's for a salad?"

After a moment's silence Gabe got to his feet and grabbed his jacket off the back of his chair. "You have a salad. I'll have a cheeseburger and french fries."

"You'll die of indigestion," she warned.

He laughed. "It's traditional. Aren't newspapermen junk-food addicts in San Francisco? In journalism school we were taught that it was as much required as the press card in the band of a felt hat."

Dana slid him a taunting glance as she passed before him into the fragrant, dusky evening. It smelled of evergreens and the sea.

"You may go back that far, but I don't."

DANA LEANED on her elbows, watching Gabe eat a piece of coconut cream pie, and thought he must have the strongest constitution she'd ever seen. Her stomach was tied in knots from hurrying through one job after another that day, and though Gabe had worked twice as hard as she had, he seemed entirely relaxed. *Of course, he's used to the pace,* she told herself. *And he's laid-back by nature.* Didn't he tear her apart verbally Sunday night without even batting an eye?

"Ready for Thursday?" he asked without preamble.

Her stomach knotted a little tighter. She looked up at him blandly. "For the routine to start all over again? Sure I am. I type the TV section until news starts coming in—"

"You know what I mean." He pushed the dessert plate away and pulled his coffee closer.

She made a production of poking at the ice cubes in the bottom of her iced-tea glass with the plastic straw. "Yes, I know what you mean," she replied without looking up. "But I don't think my relationship with my father is any concern of yours."

"Even as your friend?" he asked, undaunted by her rudeness.

She raised her eyes, their dark depths filled with a wounded look. "A friend wouldn't have taken the choice of seeing or not seeing him out of my hands."

"Did you really plan to spend the rest of your life without ever seeing him again?" Gabe crossed his arms on the tabletop and leaned toward her. "You've got to deal with this. You've got to establish a relationship with the man. If he didn't care about you, he wouldn't have called."

"What about all the times I wanted to see him and he didn't have time for me?" she demanded, her voice quiet but angry.

He fixed her with a paternal look and said gently, "That was probably a legitimate complaint when you were eighteen, but now that you're a woman, can't you be bigger than that?"

"Why the hell should I?"

"Because you can never give too much. You can never love too hard."

Thoroughly exasperated, Dana leaned toward him again. "Forgive me, Gabe, but since you're a single man whose only family is a sister, I don't think you're qualified to comment."

He admitted her point with a rueful smile. "Maybe I'm trying to change my marital status, but you're not being very cooperative."

"I thought," she said calmly, "that you weren't interested in taking a frightened virgin to bed."

"You misunderstand," he pointed out just as calmly. "I want to love you into a brave, experienced woman. I care about you."

She went back to the ice in the glass with a vicious

jab of the straw. "You could have fooled me Sunday night."

Gabe leaned back against the red vinyl upholstery, tightening jaw muscles an indication of his irritation.

"Can we take off the gloves until tomorrow afternoon?" he asked stiffly. "It's hard enough to put the paper to bed without carrying on World War Three."

"You brought it up," she reminded, slipping out of the booth.

DEE ARRIVED a half hour later and took over the typing chores while Gabe disappeared into the darkroom and Dana put together the last-minute ads, checking everything per Gabe's instructions against the run sheet, a schedule of the current week's ads and their sizes.

Dee transferred her punch tape to the printing half of the Just-o-Writer. Sure that all was working smoothly, she went to the pasteup boards and began replacing standing headlines, those used every week, in their proper places on the empty pages.

"I don't suppose Mr. Sorensen called to change his mind about the grocery ad?" she asked Dana, who sat at the art stool at the end of the row of boards.

Dana frowned. "No. That means we're in trouble, huh?"

Darlene made a horrible grimace. "Worse than that. I don't know how Gabe pulls us through week after week. With fishing all but done around here and logging slowed down to a crawl, business for our advertisers has slumped drastically. Gabe's carrying advertising accounts three and four months, even longer if they've been steady customers. Sorensen was one of the few of our accounts comfortable enough to pay regularly."

Dana stared at the ad for camping gear she was putting together for Ben Wagner's store, plagued by guilt. Sorensen had been angry when he'd arrived in the *Register*'s office, and she couldn't help but think that her smart remarks sparked his temper enough to finally force him into pulling his advertising.

"Well, don't worry about it," Darlene said, patting Dana's shoulder as though she were the older of the two. "He's been a pain in the posterior for months. And anyway, I hear your father is coming to visit. He was one of the judges on the ONPA contest board last year when Gabe won first place in several categories for newspapers under five thousand circulation."

Startled, Dana looked up at Darlene. "They know each other?"

"I don't think so," Darlene replied, moving the razor blade Dana was just about to put her arm on as she spun around distractedly. "Your father wrote to Gabe. I think he offered him a job."

"Do you know what he wrote back?" Dana asked, her voice a little strangled.

"He called," Darlene answered, reaching across Dana to retrieve a blue pencil from the cup. "They talked for a long time, but you know our fearless leader. He's happy here. He thanked him, but said no."

For a moment, the realization that Gabe and her father knew each other, if only by correspondence, threw Dana completely off balance. There was something unsettling about the knowledge that the two people in her life with whom she had the most difficulty dealing were able to deal with each other.

When Gabe emerged from the darkroom, close to midnight, Dana, now alone in the office, had all the ads ready and spread out on the makeup table.

"Good girl," he praised, pulling down his rolled-up sleeves. The night made the office cold even though it was spring. "Getting sleepy?"

"I've been sleepy for the last hour," she admitted, fighting back a yawn that would have verified her statement. "But I'm determined to see this through. What's next?"

"We place the ads first," Gabe instructed, leaning them up against the lip on the bottom of the pasteup boards. "Then we know where to put everything else. After you're here a while—" they looked at each other, a challenge tossed between them in the innocent words "—you'll know which of our accounts have been with us longest and deserve the best spots. Every advertiser is like a gift from heaven," he emphasized, "but some of them we cater to a little."

As he spoke, Gabe took Ben Wagner's ad and placed it in the bottom right-hand corner of the front page. That sparked something Dana recalled from an argument she'd once overheard in the composing room of the *Daily News*.

"Isn't it considered gauche and an offense against the objectivity in journalism ethic to let an advertiser have space on the front page?"

He grinned, slapping down the ad, then pressing it in place with a rubber roller. "If you're the San Francisco *Daily News*, I suppose it is. At the Warrenton *Register*, we're happy to have the advertiser, particularly if he's willing to pay a little more for a front-page spot."

Gabe moved to stand before page two. "Odd-numbered pages are considered prime ad locations because they get more attention. The eye lingers there longer."

"How come?"

"Imagine yourself reading the paper," he said.

She closed her eyes to oblige.

"Imagine your left arm suspended out there, probably leaning on nothing, while you're trying to read it."

"Oh, yeah."

"Those are the even-numbered pages in your left hand. However—" he placed a small ad for the local bookstore in the lower left-hand corner of the page "—page two is the feature page, and some businesses like to advertise there because they figure the intellectual types peruse it."

"Makes sense."

He moved to page three and picked out three of the ads on the table. "When placing several ads on a page, you do it pyramid style, largest on the bottom and so on." He did as he advised and stood back to look at it, his eyes narrowed. Then he picked up the Exacto knife and, gently using its point, moved a business name that Dana had placed slightly crooked.

"Sorry about that," she apologized.

"Don't be. You've done very well considering you've never made up an ad before. There." He replaced the knife and moved on to the next page. "Ideally, editorial copy should touch every ad on at least two sides. That way ads aren't competing with each other for attention."

He bypassed page four. "Four and seven will be your school story and pictures."

"Four and seven?" she questioned. "Why not four and five?"

"Because in a ten-page paper, five and six are an inside loose page. We make it the TV schedule so it can be easily removed and saved." He placed several ads on those pages as he spoke. "Restaurants like to advertise on those pages. Rate's a little higher there, too, because the subscriber consults that little sheet all week long, making it prime space. What have we got left?''

''One fairly large furniture store ad, and Darlene said to tell you she fixed the classified page and it's all ready.''

He took the ad from her. ''Then while I check to see if my prints are dry, would you write a short bio of yourself to go with your picture? We've got to introduce our new talent.''

She widened sleepy dark eyes at him. ''What picture?''

He looked back at her a moment without replying, his eyes softening while they studied hers. ''The one I took this morning while you were working on your school story. You were so engrossed you didn't even notice.''

''It had better be good,'' she warned teasingly.

''Not as good as Jack might have taken, perhaps,'' he admitted, ''but I'm not too bad.''

He wasn't a bad photographer at all, she decided half an hour later when he placed a two-column photo of her on the bottom half of the front page. Her eyes were riveted on her copy, her fingers poised on the typewriter.

''My hair's messy,'' she complained.

''Tousled,'' he said, putting a hand to it as he spoke. ''It makes you look like you've really torn at it to get to the heart of your story.''

He was right. She looked earnest and weary and somehow attractive. She had to smile. ''I like it.''

''So do I. Now get out of *my* hair so I can put this baby to bed. We might get home before we have to come back.''

Dana sat on the makeup table, her weary feet on a

chair, and watched Gabe cut and place and move and juggle until seven of the ten pages had almost taken shape. Columns fit magically under the standing heads Darlene had placed with what had looked like such random care. Well-balanced pages were taking form, completely filled except for news headlines.

She leapt off the table to take a closer look as he pasted up her pictures of the schoolchildren, bordering the pages with them, while her story ran in the middle with an impressive byline.

"Your pictures are good," he said.

She beamed, knowing he gave no idle praise. "Thank you. With a subject like that group, who could miss?"

The children fairly leapt off the page. She had managed to capture their exhilaration, their complete concentration, the thrill experienced by a winner, the loser's sadness, his feeble and then cheerful smile when consoled and teased by his classmates.

"I would have loved to take them all home with me," she laughed, then made a face at him, "but you'd have probably raised my rent."

"Darn right," he said. "Okay, that does it for tonight. I'll wind things up in the back. You might check for typos. That'll be your job in the morning while I'm slapping up the last three pages. Be back in a few minutes."

Dana was blue-penciling corrections when she remembered that Ben Wagner had called while Gabe was in the darkroom and had given her a change for his ad. It involved a change of artwork that Gabe would have to do in the darkroom. She'd better tell him now, she thought, before tomorrow morning's frantic wrapping-up pushed it from her mind.

She hurried through the back room to the black fabric door. Poking her head inside, she called his name. The radio he played while working was filling the darkness with the national anthem, and she guessed that he simply couldn't hear her. She advanced down the narrow corridor, guiding herself with her hand along the wall—as Gabe had told her to do the last time she came in—until the wall disappeared and she knew she was in the body of the room.

She shouted his name, competing with the final high notes of "La-and of the free...and the home of the brave."

Then there was quiet static as the radio station went off the air.

"Gabe?" she called her voice a trifle high. The darkness seemed to be moving around her, and she tried to reason herself into remaining calm. Sidney was safely at home. He would not fall out of some overhead shelf onto her shoulder, convincing her that the devil was loose in the dark. There was nothing in the dark, she told herself, that wasn't there when the lights were on.

Trouble is, she thought, groping for the wall that would help her find her way out again, the lights were *never* on in this place. That red bulb didn't count. Heaven knew what lurked in the corners that never saw the light of day.

"Gabe!" she called impatiently.

"Right here," his deep voice said from immediately behind her.

She spun around with a little scream, her heart lurching with new fright. The warm bulk of his body was like a radar beacon, and she put her arms around his waist, sagging against him in total relief.

"Where were you?" she demanded.

"Putting trash in the dumpster out back. What are

you doing in here?'' His arms came around her and pressed her closer, one hand making lazy, comforting circles on her back.

"I wanted to give you a message before I forgot. When you said you were going to wrap up things back here I thought you meant in the darkroom."

"Sorry. You okay?"

She sighed, feeling silly and very, very tired. "Yeah, I guess."

She felt him push her slightly away, then felt his hands at her waist. She uttered another little scream when he lifted her and placed her on a stool right behind her. He reached a hand out and the radio was silenced.

"What's the message?" he asked, his hands gently stroking her arms through the thin fabric of her sweater.

For a moment she couldn't remember who had called, much less what the caller had wanted. Her mind was filled with Gabe, his body between her jeans-clad knees, her feet hooked on the rung of the stool. He was so close she could feel his body heat, his breath against her cheek. Unable to help herself, she put both hands out to his chest and ran them lightly up to his shoulders. His muscles felt like armor plate under the flannel shirt. She moved her fingers to his neck, looking for warmth and pliability.

I'm falling in love, she realized in panic. *I can't stop it. I love his face, his mind, his body, his talent. I'm losing control.*

She felt his indrawn breath and then his now stubbly chin against her hand. "Was it..." he asked on a swallow that she felt with a sensitive thumb that rested against his throat. "Was it...personal or...business?"

Her voice was raspy. "Business...I think."

Fascinated now, she moved her fingers up to gently chart his face. They moved over his prickly jaw to the warm softness of his lips. She pulled his head closer to plant a gentle kiss there, and he did not resist. Then she pulled back to explore his strong, straight nose and his eyes. She felt the silky flutter of his eyelashes as she touched them, then the animallike toss of his head as her touch tickled. That was followed by a very predatory growl as he swooped on her lips to begin an exploration of his own.

His kiss had none of the lightness of hers; it had a forceful, aggressive quality that both flattered and thrilled her. As his mouth kept her busy, his hands swept up under her sweater, and she obligingly raised her arms so that he could pull it off. He tossed it aside, then reached around her to unhook her bra. It quickly joined her sweater.

Whatever thread of the message remained in her mind, whatever vague notion she still held of events barreling out of control, fled as his warm, gentle hands closed over her breasts. She gasped with pleasure at the newness of this delicious sensation. She had never been touched as though her body was precious, as though every inch of her skin was a path for a loving hand to follow with reverence and fascinated concentration. His hands opened and closed over her repeatedly, as though savoring the imprint of her breasts in his palms.

He was right, she thought, drugged with longing. *We should be lovers.*

Gabe tugged her arms from around him and, putting her hands at his shoulder, pulled her to a standing position. With her feet gripping the rungs of the stool, she found herself half a head taller than he. But he was unzipping her jeans, pulling them down clear of her bottom, and awareness fled again as his hands caressed the backs of her thighs and up to take two deliciously bold handfuls of her bottom.

Sensation rising in her like a stoked fire, she wrapped her arms around his neck, delighting in his possessive management of her body. He traced the line of her hips over and over until she thought she would die of pleasure. When she felt his fingertips in the waistband of her panties, she hugged him tighter, her voice a mere whisper. "Oh, Gabe."

He nuzzled her neck. "Shall we fly?"

"Oh, yes!" She held him tighter still. "I want to fling! I want to forget."

It was a moment before she surfaced enough to realize that though he still held her, the caressing had stopped. The shoulders she held had stiffened and he was pulling her jeans into place, zipping and buttoning.

"What is it?" she asked softly.

He expelled a ragged breath, and she felt her sweater and the lacy fabric of her bra pushed into her hands. "Sit," he ordered gently.

"Gabe—"

"Get dressed," he said, impatience in his voice. "We'll talk about it at home."

Reality replaced the euphoric feeling almost immediately, and she did as he asked, painful embarrassment and a chafing anger rising steadily and equally within her. In seconds, she managed to get hold of herself and dress.

He took her arm but she yanked it away.

"I'll find my own way out!" she snapped at him,

colliding as she turned into a piece of equipment. "Ouch!"

"Not through the enlarger, you won't. This way." He pulled on her as she began to head off in the wrong direction again.

Unable to shake off his hand this time, she tolerated its pressure as he led her through the narrow corridor to the back room. He freed her, opening the door to the front office. His face a stony mask, Gabe unplugged the coffeepot, turned on the message-taking device attached to the telephone, then pulled the front door open, waiting in silence for Dana to pass ahead of him.

Glaring at him, she stormed out to the van.

They drove home in silence, and it wasn't until Dana marched through the house to the kitchen and snapped the burner on under the teakettle that she spun around on him, tearing her jacket off.

"Why," she demanded furiously, "are you angry at me? You're the one who keeps talking about becoming my lover and changing me from a frightened virgin. What happened?"

"Dana." He gripped the back of a kitchen chair and said firmly but quietly, "I don't want a fling. I came here to put down roots. I want commitment and permanence."

She looked at him in confusion, sure he had misunderstood her. "I want to share your bed," she said. "I want to be your lover."

Gabe shrugged out of his jacket and tossed it on the back of the chair. Then he sat down, shaking his head.

"I'm flattered and I'm honored," he said with grim reluctance, as though he himself couldn't quite believe what he was about to add. "But... that's not enough."

"Not enough?" she repeated.

He shook his head, giving her a humorless laugh. "From the British Isles to Japan, I've written everyone else's story but my own, and I came here to do just that. I'm going to make my mark in this beautiful little place, and I want a loving woman beside me." He fixed her with that engaging grin he often used to cover the things he couldn't say. "Not a 'flinging' one."

Dana sat across from him, folding her arms on the table and leaning toward him. "Do you know what century this is, Cameron? What year? What era?"

"I know," he admitted quietly, folding his arms to lean toward her, looking into her eyes. "It's the twentieth century and the age of open marriages and free love. But not for me. Not anymore. I came here because I'm no longer a casual man. Slices of life, however incisive, aren't enough for me anymore. I want the whole pie. I want a woman who's two hundred percent dedicated to me."

Frowning, confused, Dana said, "I have a career."

He laughed. "I don't want you baking bread and locked in the house with babies. I want you ferreting out the news, scooping the local daily, calling me to fix dinner because you've got a story. But I want you loving me all that time, and when you come home, I want to see us in your eyes. Not just my reflection, but everything the two of us mean to you, because you'll see us in mine."

She shrugged helplessly, palms upward. "I...I can't do that yet."

He nodded. "I know that. But I can't be casual about you. So what do we do?"

"I won't move out," she said, angling her chin. "My rent's paid even if I didn't pay it."

He dismissed that option. "That'd be admitting defeat anyway. I could just continue to try to change your mind."

"And I yours."

"Sounds fair." He went to the stove, where the kettle was whistling.

"Cocoa or tea?"

Dana sighed and pushed wearily at her hair. "I think a double bourbon. You wear me out, Cameron."

Gabe smiled at her over his shoulder, spooning instant cocoa into two mugs. "When I wear you *down*, let me know."

She glared at him as he brought their mugs to the table. "I thought I did that in the darkroom."

"You showed me you care," he said, turning his chair around to sit astride it. "But you don't trust me yet. It takes caring and trust to make love."

Dana sipped her cocoa, then rested her chin in her hand and faced Gabe across the table. "You know you're a dinosaur, don't you? I mean, I've heard of women being rejected because they failed to give out, but never because they chose to give in."

"I didn't reject you," he corrected, looking into his cup, then up at her. "I'm just saving you from yourself. Have you ever had an affair?"

"No."

"Must be my journalist's mind after all these years, but every good story has to have a beginning, a middle and an end. You've got to know where you started and know where you're going to make the story real, to make it live. The uncertainty is what makes an affair so unsatisfying to me. All you're entitled to is the here and now because that's all you're committed to. No shared past and no common future—just today."

"I was committed to Scott and look what happened," she reminded him grimly.

"Scott was a creep," Gabe opined. "I, on the other hand, am a prince. And when you build a marriage right, no one loses. Lovers never lose."

Dana eyed him suspiciously. "Who said that?"

"I did," he said with a laugh.

Rolling her eyes heavenward, she pushed away from the table and stood up. "It's a relief that we have that on good authority. I'm going to bed."

Gabe, too, rose to his feet. "No good-night kiss?"

"Gabe..."

"Come on," he said good-naturedly. "We agreed to keep working on changing each other's mind." As he spoke, he walked around the table to her and took her face in his hands.

At the instant of contact, she felt the now familiar rush of feeling to all her extremities and that warmth at the heart of her that seemed to grow hotter still while radiating feeling.

She put her hands on his waist to steady herself as he kissed her deeply, drawing on that inner source of heat that fused them together. Then he freed her mouth and wrapped her in his arms, holding her close.

"Now think about coming home to this every night," he said. "Loving, sheltering arms that are yours alone."

She drew away, smiling a challenge. "And you wouldn't give me that if we simply lived together?"

"Good point," he said, drawing her back into his arms, holding her head to his chest with one hand while the other traced a gentle circular pattern on her back. "Think about it this way, Dana. Think about how it feels—then analyze how it would feel with the knowledge that it's yours forever. Every single day or night from this day to infinity, I will be right here, arms open, when you need to laugh or cry or just take shelter." He enveloped her in both arms and held her even closer. "Always, Dana. Not just today or tomorrow. Forever."

Dana clung, feeling hot tears in her throat. Her parents' devotion to her and Jack had always been casual at best, and uncertainty and a feeling of being lost were most of what she remembered from her years of growing up. Burdens were borne alone and fears were suffered without comfort because the loving arms every child needs had never been there for her.

She was finally coming to the realization that every woman as well as every child had that same need. But a love such as Gabe offered deserved a love that generous in return. And she simply wasn't sure, after all she'd been through, that she had it in her to give.

She drew away slightly and stood on tiptoe to plant a gentle kiss on his lips.

"I'm not sure I'm worthy of that fine a love," she said, a solitary tear falling.

He brushed it away with his thumb, his eyes dark and steady. "I am."

She smiled. "But I have to know, too. Good night, Gabe. Don't give up, okay?"

"It's a promise."

Chapter Seven

Wednesday morning was so frantic that Dana was able to do little else than try to decipher Gabe's barked orders and carry them out to the best of her ability, which she discovered to her pride was fairly respectable. She pasted up a page while Gabe did some photos for a last-minute ad, made up the ad while Gabe finished the pasteup, deflected all of Gabe's phone calls and proofread every line of copy that wasn't preset syndicated material.

Ten minutes before the noon deadline, Gabe's blue van screeched into the daily paper's parking lot in Astoria and Gabe disappeared through the loading bay in the back of the rambling modern building.

After a quick lunch during which Gabe and Dana spoke very little, they returned to the office to restore order out of the chaos left from the morning's duties. Cleanup, she discovered, was a monumental part of a job that required stacks of notes, rough copies of every story, typed galleys of every story, which were then trimmed before being pasted up, and hundreds of miles of punch tape. Wax and litter were everywhere.

Then it was time to retrieve twenty-five hundred

copies of the newspaper magically transformed from their week's labors.

Perched on the wooden crate beside the Addressograph, Dana studied her story with cub-reporter excitement. Gabe's sharp prints of her photographs were beautifully reproduced and contributed to the action and excitement of her story. Her name appeared in bold type, and she felt just as proud as she had the first time the city editor of the San Francisco *Daily News* had given her a byline. This time she had literally done it all herself, from covering the story and writing it to typing it and helping Gabe paste it up. She was grinning from ear to ear when Gabe dropped the last bundle of papers at her feet in a cloud of dust.

He smiled broadly at her expression, a kinship coming alive between them for the first time since their argument in the small hours of the morning. "Kind of turns you off big-city reporting for good, doesn't it?"

"It's like making your own potato chips," she said absently, studying her pictures one final time.

"Say what?"

She looked up into Gabe's frown of puzzlement. "They probably taste the same as store-bought ones, but the sense of accomplishment makes them that much more delicious."

He put a diagnostic hand to her forehead. "Definitely overtired. Let's get this show on the road so we can get you to bed."

His teasing mood sparked hers. "I thought we had that out last night," she said impishly.

Darlene, feeding address plates into the machine, giggled.

Gabe leaned against the antique device and fixed Dana and the girl with a mock glare.

"If you two don't have this thing out by six-thirty you can forget the pizza I promised."

Darlene yanked her stool out from under his foot. "Then move your bod, buster. We've got work to do."

"Someday," Gabe threatened his young assistant, barely holding back a grin, "I'm going to fire you."

"Sure," she said complacently, flexing her fingers, "and someday you'll learn to type with your other eight fingers. Papers, Dana."

MR. FULTANO'S PIZZA in neighboring Astoria was crowded when they arrived just before seven. Background music competed with the deafening roar of a chorus of "Happy Birthday" being sung at a long table full of seven- and eight-year-olds. The din was deafening.

Dana and Darlene settled into a table for four in a back corner and waited while Gabe placed their order.

"This is what we need at the office!" Darlene shouted across the table.

Dana frowned. "Pizza?"

"Music!"

"Oh!" Dana nodded to be polite, unsure that what she heard blaring from the sound system was worthy of the name.

"I could get more typing done," Darlene told Gabe as he sat beside them, "if we had some good tunes to work by."

"A little Barry Manilow, Neil Diamond?" he asked with a grin.

She grimaced. "Actually, I had Def Leppard and Sammy Hagar in mind."

Gabe looked at Dana questioningly. "Who's that?"

"If you like Neil Diamond, you wouldn't want to

know. She'd have to play them when you were in the darkroom.''

The sound system announced their number, and Gabe went to pick up the order.

They laughed helplessly at each other's jokes and ate heartily. Gabe went back for more Pepsi and an ice-cream-sandwich dessert that was so delicious Dana forced it down despite being already stuffed.

Watching Darlene and Gabe tease each other, she felt sorry for her own parents. They had so much, yet it was somehow never enough and never gave them pleasure.

She couldn't imagine her father, sleeves rolled up after a long day, laughing with the underlings while he ate. He had worked hard for the publishing empire he had built, but she couldn't believe he'd had any fun along the way.

Gabe, on the other hand, took great pride in his work, enjoying it and the people who were part of it. Someone was always dropping in at the office to invite him to lunch or to simply say hello. He wanted so much to make the Warrenton *Register* a success, with its anti-quated equipment that he coaxed so lovingly.

A sigh escaped her as she wished desperately that there was something she could do to help.

"Oh, Dana." Darlene caught her jacket from the back of her chair as she and Dana trailed Gabe out of the restaurant. "Your dad called while you and Gabe were at the *Astorian* picking up the papers. I'm sup-posed to tell you he'll be here around ten tomorrow morning."

Having had little time to think about Barton Free-man's visit during the past few days, Dana now con-fronted the fact of her father's impending arrival with undiminished dread and an overwhelming desire to prevent this meeting. Gabe held the heavy wooden door open for her and Darlene, and she knew when she glanced up at him that he'd overheard their conversation. His eyes were watchful, analytical. She glared at him and didn't speak until Darlene had been delivered safely home.

"I suppose you're going to dock me for tomorrow," she said, wanting to discuss her father's visit without wanting him to know she wanted to. She thought that over for a moment and, realizing it was crazy, gave herself a mental shake.

She was, frankly, terrified and, despite his high-handedness, Gabe was calm and controlled. She desperately wanted to feel calm and in control tomorrow morning.

"Depends." He shot her a smile in the dark interior of the van. The traffic lights at the intersection of Harbor and Main sparkled against light raindrops on the windshield as Gabe turned the corner toward home.

"If you're open-minded and fair, we can call it a journalistic exercise and I'll pay you for it. If you're hardheaded and hard-nosed..." His voice trailed away, leaving the obvious unspoken, with a grin.

They pulled into the driveway and Gabe turned off the motor and the headlights. He sat quietly, without reaching for the door, almost as though he sensed she had something more to say.

"I'm scared," she admitted to the dark.

Gabe turned sideways on the seat to face her in the shadows, his eyes jewellike, almost mystical. "What do you think he's going to do to you?" he asked. "Or ask of you? He's your father, Dana."

"I don't know what he wants," she said, rubbing her

arms despite the warmth of the evening and the protection of the vehicle. "That's what's scary. He's always kept his distance before. Unlike you, he's never been the hearth-and-home type."

"There's got to be some of that in all of us," Gabe said gently. "With your mother gone, you and Jack are all he has. Maybe he's looking to find something with you that he couldn't build before."

Dana tried to absorb that, but one fact kept coming to the forefront of her thoughts and she shifted uncomfortably, the vinyl upholstery crunching loudly under her movements. "He never liked me," she said.

For a long moment he said nothing; then she felt his hand in her hair, shaping the back of her head, turning her averted face toward him. She wondered if her eyes shone for him the way his did for her.

"Are you afraid," he asked on a gentle whisper, "that you won't measure up to whatever it is he wants?"

Emotion rose within her in a rush, like fire up an open draft, constricting her lungs, clogging her throat with flame. "I've never measured up before. Not for him, not for Scott." A sob erupted. "And not for you."

"Oh, Dana!" His exasperated exclamation was met with noisy tears and flailing hands that tried, unsuccessfully, to ward off the strong arms that encircled her. He hauled her into his lap.

"That's absurd! The fact that your father wants to see you shows that you mean a lot to him, and according to Jack, Scott was a bastard." He held her tightly, his cheek against her hair. "As for me, you're everything I want. But I want all of you and forever. And I'm going to get you, even if I have to wait a while."

He stroked the hair away from her face and kissed the tip of her nose. "Look. Think about this. Are you paying attention?"

"Yes." She settled closer against him, waiting.

"Remember Sunday afternoon in the basement?"

"Yeah."

"You thought something evil with talons had landed on you."

"Yeah."

"And it turned out to be a harmless, home-loving pussycat. Fear and the dark can make you crazy. Face your father squarely, listen to him and tell him what you'd like from him from now on. But, most importantly, don't make your decision about him in the dark. Think about it. Consider it from his side as well as yours. Be fair."

Exhausted, confused, but infinitely comfortable in his arms, she lay quietly, absorbing his warmth, basking in the tenderness of his hand against her temple holding her fast against him.

"Come on," he said finally, pushing her gently to a sitting position. "Let's get you inside and to bed. You don't even have to come to the office tomorrow. When your father arrives, I'll bring him home to you."

"No!" she said too loudly, then, calming herself, added more quietly, "No, I'd like to be at the office when he comes. And I'd like you to be there. Okay?"

He kissed her cheek. "Okay."

"One more thing." She caught his hand as he reached past her to push her door open.

"Yeah?"

"Say we did get married. What would we do about my money?"

"Do we have to do anything about it?"

"Well," she suggested cautiously, "it could help the Warrenton *Register* get—"

"No." He stopped her abruptly. "The *Register* lives or dies on its own merit. But I'd want to stay here with it."

She shrugged. "I like it here."

"But forever?"

What am I doing, she thought frantically, but her lips were saying, "As long as you're here."

He looked back at her evenly, a small smile forming slowly in the shadows. "Hold that thought," he said. "And let it develop."

He leaned forward to kiss her lightly, then pushed her door open.

THE FIRST THING Dana noticed about her father as she saw him alight from a gray Lincoln Continental and walk across the street toward the Warrenton *Register*'s office was how much Jack resembled him.

Barton Freeman was slightly under six feet tall, several inches taller than Jack; his dark, close-cropped hair had grayed considerably. She could see his dark eyes from the middle of the office floor where she stood. He glanced up as he sprinted youthfully across the street, and she stepped back, though she doubted that he could see her.

"Here he comes," she said ominously to Gabe, who came from his desk to stand behind her. Gabe leaned down slightly to look through the window, putting a hand on Dana's shoulder. She took hold of it, lacing her fingers through it.

"Here he comes," she said again as her father approached the door. Unconsciously she leaned back against the bulwark of Gabe's body, her own slight frame stiffening as though preparing for impact. Gabe's light laugh sounded in her ears.

"Relax. He's not packing a gun that I can see. And you're standing on my foot."

Then Barton Freeman was closing the door behind him and they were staring at each other. He was wearing a gray leather jacket over a pale blue turtleneck and designer jeans, well cut and perfectly fitted to his slim body, which showed just the barest trace of a paunch.

Freeman studied Dana and Gabe where they stood close together in the middle of the office, and his eyes finally rested on their hands, clasped tightly on her shoulder.

He glanced at Gabe with a subtle smile. "Congratulations. My daughter has never clung to anyone in her life."

Gabe extended his free hand to Freeman, his left still firmly entwined in Dana's. "I'm Gabe Cameron, Mr. Freeman. Good to meet you at last."

"And you." Freeman shook hands with Gabe. "Tired of this town yet? That job's still open."

"Thanks, but I'm here for good." He glanced at the watch on the hand Dana still held and gently but firmly pulled away. "If you'll excuse me, I've got a county commissioners' meeting to cover. Dana will show you around."

"I've got to head back to Portland by three. Do you need her back before that?"

"She's got the day off."

Dana watched with a sense of panic as Gabe shrugged into his jacket. She took half a step toward him but with a casual wave and a "nice to meet you" tossed at her father, Gabe was gone.

Silence beat like a drum in her ears. She turned to

her father with a forced smile. "Well, if I'm supposed to show you around," she said gaily, "we might as well start with these."

She swept her hand toward the Just-o-Writer. "I'm sure we've got the distinction of being the only newspaper where these antiques are still in use. And you won't *believe* what's in the back! An Addressograph and a platemaker that must go back thirty years at least. Come on, I'll show you."

She started toward the back room and her father caught her arm. "It's a neat little operation," he said, his eyes roving her face, seeming to absorb every detail of Dana's features as though he'd been starving for them. "I can tell that from this office, and I knew it before from the depth of Cameron's reporting and the quality of his writing. What I came the extra hundred miles to see, Dana, is you."

She did a nervous pirouette. "Here I am."

He smiled at her working garb of jeans and a gray sweatshirt with a cartoon sketch of Shakespeare on the front. She had dressed deliberately as though it were any other day.

"Straining to see through the screen you're putting up against me, I'd say you look well. At least you did before Cameron left."

"I am," she said. But it wasn't entirely true, and the doubt was obvious in her voice.

"Want to take a ride?" Freeman suggested.

"Where?" she asked suspiciously.

"I thought you could suggest someplace where we can talk."

Knowing she could not avoid it, Dana suggested unenthusiastically, "The beach?"

His expression was doubtful. "The beach?"

She felt a smile form. "Californians go to the beach for sun. We Oregonians go for the drama and excitement."

He looked out the window, where the spring wind blew dust and blossoms in a whirlwind down the middle of the street. "We should certainly have that today. Let's go."

A completely different mood prevailed at Fort Stevens this day than the sunny atmosphere on the day she had been there with Gabe. But the weather had changed, she remembered, and they had been drenched and had a delicious dinner in front of the fire at home. Then her father had called and she and Gabe had had an argument. It brought a frown to her forehead to realize that that argument had never really ended.

She directed her father to the parking lot Gabe had used, then up the trail to the top of the sandy rise. Surf crashed, gulls called and the wind blew; she looked challengingly into her father's eyes. They were slitted against the wind, as dark as hers, and as challenging.

"Too cold for you?" she asked.

"You?" he countered.

"Nope."

"Then lead on."

Dana went ahead of her father down the trail, waiting at the bottom for him to catch up. "Reminds me of the Irish coast," he said, pausing to catch his breath.

"Got holdings there, too?" she asked. It was a snide remark and she knew it, but she was unable to hold it back.

He looked into her face, his eyes registering her intention. "A fishing cottage, as a matter of fact," he replied politely.

His good manners shamed her and she said, turning to lead the way down the beach, "I've always wanted a genuine Aran sweater."

"I'll bring one back for you," he said, trudging along beside her. "I'm going at the end of the summer. Slow down!" He stopped her with a hand on her arm and an apologetic laugh. "I try to keep fit, but I'm close to sixty, remember."

"Sorry. How about stopping here?" She indicated a small fort built of driftwood several feet from where they stood. "We should have brought some hot dogs." A neat fire ring remained from the previous inhabitant's visit. Dana sat on the cold sand against one of the log walls, then thought belatedly of her father's obviously expensive jeans. But with only a second's hesitation he sat across from her and leaned back against the driftwood, stretching his legs out.

It was coming now, she knew. The confrontation. She tried to appear composed, but she was sure her knees drawn up against her chest, her arms wrapped around them in a protective attitude, indicated otherwise.

"Why'd you leave the *Daily News*?" her father asked bluntly, his dark eyes fixed on her face.

"I told you," she replied shortly. "To get away from Scott."

"You've been divorced over a year."

"I know. But I needed...new surroundings, something different in my life. And Jack had offered me this job right after Scott and I separated."

"And it was good to get away from me?" he suggested.

She looked at him evenly. "You don't try to get away from someone who's never there."

"At the *News*," he said quietly, "I thought you'd appreciate not being treated like my daughter."

"At the *News*, yes," she replied coldly. "But at home being treated like your daughter would have been nice."

There was silence for a long moment, the whistle of the wind outside the crude shelter a counterpoint to the tension.

"It was never that I didn't care," he said finally.

"Yes, I know. Only that you didn't have time. I'm sure there's a difference there somewhere."

"You've come to hate me," he observed. His face was pinched from the cold, his dark eyes standing out against his pallor.

She noted his pain with a feeling of uneasiness. "I don't know." She couldn't deny his claim, but she knew it wasn't entirely true, either. "I don't see you often enough to know."

"Well, I'm here now," he said. "And I'd like to explain about...us...about your mother and me. Can you be open-minded enough and forgiving enough to listen?"

Be fair, Gabe had said, she recalled. *Fear and the dark can make you crazy. Don't make your decision in the dark.*

Dana straightened her legs and sat up. "I'll try," she acceded. "Go ahead."

Barton Freeman closed his eyes and leaned his head back against the rough driftwood. He jammed his hands into his jacket pockets, and Dana sensed his withdrawal from her into the past. A line appeared between his eyes, and she realized that looking back was as painful for him as it was for her.

"Your mother was the most beautiful woman I'd ever seen," he began. "She was small and fair and so cool and controlled." He opened his eyes to look at Dana and smiled in self-deprecation. "I often wondered later why that appealed to me so much. Maybe because I was so aggressive and brash. She was like a cool hand in the heat of battle." He frowned, a deep inverted V appearing between his eyebrows. "It didn't take long to realize, though, that she was ice clear through, and that nothing and no one could warm her. When she was pregnant with Jack I thought she would change, but she didn't. She was able to push him aside and then you with the same uncaring, unfeeling detachment with which she kept me away."

He shifted uncomfortably and raised a knee, resting his arm on it. "At first it was a challenge to try to get through to her. After a while, all I wanted was to get away from her. But by then there were you and Jack."

"Why didn't you take us away from her?" Dana had asked herself that question a thousand times and was surprised to hear herself speak it aloud.

"Several reasons. First, she wasn't raising you, the household staff was, and I knew they were caring and competent, if not really family. And second, what I'd dreamed of all my life was finally taking shape. I was building a news network, so to speak, that was doing the job journalism is supposed to do. Everything I touched turned to gold, and it was almost beyond my control. It was like running three inches in front of a freight train; I had to keep running with it or be run over by it and lose it." He shook his head.

"I've thought about the past a lot recently. And I'm ashamed to admit that, though I knew I wanted love from your mother, I didn't realize how important love is to someone, how very much it colors every move you make, every breath you draw." He looked at her regretfully. "I never had love, being orphaned as a child, then married to your mother. I had no idea of what I was depriving you and Jack. I stayed away from home because it was easier for me; then, as the two of you grew up hating me, it became too hard to face you. I thought of myself and I'm sorry, but I plead ignorance." He sighed heavily. "Am I too late to make peace, Dana?"

Confused, panicky, a little sad, Dana knotted her fingers and looked away. The hatred she'd held so long was more comfortable and familiar than forgiveness, acceptance and starting over in a new relationship.

When she didn't reply, Freeman got slowly to his feet and dusted the sand off his jeans. He looked down at Dana with a wry smile. "It's all right. I can't ask you to love me when I've given you so little. But I've always had love for you and Jack though I've never shared it with you. And I will continue to love you both whether or not you can return what I feel. Remember Janine Franklin?" he asked.

Dana frowned, accepting his hand up. That seemed like a non sequitur until she saw the expression in his eyes and suddenly some loose ends in their conversation began to fall into place.

"Your secretary?" she asked.

He nodded. "We're getting married in August and we'll be honeymooning at the cottage in Ireland. Janine's taught me a lot about loving and accepting love. She said she's loved me for years, when I never knew it." He looked awed, and his expression touched Dana in some secret corner of her being she didn't know was there. "Imagine. Continuing to love for ten years when your love isn't returned. She said it never hurts to love someone, even if the one you love doesn't or won't love you back. She says it's like regenerating cells or pumping air through your lungs or blood through your arteries. It's life-giving to love.''

Lovers never lose. Hadn't Gabe told her that?

Something unfolded inside her and loosened, releasing feeling to every limb, accelerating her heartbeat. She looked into her father's eyes and saw it: the regeneration, the renewal.

She resisted an instinctive urge to reach out to him and lowered her eyes instead, clearing her throat.

"Maybe..." she began cautiously. "Maybe you could stop by after the convention." She looked up at him and found his eyes wide and surprised and welling with emotion. She looked down at her feet and awkwardly shuffled sand. "I'm sure Gabe wouldn't mind. That is, if you can get away. I realize—"

"I can get away," he interrupted quietly. Then he glanced at his watch. "Hell! Where does the time go? In a dull board meeting or a lonely hotel room it can stretch forever."

"We'd better start back," Dana suggested, turning away from him, unable to bear his pain because she was unable to ease it—at least not yet. She was still protecting her own feelings, holding in place the bars Gabe had talked about.

"No, I think we've got time for a quick lunch," Freeman amended with a cautious smile.

As THEY LEFT the Buccaneer Restaurant on their way back to the house, Freeman glanced at his daughter with a half smile.

"Will you misunderstand if I ask you if there's anything I can do for you?"

The moment those words were spoken a light went on in Dana's brain. There *was* something he could do for her.

"Do you still hold stock in Top Test Tires?" she asked, turning sideways in the plush leather seat of her father's rented car.

"Fifty-three percent."

"The Warrenton *Register*'s in a little financial trouble," Dana said. "Could you send a little co-op advertising to our local Top Test dealer?"

He gave her a slanted grin that suddenly made him appear years younger. "What did you have in mind?"

She shrugged, embarrassed. "Maybe a full-page weekly through the summer. Something like that."

Freeman whistled.

"Oh, I'll pay for it."

He gave her another look, the grin gone. "When do you want it to start?"

"Is the next edition too soon?"

He turned back to the road. "I'll see to it."

"Thank you. Gabe needs help, and I know he'd never take an offer of a loan, but some good healthy advertising is another story."

Freeman pulled up in front of Gabe's house and glanced at the digital clock on the elegant dashboard. It was 3:45 P.M. Dana knew enough about the kind of life he lived to realize that the hours he'd spent with her that afternoon could affect his schedule for the next several days.

"I know you've got to run," she said hurriedly, gathering up her jacket and purse. Then she stopped to look at him, really look at him, and with surprise she saw herself, as well as Jack, in his face.

"I'll come by sometime this weekend," he said, the tone of his voice uncertain, as though he were afraid her earlier offer might have been withdrawn.

"I'm glad you came," she said, emotion rising up to snatch her voice away.

"So am I. And you'll let me know when you hear from Jack. I'd been hoping to see him, too."

"I know. Maybe I'll have heard from him by the time you come back. Well..." She fiddled with the door handle, unable to look at him again. He was waiting for something more, something she couldn't give just yet. She stepped out of the car, calling a hasty goodbye.

Chapter Eight

The front door opened as Dana walked slowly up the porch steps. Gabe appeared in the doorway in jeans and his Stanford sweatshirt.

Seeing him there, she felt the crush of emotion that was stifling her breath beginning to build to explosive force.

His blue eyes did a cursory examination of her face; then he opened his arms. As the dam burst, she ran the rest of the way to fling herself against him. He swung her up and carried her inside, kicking the door closed behind them. He sat on the sofa with her cradled in his arms.

"What happened?" he asked.

She told him everything, from her terror when he'd left her and her father together in the office, to all her father had told her about her mother, to his feelings of anguish and finally his declaration that he loved her, Dana, and that he would love her always.

By the time Dana had reached that point in her narrative, evening had fallen and they sat in a long shadow, stillness all around them. She remained in Gabe's lap, her head pillowed on his shoulder, his arms clasped loosely around her. The only sound was Sidney's loud purr as he slept curled up contentedly on Dana's knees.

"Did you tell him that you love him, too?" Gabe asked. "You do, you know."

She stroked the cat's silky black fur. "I couldn't. I knew I should. I knew I was being selfish. But I couldn't. And when he drove away..." Her face contorted and she drew a sobbing breath. "I felt the way I used to when I was little and watched him drive away—always driving away—only this time he had told me he loved me."

He rubbed her arm while she fought back another bout of tears.

"God!" she exclaimed impatiently. "I don't know why I can't stop crying."

"I do." Gabe brushed the hair from her tear-dampened cheeks. "I think the bars are coming down."

Dana remained curled in her haven several minutes more, then she stirred reluctantly. "It's my turn to fix dinner, isn't it?"

"How about Chinese?" Gabe suggested, steadying her as she got to her feet.

"Thanks for your confidence," she said dryly, "but what I had in mind was meatloaf."

Gabe laughed and stood up also. "I meant I would go pick it up at the Chinese restaurant and bring it home."

"That sounds wonderful."

"Do you like all the usual stuff?"

At her nod, he patted his pocket, heard the jingle of keys and went to the door. "Give me about twenty minutes, then put on the kettle."

On her way to the kitchen, Dana reached the spot near the table where Gabe had held her in his arms the other night to conduct that "experiment" that was meant to prove to her what marriage to him had to offer.

She remembered his promise that he would always be there for her; then her mind replayed her desperate flight up the porch steps and into his arms as her father drove away. He had been there and he had held her while the raw emotion erupted from her and was washed away. He had kept his promise.

But she couldn't think about that right now. Confusion rang in her brain from the events of the day, and she set about the simple kitchen chores, hoping to reestablish balance through familiarity.

Dana had made tea and set the table by the time Gabe appeared with six take-out boxes of various sizes. The aroma as he entered the kitchen stopped her in the midst of carrying the teapot to the table. She stood in the middle of the room, her eyes closed, inhaling deeply of cooked onions, peanut oil and sweet-and-sour sauce.

To her complete surprise, her lips were covered by a pair of warm, mobile lips, and she opened her eyes as Gabe drew away, the delightful kiss imprinted on her lips.

He opened the cartons and the blend of aromas became downright debilitating.

"If you don't snap out of it and pour the tea," he teased, sitting down. "I'm going to eat it all before you even pick up your fork."

The size of the servings he was heaping onto his plate spurred her to immediate action. She swiped the fried rice out from under his hand and helped herself to a more than generous portion. She followed that with fried shrimp, sweet-and-sour pork, shrimp chop suey and egg rolls. She reached for the sixth carton, which was still closed, and Gabe slapped her fingers with his fork.

She looked up at him, feigning hurt surprise, and he said imperiously, "You don't touch the fortune cookies until you've cleaned your plate."

"Somebody made you emperor?" she challenged.

He nodded gravely. "It comes with the number seven combination. Would you get the soy sauce?"

She narrowed her eyes at him. "You aren't under the misapprehension that the number seven also comes with a coolie wife, are you?"

Gabe's eyes rose from his plate to settle smokily on her grin. "The position of empress is open."

With a dry glance at him, Dana changed the subject.

"Shouldn't we have heard from Jack by now?" she asked, dipping a lightly battered, crescent-shaped shrimp into the tangy sauce.

Chewing, Gabe shrugged and took the carton of shrimp she had placed next to her plate. "Not necessarily," he said finally, passing back the empty box with a wink. "He never was much of a letter writer. He probably got some hot story and has forgotten all about us. I'll let you know when to worry."

"You're too late. I've already started."

"Well, you're premature. Did I tell you I found out an interesting tidbit about Sorensen today?"

Dana looked up, an egg roll halfway to her mouth. "No," she said. "What?"

"I'm not entirely sure what it means, but I saw him with Daniel Bradley this afternoon. Bradley works for Capricorn Development."

Dana frowned, nibbling on the egg roll. "What's that?"

"They build shopping centers. I wouldn't have known

him except I once did a story for the *Times* about the company he works for. It's interesting to speculate why he was here."

Dana thought about it. "To sell a spot to Sorensen and his grocery store?"

"I doubt it," he replied. "In a small town, without a major chain supermarket, they usually bring one in. Sorensen does well, but I doubt that he could afford the kind of space he'd be asked to fill or what it would cost him to move into and equip a place that size."

"Could he have a reason for wanting to see the shopping center go in where you want to see them put the Work Corps?"

"Something like that. I've been thinking about this all afternoon, and I wonder if it isn't simply that Sorensen was hoping to sell his land across the highway from the old school to Capricorn Development. If they're serious about building in Hammond, that's probably the best spot available." He dipped his last bite of shrimp, popped it into his mouth and chewed thoughtfully. "I'll just bet he's afraid of having to take a lower price for the property if the Work Corps goes in instead of the condominium he'd like to see there. The condo would no doubt be a more profitable neighbor for a shopping center than a group of young people with limited spending power."

"I thought you said the property was in his mother-in-law's name? What does he stand to gain by the sale price? Don't tell me she has him on commission."

Gabe laughed. "Nobody underestimates Beatrice Phillips. I'm not sure why, but rumor has it that she just tolerates him for her daughter's sake. She probably considers the property his when taxes have to be paid and hers when there's a decision to be made on it."

Dana's eyes lit up. "Have you checked building permits, applications for zone changes, even the water department's work schedule? Evidence of anything being done on Sorensen's property would give us a clue."

Gabe made a face at her. "I had a paper to run while you had the day off, remember?"

Dana frowned. "Who insisted that I take it off? What's on your agenda tomorrow?"

"I'll be tied up most of the day. The commercial fishermen, the sports fishermen and the Indians upriver are having it out over fishing rights at the Thunderbird's meeting room. Why?"

"I'd like to work on this. Please, Gabe," she added when he glanced at her doubtfully. "I've done all the routine stuff without complaint."

"We shouldn't both be away from the office all day," he said.

"I won't be gone more than two hours," she cajoled. "Come on. We shouldn't put out a dull paper, either."

He was watching her with a smile that was indulgent and amused.

"It wouldn't hurt you to delegate a little," she said, pressing her advantage. "I hear you banging away in your office upstairs till three in the morning."

He pushed his plate away and leaned forward on his elbows, a predatory gleam in his eyes. "Sorry. I didn't realize I was keeping you awake."

"It wasn't you," she said in an attempt to pacify. "It was your typewriter."

"Are you sure you weren't plagued with thoughts of us before a minister?" he asked.

"No."

"Of the two of us walking along the beach with a pair of frisky children running ahead of us?"

"No."

"Of you and me Christmas shopping for dolls and electric trains?"

"Stop it!" she shrieked at him, in the throes of an anger even she knew to be disproportionately strong considering their mild exchange. She was on her feet, her cheeks hot; and he was watching her with eyes that read her like a brain scan. She knew he was deciding that his fanciful observations were right on target.

She turned away from him and stalked across the kitchen, her arms folded across her small chest. No one had ever understood her to that degree before, and she wasn't sure she liked it.

"I don't want children," she said peevishly, refilling the kettle.

"But I do."

She slammed the kettle on the burner, snapped it on and then stalked back to the table. "Well, I don't, so I think that formally terminates this relationship!"

"Why?" he asked mildly.

"Because if you want children and I don't—" she began hotly.

"Why don't you want children?" He corrected her interpretation of the question.

"Because they want and need—" she shrugged helplessly and turned away again "—things... I can't give. We've been all through this."

"Once you make up your mind to give love," he told her quietly, "it multiplies and suddenly there's enough for everyone—husband, father, children—"

"That's a fantasy."

"No, it's not," he said, his voice right behind her ear as his hands settled on her shoulders. "I have that kind of love."

She turned on him, fists clenched, hot tears standing in her eyes. "Then don't waste it on me, because I haven't!"

"I hate to keep editing you, cupcake," Gabe corrected her again with that infuriating imperturbability. "But I can see it in your eyes when you talk to me. I feel it in your hands when you lean over me to take copy from my desk or squeeze past me when we're pasting up. I feel it in your body when I hold you. You have love to give me." He framed her face in his hands and leaned down to kiss her softly. "We've just got to get the damn bars out of the way."

She wanted to scream in exasperation, and she wanted to melt in his arms and test his theory. But a woman could take just so much in one day.

Her arms hung limply under his hands. "Do you want more tea or not?"

With a look of acceptance, he gave her arms a final squeeze and let her go. "Sure. We've still got our fortune cookies."

He reached back to the table for them and offered her the carton. "Here, you first."

Poking into the box for a cookie, Dana selected one, broke it in two and pulled out the small strip of paper. "'You will live a long life,'" she quoted, glancing up at him with a derisive smile, "'rich in love and joy.' What does yours say?"

Gabe put the cookie between his strong teeth and bit down, snapping it in half. Neatly pulling out the fortune, he chewed while frowning over the message.

"'You will meet a small, dark stranger,'" he read, "'who will turn your life upside down, foul up your darkroom, frighten your wildlife, screw up the typing—'" he turned the small paper over and pretended to read from the other side "—and destroy your sanity. You—"

With a laugh and a "Give me that!" Dana tore the fortune out of his hand.

"'You will marry,'" she began to read, then finished in feeble tones, "'the lover of your dreams.'"

"That's you, cupcake," he said, wincing down at her as though she were a live bomb about to explode. "But I didn't think you'd want to hear it."

Dana sighed defeatedly. "You're right, Gabe. Good night."

"No good-night kiss?" he asked of her retreating back.

She spun around, her eyes stormy. "Cameron…" she warned.

He raised both hands in a gesture of surrender, valiantly fighting a grin. "Good night."

Without replying she spun on her heel and left the room.

SOMETHING AWAKENED HER in the early hours of the morning and she sat upright in bed, trying to determine what it had been. She was hurrying quietly along the hallway to go downstairs to check Sidney when Gabe's door opened, startling her.

"Oh," she said in relief, something very reassuring about his presence in the dark of the night. "Did something wake you, too?"

His shadowy figure looked down at her in the almost complete darkness, and she sensed something different in his manner. Something was wrong. Unconsciously she stiffened.

His hand closed over her arm, and he pulled her into his room. "The telephone woke you," he said softly, pushing her through the dark until her knees backed up against something soft—his bed.

She sat, and he walked farther into the room until a small pool of light brightened the left side of his bed. As he walked back to her, clad only in gray pajama bottoms, she had a vague impression of a brown bedspread thrown back, of the warm sheet under her legs. Her heartbeat began to accelerate.

"What's happened?" she asked. Her voice sounded disembodied in the quiet shadows. "Is it my father?"

Gabe shook his head. "No."

"Jack?"

Gabe sat beside her, his eyes both troubled and sympathetic. Fear stabbed at her; tiny, sharp thrusts aimed repeatedly at her stomach.

"Yes. He isn't dead or hurt—as far as they know," Gabe said, putting an arm around her shoulders and pulling her close. "But he's been out of touch with his bureau for more than a week. They're considering him missing."

Dana swallowed, not sure whether to be relieved or frightened. "But is one week so unusual in a place so remote?"

Gabe drew a deep breath. "Normally, no. But the Jeep he was riding in was found abandoned outside of Kabul."

As ominous as that news was, Dana still sensed something unspoken. "Is there more?" she asked.

There was silence for a moment, then Gabe said reluctantly, "Yes."

She clenched her hands together. "What?"

"His driver was found about a mile from the Jeep," he said quickly, as though anxious to get it over with.

"Dead?" she guessed in a small voice.

"Yes."

He put both arms around her then, one hand rubbing her bare shoulder. "But Jack might not even have been with him at the time; no one seems to know."

Dana shivered, welcoming the warm haven of Gabe's embrace. Horrible pictures flashed across her mind, and she shrank away from them against his chest. She would not allow herself to think of her brother dead or injured and in pain.

"I know it's hard," Gabe said gently. "But try to think positive. He's out of touch, but we're not sure anything worse has happened than that he simply can't get a message out from wherever he is."

Tears were starting to come, and she seemed unable to stop trembling. An image of Jack as she had last seen him—his bright, open face—swam before her, and she clung to it, swallowing hard. She stiffened, fighting for control.

"I should call my father."

"It was your father who called us. He's going to Paris to see what he can do. He told me not to wake you. I was going to tell you in the morning. You're shivering. Come into bed." He caught her under her arms and pulled her up to the pillow, covering her with a silky sheet and soft blankets. "Don't fight it. I can feel you stiffening up like a board. That's not healthy, and you can't keep going that way."

The light went out and he was in bed beside her, drawing her into his arms. "Cry if you want to," he said, settling her comfortably against him.

"I don't want to," she said stubbornly.

"Then relax," he ordered, "and try to sleep."

"If those Russians have hurt my brother..." she threatened shakily.

"I'm sure even the Kremlin knows better than to cross you, cupcake." Gabe planted a kiss on her forehead; despite her statement, the warmth and comfort of his body forced her to lean on his strength, and that made the tears fall in earnest. In all the years she'd spent at home, and then with her husband, no one had ever been there when she was in need of comfort. She had wept and worried alone.

Now the luxury of Gabe's shoulder allowed her to weep until exhaustion finally closed her eyes.

FOR THE REST OF THE WEEK Dana had little time to dwell on Jack's fate. Another issue of the Warrenton *Register* was under way without the valuable assistance of Darlene, who was home with the flu.

Concerned about the calm and stoic manner with which Sheila had taken the news about Jack, Dana made a point of calling her several times a day at work and at home, to see how she was faring. Gabe's caring, comforting arms had helped Dana through those first frightening hours and she was worried about Sheila, who had no arms to go to for shelter.

Since the night Dana had slept in Gabe's arms, he had carefully kept his distance. He was thoughtful, helpful and friendly, but rarely affectionate and never physical in his treatment of her.

The only explanation for his behavior that she could think of was that he had changed his mind about his feelings for her, and she found herself unable to consider that for very long. She tried to abide by the unspoken rules he had set down. Yet there were times when it was all she could do to keep her hands at her sides. That springy, silvery hair beckoned to her fin-

gers; the frown line between his eyes invited the sooth-
ing touch of her lips.

Though Gabe never mentioned either, she knew he
was worried both about Jack and about the Warrenton
Register's financial position. The loss of Sorensen's grocery ad had taken a sizable chunk out of the newspaper's income. She smiled to herself at the realization
that the next edition would have a new full-page ad.

And the whole plan might have worked had Barton
Freeman not gone overboard in his eagerness to please
and assist his daughter.

It was Saturday afternoon, and Dana was adding
freshly peeled and sliced vegetables to a partially
cooked, deliciously fragrant pot roast. She filled the
sink with sudsy water, then stopped to admire her roast
one more time before turning to the tedium of doing
dishes. She heard the front door slam and called a
cheerful hello over her shoulder.

"You're home early," she noted, hefting the roast to
return it to the oven. But biting fingers grabbed her
arm and yanked her around, depositing the roast and
half the vegetables in the sudsy water. The rest of the
vegetables rolled noisily on the kitchen floor.

Dana looked up into Gabe's icy blue eyes, her own
widening in alarm. Her heart rocketed in her breast and
the roasting pan fell to the floor with a terrible clatter.

"What—" she began, drawing away from him, unsure who this angry stranger was.

He interrupted her by shaking a sheaf of papers in
her face, his grip on her tightening painfully. "What in
the hell is this?"

She knew what it was instantly. As he waved the
papers in her face, then slammed them with an angry

thwack on the kitchen table, she caught the Top Test Tires logo on the top of a slick white sheet of paper and knew the promised ad had come through. Her father must have called in his instructions from Portland the day he visited.

"Looks like an ad," she replied calmly, playing for time, unsure yet just what the root of his anger was.

"Dana," he threatened, his grip on her tightening further. But she looked into his furious, ice-water gaze and told him quietly, "It really is hard to think when your arm is being broken."

He dropped her arm in disgust and pointed to a kitchen chair. "Sit down!"

"Yes, Your Grace." She complied with exaggerated immediacy.

He gave her a murderous glance before throwing open the ad slicks and the run sheet that had arrived with them. Dana swallowed. Her father may be a genius, but he wasn't long on subtlety.

It was an ad for Top Test Tires all right, but instead of one full page it was a double truck, two facing pages, and the directions said it was to run weekly for the next six months.

Dana looked from the ad to Gabe, who was pacing in front of her. "I was right," she said. "It's an ad. For tires."

"And where did it come from?" he asked, his voice like tearing velvet.

She appeared to study the slick. "Says here their administrative offices are in—"

He snapped her chin up, trapping it between his thumb and forefinger, his fingertips biting into the thin flesh of her jaw. "I know your father owns Top Test Tires."

"My father owns a lot of things," she replied, making her voice dramatically stiff because of the way he held her.

"Well, he doesn't own me!" he shouted at her, dropping her chin with a snap. "If I can't have your trust, I sure as hell don't want your money! I told you before that the *Register* makes it on its own merit or it folds."

Horrified by his reaction to her innocent effort to help, Dana rose, stopping him with a hand on his arm as he would have stormed past her. "Gabe, I'm sorry. I care—"

"Buying and caring are not synonymous!"

"I only meant to—"

"You meant to buy me!" he snapped.

"I did not!" she shrieked at him, temper now overtaking her surprise and confusion. "I lost you Sorensen's ad! I just wanted to replace it."

"With a double truck at prime rate for six months? Dana..." He pulled her hand from his arm, grasping her wrist and shaking it. "A two-page tire ad in a town of twenty-five hundred? To run every week for six months? The L.A. *Times* doesn't get ads like that!"

"He wanted to help me." She yanked out of his grasp and turned away from him. "I wanted to help you. That's all it was."

"Don't give me that!" He spun her around again, and she looked with shock into his eyes, unable to believe that this monster was Gabe Cameron. He held her forearms in a grip that brought her up on tiptoe.

"You're not going to get by me with those teddy bear brown eyes and your father's money. That ad isn't running, not even once. Just do your job, Brenda Starr, and leave the ad selling to me." Gabe stormed from the room, tossing the ad, torn in two, on the sofa as he passed.

Dana sank into a chair at the table, kicking angrily at a potato that rolled into Sidney, who was hiding behind the stove. She wanted to cry, but the frustration went too deep for that. Her gesture had not been entirely innocent, but it certainly had none of the treacherous undertones Gabe had read into it.

Sidney jumped into her lap and she stroked him gently, his purr rising immediately and loudly. Dana looked sadly around her at the vegetables littering the floor and the succulent roast now drowning in a sink full of dish detergent. Her brother was missing and possibly dead several thousand miles away; her father, newly rediscovered after all those years of tension, was having his effort to help her thrown back in his face; and the man she loved—God help her, the man she loved!—was convinced she was a manipulator and had put her firmly, painfully, in her place.

The first brave steps into her new life, she told Sidney, appeared to have been taken in a backward direction.

DANA HEARD GABE come home early the following morning. He did not appear for breakfast or lunch, and when she heard no activity from his room all afternoon she went upstairs to investigate.

She stared at his closed bedroom door and stood very still, listening for movement from within. There was none. She rapped lightly on the door. There was silence for a moment; then Gabe's voice replied testily, "Yeah?"

"Are you okay?" she asked.

Another silence. "More or less," he finally answered.

"Can I come in?"

"No!"

She would have turned away, but despite the shout, there was an unfamiliar weakness in his voice. Dana let herself in and closed the door behind her. Gabe was lying on his back in jeans and a sweatshirt, his feet bare.

She sat on the edge of the bed and put a hand to his forehead. It was hot and he was pale, except for a bright flush across his cheekbones. He opened his eyes as though it required great effort. They were feverishly bright, and she guessed that he had caught Darlene's flu.

"When I marry you," he said weakly, "I'm going to... beat you."

She shook her head, unbuttoning his shirt. "Sorry. That's no longer legal."

He made a disgusted sound. "Pity... the way all... the old traditions... die."

"Life is hard," she agreed, opening dresser drawers to find pajamas. She brought a dark blue pair back to the bed and sat down again to ease his shirt off.

"What—" He began to raise his head in protest, then immediately regretted it. He sank back against the pillow with a groan.

"Take it easy, chief. You'll be more comfortable out of these clothes and settled for the night." She guided his right arm into the sleeve, then eased her hand under his back. "Put your arm around my neck," she instructed in a businesslike tone.

"Are we... changing my clothes," he asked with a thin grin, "or my mind... as we agreed the other night?"

"I wouldn't pick on someone in your condition,"

she said, straining to lift his weight off the pillow while slipping the shirt around his back and his other arm into the second sleeve.

"I appreciate that," he said wearily, sinking back to the pillows when the task was completed. She fastened the buttons.

Undoing the belt at his waist, she felt grateful for his weakened condition and closed eyes. "Lift up," she ordered and, when he complied, slipped the jeans down his long, strong legs. Then she reversed the task with the pajama bottoms. His feet were icy cold, and she rummaged around until she found a pair of socks and put them on him.

"I'll have to bother you one more time to get the blankets from under you," she said apologetically. "Then I'll let you sleep."

"Deal," he replied.

That finally accomplished, she pulled the blankets up to his chest and felt his forehead once more. "How do you feel?"

"Like hell," he admitted raspily. "But a good night's sleep and I'll be up tomorrow."

He was not better the following day, or the day after that. Dana helped him most of the night while he was violently ill, her pain over their argument forgotten in his genuine need of her.

At the office the following day she typed everything she could get her hands on with the intention of simply getting enough filler material to cover the usual ten pages. When Darlene arrived in the afternoon, Dana handed her a camera and explained about Gabe. "Take lots of pictures," she directed.

"Of what?"

"Anything. Dogs. Kids. Flowers. We'll think of a theme later. We just need to fill space."

Darlene frowned. "Who'll develop the film and make the prints if Gabe is sick?"

Dana groaned and rested her head on her arms, folded atop the Just-o-Writer. "Get the pictures and I'll try to solve that problem tomorrow."

It was after six when she arrived home. She fixed soup and a sandwich, relieved to find that Gabe was sound asleep. She took a leisurely bath and tried to clear her mind of the problems it would be unhealthy to think about—her brother, her father, her relationship with Gabe.

On the other hand there were a lot of things she should think about. Like how to handle the darkroom work tomorrow. Perhaps the young man at the camera shop would have a suggestion. She made a mental note to call him first thing in the morning.

The next day followed much the same pattern, and she went home at noon to try to force some broth down Gabe's parched throat. But he seemed more interested in sleeping than eating, and she finally consoled herself with the thought that such a normally healthy specimen wouldn't starve in two days' time.

Back at the office she did more typing and, while the tape ran through the reader, began to plan the page layouts. Without knowing what was on Darlene's roll of film and how much of it would be usable, the page dummies would be subject to change, but at least it was a start.

The young man from the photo shop arrived after closing time and within an hour and a half had Dana's desk covered with more photos than she could use.

Darlene had shot a close-up of a sprig of forsythia in bloom; a little girl hanging upside down from the monkey bars at school; a young couple walking hand in hand; a dog in midair, catching a Frisbee.

"We could call it 'Spring' or something," Darlene suggested shyly, obviously pleased with her accomplishment.

"You saved our hides, young lady," Dana praised, then patted the young man on the back. "Not to mention you. How much do we owe you?"

The young man shook his head. "Nothing. I owe Gabe. And I'm a pushover for a pair of pretty girls in distress. Anything else I can do?"

"I think we've got it made," Dana said.

When the man left, Dana set about readjusting her layout to fit the spread of photographs. She was just considering breaking for dinner when Darlene's mother arrived with a noodle casserole and a two-liter bottle of Pepsi.

"Mom, you're wonderful!" Darlene hugged the small blond woman.

"Darlene told me what you two are up against." The woman smiled sympathetically at Dana. "I called Darlene's counselor at school and she's excused from classes tomorrow to help you out. Anything else I can do?"

So that was where Darlene got her competence. Dana shook her head in wonder. "You seem to have taken care of everything. You couldn't by any chance whip up an editorial, could you?"

Mrs. West laughed. "I'm afraid not."

"I don't know how to thank you. Darlene can spend the night with me."

"That's fine, and helping is what mothers are for."

Yes, Dana thought dryly. Some of them.

It was 3:00 A.M. when she finally stopped out of sheer exhaustion. But she and Darlene had four pages fully made up, two nearly finished and four well on the way to completion. Darlene's pictures covered the center-fold page, and Dana set a byline for her in bold type.

She put an arm around Darlene's shoulders as the girl admired her work on the pasteup board.

"You did very well, Dee. Are you planning a career in journalism?"

Darlene smiled tiredly. "I'm not sure. I love the work, even in this tiny operation. But I'm not sure it's worth it. Gabe fights like this every week to get it out, and now—" she shook her head dispiritedly "—he's on the brink of losing it because of that rat, Sorensen. Gabe's done so much for this town. But their gratitude can't keep him in business."

"Well, we kept it going for one more week," Dana said bracingly. "Let's go get a few hours' sleep."

At home Dana led Darlene to the bathroom then went to check on Gabe. His sheets and blankets were hopelessly twisted, and she tried to straighten them without disturbing him. His face was a little cooler to the touch, and one piece of the toast she had left on his bedside table at noon was gone. Dana leaned down to kiss his forehead, stroking back the thick, wiry hair. She laid her cheek against his for a moment, then left the room.

She settled Darlene on the sofa in Gabe's office, then took her turn in the bathtub.

By 6:00 A.M. she was dressed and about to wake Darlene when she heard a thud from Gabe's room. Her plaid shirt still unbuttoned over a pair of jeans, she raced to the foot of his bed to find him sitting up, legs over the side. In his hand was one shoe. The other had apparently fallen to the floor when he tried to put it on. He was holding his head weakly in his free hand.

"I don't think you're ready to get up, Gabe," Dana

said, taking the shoe from him and trying to push him back to the pillows.

He resisted her, but with effort. "It's Wednesday," he said feebly. "God, it's ... Wednesday! And I haven't—"

"I have," she said firmly, pushing against him a little harder. He fell back against the pillows, and she swung his legs back onto the bed and covered him. "I have six pages completely pasted up," she fibbed. "And four in better shape then you've probably ever had them on a Wednesday morning."

He fixed her with a worried look as she fluffed his pillow. "With what?" he asked uncertainly.

"Well, it won't win you a Pulitzer," she said frankly, "but it's not bad, either. I'll bring one home tonight and if it doesn't give you a relapse I want a raise. Feeling better today?"

"Yes. But I feel as though my bones have been removed."

"You haven't eaten in three days. Want to try some toast and a soft-boiled egg?"

"Have you got time?"

"I have to wait until Darlene's ready anyway."

"She's here?" He looked up at her in confusion.

"It's a long story. Want to try a cup of tea, also?"

"Yeah." He grinned, looking a little like his old self. "And button your shirt before you come back or it may be Thursday before you go to press."

DANA AND DARLENE met the noon deadline with half an hour to spare. Even the mailing went off without a hitch, although it did take longer with just the two of them. It was almost nine o'clock when Dana dropped Darlene off.

At home she closed the front door quietly, then tiptoed across the living room and up the stairs to the bathroom. She was famished, but even more than that she was bone-tired. Two sleepless nights nursing Gabe and three fifteen-hour days at the office were finally taking their toll. She filled the tub and stripped off her clothes, grateful for the quiet sounds of the house. Gabe must be sleeping peacefully.

Sinking into the hot water, Dana leaned her head back on the cold enamel of the tub and let herself relax for the first time since Sunday evening. She had done it, she congratulated herself. The Warrenton *Register* would be in every local mailbox tomorrow.

She gave the bar of soap a desultory toss, wondering where she would be tomorrow. After Gabe's reaction Saturday, there seemed little future for her here.

That strange diabolical meow that was finally growing more friendly than threatening to Dana's ear preceded Sidney into the bathroom. Tail held high, the cat leapt onto the closed commode, purring loudly.

Laughing at him, Dana raised a foot out of the water and scratched his chin with it. He leaned into her dripping foot, his purr rising an octave and increasing several decibels in volume.

Cross-eyed with ecstasy, Sidney leapt onto the narrow side of the tub. His purr increasing even more, he ran gingerly along the rim to her head, where he rubbed against her hair while she laughed, petting him with a wet hand. "You should be keeping your master's feet warm," she chided. "No...Aaah!" She screamed as Sidney lost his precarious footing and fell into the hot water.

His feline sensitivities offended by the water, Sidney's personality changed suddenly from gentle house cat to maniacal killer. He wanted out of the tub and had no compunction about using Dana as his path to safety.

But his efforts to evacuate were hindered by the slick side of the tub that had entrapped him and the shrieking, writhing body on which he scrambled, screaming loudly all the while.

Mercifully, Sidney's loud pleas for help were answered by his master. As he was lifted firmly under the belly and deposited, drenched, on the bathroom rug, he thought with new profundity that one could always trust another man. Though his master was less inclined to stroke and pet him than the new arrival, he also knew better than to lure him to the brink of drowning. With a suspicious glare over his shoulder at Dana, who sat huddled at the back of the tub, her eyes wide, her cheeks pink, Sidney stalked away, leaving a trail of sudsy water as he passed.

"Are you all right?" Gabe pulled Dana to her feet, a laugh about to burst from him until he noticed the fiery scratches that crisscrossed her stomach.

Rendered mute by the wiry gray hair grazing her breasts as he bent to inspect her injuries, Dana said nothing.

"Come out of there and let's put something on those." He lifted her onto the rug and turned to take a small jar off the blue-tiled counter.

While his back was turned, Dana snatched a towel off the rack, holding it at her breasts, trying hard to get control of herself. With the excitement of Sidney in her bath and Gabe's casual appearance in the room, looking alarmingly fit again, and his clinical assessment of her wounds, she felt as though she was spinning like a top. Only a moment ago she had been having a nice quiet bath!

As he turned back to her, Gabe's eyes went to the

towel clutched in front of her, then to her bright eyes, his own lit with amusement. "Little late for that, isn't it?" he asked. Then his tone became no-nonsense. "Come on, drop it. This'll only take a minute."

"But..." As she began to stammer, he took the towel from her and let if fall to the floor. With complete detachment he dabbed at a long scratch on her left breast, carefully covered the painful ones crisscrossing her stomach, then traced the path of the longest one on her thigh. Every muscle leapt under his hand, and she stood silently mortified, knowing he could feel her body's reactions to him. And that, she realized as awareness began to return to her, after all the things he had accused her of Saturday afternoon!

When he had finished and straightened to look into her face, her hurt dark eyes were watching him. The light in his eyes flickered and his expression sobered. Capping the jar, he replaced it, then handed Dana her towel, leaning a hip on the counter to watch her wrap it around herself. Her color high, she tucked the end of the towel in at her breast. She was unprepared for the warm hand that pulled her in between his knees and kept her close inside the circle of his arm. Her eyes flew up to his, startled, waiting.

"I'm sorry about Saturday afternoon," he said gravely, brushing the damp ends of her hair off her bare shoulder. "I'm surprised you didn't just leave and let me put the damn thing out myself, alive or dead."

She angled her chin. "That wouldn't have been very professional," she pointed out softly.

"It would have been what I deserved." He gave a shrug that was as close to helpless as she had ever seen him. "All I can say in my defense is that I was tired, that I've got a lot on my mind...." He gave her a wry smile. "Having your delicious little body near me all the time has me as frustrated as a fenced-in bear."

"You won't have to worry about that anymore," she said softly, praying that tears wouldn't form. She really was too tired for this.

"Oh?" The one small syllable was swift, guarded.

"Now that the paper's out and you're feeling better, I think I'd better go."

"No," he said, without letting a pulse beat fall between them. "You're not going anywhere."

Impatient, Dana pushed at his chest. "I won't fight with you," she said wearily. "I'm tired and I'm hungry. Will you please let me go!"

When he continued to hold her, she slapped at his chest, and as he grabbed her hand to hold it away, she cried out in pain. Frowning, he pulled her hand toward him. He turned her hand palm up and saw a series of swollen red marks. An inspection of her other hand revealed the same.

"What the hell is that from?" he demanded.

"It's nothing." She pulled her hands away and hid them behind her back, but his arm around her waist refused to free her. "It's just from carrying the papers," she explained. "The twine is rough and they're heavy bundles."

"God!" he said angrily, reaching for the trusty gray jar again.

"They'll probably be gone in the morning," she said reasonably. "Darlene's got them, too, and I'll bet her mother isn't making half the fuss you're making."

"Her mother isn't the reason she's got them. Give me your other hand."

Dana obeyed, secretly enjoying the erotic sensation

of his fingertips in her palm. Why did life have to be so complicated?

"If it'll ease your conscience," she sighed. "We were both happy to do it for you. Even Stan from the photo shop, who developed the pictures, wouldn't let me pay him. He said he owed you. You're a damned paragon, Cameron. Seems we all owe you for something or other."

He tightened his grip on her, his rough hand caressing her bare arm. With his gray hair combed into order and his jeweled eyes serious, he looked like a stranger.

"And what do you owe me?" he asked.

She looked down at her fingers, fiddling with the selvage end of the towel. "I wouldn't know how to add it up. If I had to translate it into numbers, the figure would be astronomical."

Gently he lifted her chin. The look with which he fixed her was half genuine perplexity, half fascination with something in the depths of her eyes. "How do you figure?" he asked.

With her swollen hand, she took the hand that held her chin and turned her lips into it, then rested her hot cheek against it. "Because you've taught me that love is still alive in me, that a lonely childhood and a loveless marriage haven't killed it. Because of you I know I'm still a whole human being."

She sighed heavily, relief and apprehension settling in her side by side. Before she could stop herself, she asked defensively, "Do you still want to marry me?"

Gabe stared at her for a moment, surprise registering in his eyes. Then he framed her face with his hands, running his thumbs lightly over her flushed cheekbones.

"I do love you," he said heavily, his eyes like the ocean in a storm. "And I still want to marry you. But do you love me?"

She didn't have to think a minute. "Yes, I do."

His look became wary. "But do you trust me?"

"I guess after Saturday afternoon," she said with a slight smile, "I can safely assume you're not after my money."

"True," he said, laughing. Then he asked with a quirk in his grin, "Has it occurred to you that this is a strange conversation to be having in a bathroom?"

She opened her mouth to reply and her stomach growled loudly.

He held her to him and laughed. "It's occurred to you. Shall we retire to the kitchen and fix you a steak?"

"I couldn't eat that much," she protested as he snatched his terry-cloth robe from the hook on the door and helped her into it. Then, belting the robe, he deftly reached inside it and yanked the towel from her.

Dana raised an eyebrow at him. "You do that very well."

"Comes from all those years of editing copy," he said, pushing her before him out into the hall. "You learn quickly to dispense with what isn't necessary."

Chapter Nine

Dana ate not only the steak but a respectable helping of cottage fried potatoes, green beans and a plump whole-wheat roll. Sipping a glass of milk, Gabe sat across the table looking through the current copy of the Warrenton *Register* while Dana continued to feast.

She had carried her empty plate to the counter and poured herself a cup of coffee when Gabe closed the paper, folded it and put it aside.

He looked at her with respect in his eyes.

"Layout's nice and clean." He sat back comfortably and smiled at her. "No typos that I could find, and you did a good job with the photo page."

"Darlene took the pictures."

"I saw the credit line. We'll have to give her a bonus."

Dana looked down at her cup. "I'm sorry about the tire ad."

He shrugged. "When I got over being angry, I appreciated your concern and your eagerness to help, but I was too sick to tell you." Folding his arms on the table, Gabe leaned toward her, the clean flyaway tips of his silvery hair sparkling. "But I'll make it up to you after we're married. Come sit with me and we'll discuss it."

A strange feeling somewhere between shyness and excitement made her lower her eyes as she walked around the table to his chair. As he pulled her down to his knee, her arms went automatically around his neck and she found herself looking deeply into his eyes. She caught the warmth and laughter there instantly and was sure she heard the "click" of her life finally snapping into place in the complicated universe.

"We've got to get married before another deadline," he said, kissing her chin. "What do you think?"

That was a little sooner than she'd considered, but the prospect excited rather than frightened her.

"This weekend?"

He nodded. "That's what I had in mind."

Dana frowned for a moment, thinking of Jack and her father. "Do you think Jack and Dad will mind if we go ahead without them?"

He hugged her to him. "No, I don't. They both love you and want you to be happy. But..." He held her away and looked into her eyes. "You're sure this is what you want? I have done my best to bully you into marrying me."

"I'm sure." She gave him a smile that was weary but warm and very genuine. "Can't you see us in my eyes?"

He looked at her deeply and she saw the flare of emotion in his eyes. Then he refocused to smile at her. "Yes, I can."

"I missed you abominably while you were sick," she told him, enjoying the release she felt at being able to be honest with him at last. "I fretted over you and slaved over the *Register* because it's yours and I wanted it to be as good as Dee and I could make it. And every single moment of those three days you were on my mind.'' She sank wearily against him, nuzzling her nose in the warmth of his neck. ''I'm so tired,'' she said, yawning. ''You won't think my declaration of love any less sincere if I fall asleep while making it, will you?''

Laughing, Gabe stood up with her in his arms and made his way through the living room and up the stairs. In her dark bedroom he deposited her on the cool bedspread and kissed her gently.

''Can you get out of your things okay?''

She smiled drowsily. ''Want to help me?''

''Yes.'' He chuckled, pulling her shoes off. ''But you're exhausted, and I've been waiting for you too long. I'd better stop at your socks.''

Dana settled into her pillow as he pulled the other half of the spread over her. ''Always a gentleman,'' she praised, no longer able to keep her eyes open.

''No, I just know my limitations. Good night, cupcake.''

Dana felt Gabe's lips on her forehead as sleep overtook her.

SOMETHING WAS WRONG, Dana decided the morning of her wedding. She felt headachy and weak, and the mere thought of the brunch that would celebrate their marriage made her nauseous enough to feel faint. *Only I,* she thought dryly, *could catch the flu on my wedding day.* She could just imagine the glee with which Gabe would react to the news, not to mention her own disappointment.

Skillfully applied makeup and avoidance of Gabe's eyes got her through the ride to church and most of the brief ceremony, until the minister declared them man and wife and Gabe leaned down to kiss his bride. His eyes ran quickly over her face, seeing the pallor under the pink blusher and the overbright gleam in her eyes. He kissed her gently, then straightened, a faint grin on his face.

She wanted to overrule his decision that they skip the brunch and go straight home, but she was feeling increasingly worse by the minute.

"I wish you happiness," Sheila said with a catch in her voice as they separated on the church steps. She drew away, her blue eyes brimming. "When Jack comes home, I'm taking him to that same altar under whatever conditions he sets down."

Dana smiled wanly. "Now don't be too easy on him."

"If I was sure he was coming back to me," Sheila whispered, "I wouldn't care where he went or how long it took him." Sheila's composure cracked for an instant, but she made a firm effort to pull herself together. "Well, you don't want to hear this on your wedding day. You be good to her, Gabe. And don't worry about a thing tomorrow. I'll see that Dana has lunch, or at least tea and toast or something, and I'll leave your dinner in the refrigerator and be gone before you get home."

Gabe grinned at his sister. "Want to hire on permanently?"

"Thank you." Her smile thinned. "But I'll have my own man to take care of soon enough. 'Bye, you two."

Gabe took Dana home and she settled comfortably into the hollow of his shoulder, twining her arms around his neck as he carried her upstairs.

He looked down at her worriedly. "How do you feel?"

She swallowed a wave of nausea. "You'd better deposit me in the bathroom instead of the bedroom. And—I hate to tell you how to drive, but—hurry!''

She was violently sick all night long; Gabe was up and down with her, bathing her face after the bouts of vomiting, holding her gently against him when they were in bed. By dawn she was exhausted and fell into a fitful sleep.

The next two days followed the same pattern. During the day she would wake to find Sheila smoothing her blankets or trying to cajole her into drinking a cup of tea. At night the nurse was Gabe, and the comfort of his arms always brought relief from the nauseous misery she suffered all day long.

She began to feel human again by Wednesday afternoon. Though still weak, her stomach seemed finally settled, and the roar in her head was down to a mild thump. With Sheila's help she got up to bathe and had considered getting dressed, but the effort proved too much and she finally went back to bed.

Dana awoke to darkness and reached instinctively for the broad waist she had clung to the past few nights. But all she met was the bare expanse of sheet.

"Gabe?" she asked weakly, feeling much more bereft than the situation warranted.

"Are you awake?" Sheila's voice spoke softly from the doorway.

"Yes," she replied softly. "What are you doing here?"

"Gabe called. The Addressograph broke down." She came to sit on the edge of Dana's bed. "He and Darlene are writing all the addresses by hand. He asked me to come back and keep an eye on you."

"Any news of Jack?" Dana was almost afraid to ask.

The older girl drew a ragged sigh. "No. I hope he's taking care of himself."

"Gabe says he's a survivor. Sometimes I think Gabe knows Jack better than I do, even though I'm his sister."

"Gabe understands everybody. It's that analytical eye."

Dana made a cynical sound. "If only he was so easy to understand."

"Nothing is easy to understand." Sheila stood up and sighed again, with acceptance this time. "Jack is everything I swore I'd never get mixed up with again, but if he walked in the front door right now I'd go against everything I've ever said and marry him, world traveler or not."

"Any day now he will," Dana said firmly. "But I want to return the favor and stand up for you, so wait until I'm better."

"Okay." Pulling the blankets and tucking them carefully around her patient, Sheila fluffed the pillow, then turned toward the door. "Do you want anything? Tea? Toast?"

"No, thanks. You'd better get some rest, too. If I need anything, I'll call you."

IT WAS MORNING when Dana woke again. Gabe was emerging from the bathroom, a pale blue sweater in his hands. He crossed the room to the dresser, unaware that she was awake. He snatched a comb from its top and, bending his knees to look into the mirror, ran it through his wet, steely gray hair. Then he pulled the sweater over his head, turning toward the bed. His head rose from the V neck of the sweater as he tugged the garment down. His gaze fixed on her face, which was highlighted with a little more color that morning, and he gave her a strangely watchful smile.

"Good morning, cupcake. How do you feel?"

The blue of his sweater deepened the blue in his eyes, and her glance went to the small patch of chest hair visible above the V. A spiral of warmth moved in her chest. But he seemed wary, not his usual open self. She smiled casually back at him.

"Recovered, I think. I'm hungry, and I'd love to have a bath."

His manner became cautiously offhand; instead of reducing the tension that crackled between them, his behavior seemed to increase it. Gabe sat in the chair by the bed pulling on socks and shoes.

"Go ahead and take your bath. I'll fix breakfast."

As he tied those foot-long Nikes, she watched the muscles in his forearms and the broad back bent over the task. When Gabe straightened, her eyes surprised his and, seeing their appraisal, he let his casual manner slip and his eyes grew warm. Confused, she dropped her eyes; after a moment he stood and crossed the room to the door.

"Eggs and toast?" he asked.

Despite the confusion she felt, her hunger was a force to be reckoned with, too. "And bacon and potatoes," she requested.

He raised an eyebrow. "Is that wise?"

"I don't know," she admitted. "But it sure sounds good. And I'm tired of dry toast."

He nodded. "All right. How long will you be?"

"Fifteen minutes."

In the bathtub, Dana lay back and analyzed this strange and sudden tension between them. She knew what it was, of course. The heat that now invaded her body under every skin cell that covered it had nothing to do with the warm bathwater. It had to do with loving

Gabe and wanting him—and that wanting had been stretched to the snapping point by her four days of being ill.

Dana heard the rattle of crockery from the kitchen and the distant ring of the telephone in the next room. She wondered idly if she should try to answer it, since Gabe was busy with breakfast. But it rang only once, and she knew he had picked it up downstairs. Good, she thought, relaxing in the hot water. Five more minutes and she might be able to face the day.

But that was not to be. She heard Gabe's footsteps on the stairs, then along the hall. Looking up as her door opened, Dana watched in surprise as he walked in and pulled her, dripping, to her feet and wrapped a towel around her.

"Telephone," he said casually, ignoring her indignant expression.

"Can't you take a message?" she demanded.

"You can take it in our room," he said.

"Well, really . . . !" she grumbled as he bustled her through the connecting door, pushed her to a sitting position on the edge of the bed and placed the receiver in her hand. With a small, mysterious smile over his shoulder, he left the room.

Wondering if it was Sheila or Darlene with some problem at the office, she said abruptly, "Hello!"

"Hi, babe!" the caller replied. The breath stopped in her throat and she felt her heart begin to pump.

"Jack!" she screamed. Then afraid to believe it, "Jack?"

"Yes, it's me!" he replied. "I called as soon as I heard they'd declared me missing. I was just on to a good story. I was with the Mujahideens, and I've got some incredible pictures! I just got back to Kabul yesterday. You must have been frightened. I'm sorry."

"Your driver was found dead," she said, her voice trembling.

"Yeah, I heard. I don't know what that was all about. We'd parted company a few days before, when I went into the mountains. Are you okay? Getting along with Gabe all right?"

"Yeah," she said hesitantly. "Did...did he tell you?"

"Tell me what?"

Deciding the news of their marriage wasn't something for a many-dollars-a-minute phone call, Dana changed the subject with another question. "When are you coming home?"

"I'm taking my film to the Paris bureau, and I want to hang around long enough to see what I've got. Then I'll be home. Probably a week or so."

"Have you called Sheila?"

He hesitated a moment. "I thought you might do that for me?"

"No," she said.

There was a moment of silence, then he cajoled, "Do you know what this call is costing me?"

"She's been crazy with worry, Jack," Dana told him firmly. Glancing up, she saw Gabe standing in the doorway, leaning against the jamb. "Charge the call to Gabe." She winked at him. "But call her."

"What if she's mad at me for being alive?"

"Jack!"

"Well, if she was really worried and I turn up without a scratch, she'll probably beat me up herself."

Dana smiled into the phone. "After what she told

me last night, you might not find that so unpleasant.''

Even across several thousand miles and over a telephone, she heard his voice sharpen. "What did she tell you?"

"Call her," Dana replied heartlessly, "and find out for yourself."

"All right, all right, I'm coming," she heard him respond as though to someone beside him. "Look, I've got to go," he said. "And I'll call her. Take care, and I'll see you in a week, more or less. I love you, babe."

"I love you, too, Jack," she whispered back as the line went dead. She replaced the receiver and felt the weight of worry fall from her as if she had dropped a weighted pack. With the release came a rush of emotion held fiercely in check since she'd heard he was missing.

Gabe sat beside her on the bed as she turned to him, tears streaming down her face, still pale from the past four days.

"He's all right," she whispered in wonder. "He's... coming home."

Dana began to tremble, partly in reaction and partly from her still-damp body being exposed to the cool morning draftiness.

Gabe pulled the towel from around her, yanked the spread out from the pillows, and pulled the top of it around her shoulders, securing it with his arm.

"I'm so happy," she sobbed, her nose burrowed in his shoulder, her arm hooked around his neck. "He's fine. He isn't hurt or... or anything! And..." She lifted her head to look into Gabe's eyes. They were warm and deep, and she smiled, knowing that the awkward mood was gone. "And... I'm married to you. God, what blessings!" Leaning backward on the arm hooked around his neck, she brought him with her to the mattress. The spread slipped from her shoulders and she felt rough denim against her legs, the prickly wool of Gabe's sweater covering her from her stomach to her breasts.

His mouth closed over hers and, as her lips moved against his, she felt his warm, strong hands roaming over her body. She shuddered with longing. This wildfire in her veins was new, this spontaneous response something she'd never experienced before; but she knew her feelings were right. With a single-mindedness that chased every fear away, she wanted to love Gabe and be loved by him.

Gabe rolled off her and she tried to pull him back, hoping he was not using some knightly moral fortitude on her behalf.

"What are you doing?" she asked, clutching the sleeve of his sweater.

His eyes were clouded with desire as he grinned at her. "You seem to be unaware of it," he said, "but I'm overdressed."

"Oh." She grinned back. "Shall I help?" Without waiting for an answer, she slipped her fingers up under his sweater, pausing to plant kisses in the mat of hair on his chest. He lay back docilely while she pulled the sweater up, free of his arms, and tossed it aside. Then she moved to his belt buckle and unfastened it, working it slowly out through the belt loops while kissing his flat waist. She unbuttoned and unzipped his jeans.

As Gabe sat up to remove them, she knelt behind him, kissing his ears, nipping the cordlike muscles in his neck. She caressed the line of his shoulder and down his back, leaning her head against it to reach around his waist. The jeans kicked aside, Gabe slipped

out from under her arms and fell back against the pillows, pulling her down across him. She felt the silky
cool sheet against her body as he drew the covers up
over them. But it was the velvety warmth under her
that consumed her.

One hand held her to him while the other hooked
her knee up against his side, then moved to stroke the
line of her hip and return with silken caresses to the
back of her knee. His exploration began gently, his
fingers barely skimming her, then changing to possessive firmness as she pressed even closer to him, trans-
ported by his coaxing hands. Her mouth descended on
his with a little moan of pleasure, and she gasped as he
turned, tucking her under him. He looked down at her,
his bright blue eyes electric with passion. They roved
her face, and though she wasn't quite sure what he
looked for, he seemed pleased with what he found.

"I love you, Dana," he said gently. A hand came up
to cup her breast, and she arched against it with a helpless little smile.

"I love you, Gabe. I'll be so good for you," she
promised, and she reached around him to bring his
body down on hers. The contact brought a tremor from
deep inside her, as if the earth were about to break
apart while the underworld shifted. The tremor intensified as he teased her breasts with his mouth, then rested his face between them as he reached down to stroke
her legs apart, one hand moving silkily along her inner
thigh.

Though not afraid, Dana stiffened as he shifted to
enter her, expecting pain because she knew it had to
be. Instead, it was a mere moment of white-hot heat,
and then he began to move on her, not with Scott's
hurried, painful thrusts, but in a gently rhythmic coax-

ing, probing for that little core of her still trembling to break through. Fascinated for a moment by this new experience, she lay completely still, letting all her sensors absorb and assimilate. Then, prodded by the tremor building inside her, she began to move with him, hesitantly at first, until his strong arm reached under her to enfold her against him.

She writhed spiritedly, lustily, until the tremor became a storm that broke over both of them. Clinging to Gabe as wave after wave of sensation washed over her, she heard her own little cries as though from far away, her entire being concentrated on the bursting storm. Then her cries became soft sighs expressing the most incredible feeling of well-being she had ever known.

Gabe moved to lay beside her and hold her close, brushing her disheveled hair back and pulling the covers over her shoulders.

Dana clung to him, unable to speak.

"Told you," Gabe said quietly, kissing her hair.

"What?" she whispered.

"That we'd fly."

That about described it, she thought.

"Are you okay?" Gabe asked, pinching her shoulder.

She heaved a deep sigh. "Yes."

"Good. In a few minutes you can get up and fix breakfast."

"Sorry," she said, nuzzling his chest. "I'm helpless when I'm sexually satisfied."

"Now you tell me. We'll have to hire someone."

She kissed his shoulder. "To cook or to keep me sexually satisfied?"

The smack on her bare bottom stung. "Ow! Just kidding. Oh, Lord, Gabe." Resting an arm on his chest, she propped her chin on it and looked into his eyes, her eyes heavy and grave. "Would you be embarrassed if I told you that I've never felt in my life the way you made me feel?"

He smiled, stroking her hair back. "No. It pleases me. And you are absolutely delicious." His hand swept across her shoulders, down over her back and beyond. He turned, pinning her to the mattress with his weight, his hand already raising a new series of volcanic tremors inside her. "Hell with breakfast," he murmured.

Chapter Ten

"Gabe!" Dana called through the darkroom curtain.

"Yeah?"

"I'm leaving for the courthouse, and I'll be having lunch with Sheila!"

"I can't hear you!" he shouted back.

Dana shouldered her purse and followed the narrow corridor to the center of the room.

"I said—ouch!" A stinging pinch on her bottom spun her around into a pair of waiting arms that made the sun shine for her everywhere, even in the Warrenton *Register*'s darkroom.

"You beast!" The giggle underlying her accusation negated its sting, and Gabe hugged her to him with a laugh.

"If that was supposed to convince me of your indignation, it failed miserably."

She put her hands up under his shirt and felt the involuntary contraction of his muscles in response. "That's because you've made me shameless and insatiable," she said, kissing his throat. "I came in to tell you—"

"I heard you," he stopped her, reaching down to nibble at her lips. "You're going to the courthouse and then you're having lunch with Sheila."

"Gabe!" She pushed at his shoulders. "Then why...?"

"If you have to ask," he said, pulling her back against him with flattering force, "you aren't paying attention to what I'm doing." Then he lifted her onto the stool.

"I am paying attention," she said, laughing. "But Ben's waiting to take you to lunch."

He groaned. "Well, there'd better not be anybody but us for dinner or someone's going to be very embarrassed." Gabe's lips found hers in the dark and their touch was light but promising, then he lifted her down again.

"I'll see to it," she promised. "'Bye, sweetheart. I'm going home after lunch to fix something special for dinner. Think you can handle things here without me?"

"No," he said, more gravity than humor in his voice now. "And I'll never be able to again. I'll be home about six."

"I'll be ready." Dana kissed him fervently, then allowed his hand to direct her to the narrow corridor leading to the back room.

"Be careful," he warned. "Don't do anything...impetuous."

"In the courthouse?"

"You could get in trouble in a phone booth."

DANA HAD PERUSED the county records for over an hour before she uncovered the tidbit of information that Gabe apparently had missed. Sorensen's home and the lots located across from the proposed Work Corps site were, as Gabe had said, all titled under the name of Sorensen's mother-in-law. However, there was record of another small plot located on the state highway several miles south of Warrenton. Sorensen had purchased it a year earlier in his own name. Dana frowned down at the open file, wondering what the information could mean.

A glance at her watch told her she would have to hurry to be on time for her lunch date with Sheila. Dana closed the files and thanked the clerk behind the counter for her assistance. As far as she could judge, her discovery was a totally useless piece of information. It was several miles from the property in question, and she could find nothing to relate that information to the dispute between Sorensen and the Warrenton *Register*.

Sheila already occupied a booth at the Marketplace when Dana rushed in several minutes after noon. Sheila's smile was bright but a little forced.

"Hi!" Dana greeted, slipping into the booth. "Sorry I'm late."

"That's all right. I'm off this afternoon, so I'm not on a strict lunch hour." Sheila took a sip of wine and looked at Dana over the rim of her glass. "Your radiance is disgusting. Does Gabe really make you that happy?"

"Yes!" was Dana's emphatic answer. Then her eyes narrowed on her sister-in-law. "Do I see a little kink in your smile?"

"Probably. With Jack coming home any day I'm... I'm..." Sheila pushed the long menu aside with an irritated flick of her wrist. She sighed heavily. "Of course, I'm thrilled to death that he's all right, but he was so... so distant on the phone."

"He *was* distant!" Dana leaned across the table and frowned at Sheila. "He was thousands of miles away. Can you imagine what phone connections are like in Afghanistan?"

She shook her head. "It was more than that. He was deliberately trying to be noncommittal. I know him."

"So do I. And I think you're imagining things. Just wait and see."

Sheila rolled her eyes. "Don't you ever get tired of looking on the bright side? You've no idea how satisfying a deep blue emotional funk can be."

"Right now I'm riding a pure white high and I'm not coming down for anyone. What'll we have? I'm starved!"

Over stir-fried vegetables and lightly seasoned brown rice, Dana and Sheila talked about love and men and life.

Turning lighthearted with a sinful dessert, they finally pushed empty plates away and looked at each other uncertainly over the debris of their lunch. "Let's go shopping, or something," Sheila suggested.

"I'd love to." Dana scooted out of the booth, delving into her purse for her wallet. "But I want to do a little sleuthing this afternoon. If you haven't any plans, why don't you come with me?"

Sheila followed Dana to the cashier. "Where are you going?"

"Just outside of town." Dana paid their bill; then they walked together out into the sunny afternoon. "Where's your car?"

"Being repaired. I was going to bum a ride back to Warrenton with you. Nothing serious. A broken fan belt or something. Where outside of town?"

Dana fished in her purse for the address she had written down and showed it to Sheila. "Come with me. You can navigate."

It was a beautiful sun-dappled afternoon with large white clouds thrown at random across the sky. The air was perfumed with spring. They passed a field of sheep with new lambs cavorting in stiff-legged dances in the jewel-green grass.

Dana explained to Sheila the purpose of her investigation, and Sheila admitted that she'd been keeping up on Gabe's editorials.

Sheila looked a little worried. "Does Gabe know what you're doing?"

"He knows I had lunch with you. He doesn't have to know that I had plans for later."

"I wonder how Milly Sorensen feels about all this?" Sheila speculated thoughtfully. "She works at the college, you know, and she's such a mousy little thing. She always looks as though she's on the verge of hysterics. Look at the daffodils!"

They exclaimed together over the deep yellow border of small trumpets along the side of the road; then Sheila continued, "I guess her mother is the domineering type. Milly's grandfather was wealthy and her mother used his influence to get everything she wanted."

Dana grinned at the road. "Reminds me of me."

Sheila glanced teasingly at her profile. "I didn't want to point out the likeness. Anyway, she was convinced that Sorensen was after her daughter for her money and kept everything in her own name. But she did give him a stake to start the grocery store. Which he's managed very well."

Dana's eyes left the road to look at her sister-in-law in surprise. "How do you know all this?"

"The most reliable source: gossip! There!" Sheila pointed to the right and Dana turned onto a rutted road that led through an evergreen woods. Pulling over, she stopped, considering what to do. The last thing she wanted was to be seen.

"We'd better go the rest of the way on foot, just in case."

As she opened the door on the passenger side Sheila asked uneasily, "Just in case what?"

"Never mind. Come on."

Staying in the shadows at the side of the road, they crested a rise and spotted a small yellow cottage surrounded by crocuses and daffodils.

"Does that house look to you like something Sorensen would own?" Dana asked Sheila who was hiding behind a spiky tree trunk and straining to see.

As she spoke, the front door opened and a woman stepped out onto the porch. She wore a black peignoir with a deep neckline and she reached to pluck a small purple flower from a window box that was full of them.

Sheila inhaled so loud that Dana reached up quickly to cover her mouth.

"What's the matter?" she whispered, lowering her hand.

Sheila's eyes were large as saucers. "That's Margie Crowell!"

The name rang a bell in Dana's brain, but she couldn't place it.

"The mayor's wife!" Sheila informed her. Then, "Oh, Lord! There's Sorensen!"

Sorensen emerged from the house, pulling on a pale blue jacket. The woman snapped the stem off the flower and put the blossom in the buttonhole of his lapel. He gathered the mayor's wife in his arms and gave her a kiss that made Dana decide in revulsion it was time to leave.

Grabbing Sheila's arm, she ran for the car.

They were on the highway headed away from town when Sheila, leaning over the back of her seat to see through the rear window, verified that Sorensen had pulled out onto the highway and was headed back toward Warrenton.

"Well," Dana said, turning into a restaurant parking lot to turn around. "That was interesting. Useless as far as the Work Corps issue is concerned, but interesting."

"But the mayor's wife!" Sheila said in disbelief. "Isn't it scary that the wife of a public figure would have such poor taste?"

"Terrifying. I wonder if Sorensen's wife knows? Or even suspects?"

"I don't know. But I can tell you his mother-in-law doesn't know. He'd have the rug pulled out from under him so fast..."

Headed back in the right direction, satisfied that they hadn't been seen, Dana glanced at Sheila. "Want to come home with me for a cup of coffee? I'm fixing a special dinner but I don't have to put it on for an hour yet."

"What's the occasion?"

"Nothing. I'm just trying to impress Gabe with my domestic abilities."

"Why? He seemed very impressed with your professional ones last time I talked to him."

"Gabe's home," Sheila noticed a short time later as Dana pulled into the driveway behind the van. "We'd better skip the coffee. I'll walk home."

Dana caught Sheila's arm as they got out of the car. "Don't be silly. He probably just forgot something. He said he wouldn't be home until six. Come on, we've got plenty of time for a cup of coffee."

The sound of raucous male laughter stopped them both inside the front door.

"And there I was," a masculine voice said, humor

heavy in it, "in this sheepskin vest that had more fleas in it than a dog team, and she says to me—"

"Jack!" Sheila gasped on a whisper.

Unattended, the front door slammed closed and whatever "she" said was lost. Then there was silence, and Jack stood in the doorway to the living room.

Dana could feel the tension in Sheila and knew Jack saw nothing and no one but the tall blond girl. For an interminable moment the two simply stared at each other. Resisting the urge to shove Sheila and yank her brother forward, Dana simply stood still and waited.

Sheila and Jack began to walk toward each other. Then Jack stopped and Sheila, too, paused.

Dana held back a moan, thinking defeatedly that her stubborn brother would stand there till hell froze over waiting for Sheila to come to him; and Sheila, afraid to be hurt again, was unable to go to Jack.

Then Jack took one firm step and another, and strode purposefully toward Sheila, who ran the last few steps that separated them, flying into his outstretched arms.

The breath left Dana in a rush and she felt suddenly light-headed and weak.

"Sit down, Dana." Firm hands pushed her into a chair.

She stared openmouthed at the man. "Dad!" she exclaimed. Then, hearing what she had said, corrected herself. "Barton."

"I picked Jack up in Paris, and it seemed like a good time for a family reunion. Gabe says I can have your old room tonight." He looked over his shoulder at Jack and Sheila still locked in each other's arms. "I don't think we have to worry about where he's going to sleep." He turned back to her with a cautious smile. "You don't mind, do you, *Mrs.* Cameron?"

Dana smiled back as her pulse began to behave normally. "Of course not."

Their conversation was halted as Gabe handed Dana a shot of brandy and sat on the arm of her chair. His eyes were loving and concerned.

"You okay?" he asked.

She nodded, grimacing as she sipped. "I think so. I'm just—surprised."

"You should have seen me when they walked into the *Register* office together." Gabe urged the glass to her lips again. He glanced up at the couple still embracing and said with mock grimness, "I wish they were more pleased to see each other."

Jack and Sheila finally stood apart, looking sheepishly at their audience. Jack came to lean over Dana and give her a hug. "Hi, sweetheart."

"Oh, Jack!" She hugged him fiercely. "It's so good to see you in one piece. Are you feeling as good as you look?"

"I feel great! I got the story of a lifetime. Even *Newsweek*'s Paris bureau called me about a feature."

"Really?"

"Yep. And Gabe's going to do the text for a pictorial I've got in mind on the tribesmen I camped with."

Dana smiled at her husband. "In your spare time?"

He ruffled her hair. "Now that I have such an efficient veteran of the San Francisco *Daily News* on staff, I practically have time to waste."

"What I really want to know—" Sheila folded her hands on Jack's shoulder, her eyes smiling at him "—is what 'she' said when you stood there in your flea-ridden sheepskin vest."

Jack glanced at Gabe and then at his father, all three exchanging a grinning look. "Well, I'll tell you," he said, looking intimately into Sheila's eyes. "I'll pose the very question to you—later."

Sheila swallowed, fighting a blush. "I see. Yes... well..."

"Dad." Jack squeezed Sheila's shoulder and drew his father to her. "I'd like you to meet my fiancée Sheila Mitchell, Barton Freeman, my father."

Freeman took Sheila's hands, and Dana saw a quiet charm in him she hadn't known he possessed. He spoke to her for a few moments, Jack looking proudly on. A feeling of unreality took hold of Dana. Jack was home, safe and sound; their father, from whom they'd been alienated for so long, had gone to Paris to pick him up and was now chatting companionably with Sheila. If appearances could be trusted, it looked very much as though the girl's reservations about Jack had been unfounded. Everything seemed to be working out with a "happy ending" certain for everyone.

Then to what could she attribute her vague feeling of uneasiness, this curious uncertainty that lay over her relationship with Gabe like a fine netting? Love, understanding, compassion all came through, yet something vital was blocked, preventing their happiness from being complete. Was it trust, she wondered? Weren't the bars all gone?

She glanced up at Gabe and with uncanny perception read the same thought in his eyes. For a moment they measured each other. Then with infinite tenderness Gabe combed her hair away from her face with his fingers and kissed her.

"What do you want to do about dinner?" he asked.

"Dinner's my treat," Freeman said. "Let's do it up big. We've got a lot to celebrate. Where'll we go?"

The matter was debated and discussed at length. Jack

and Sheila finally left for her apartment to change, and the other three began to prepare for a festive evening.

Dana's father, bathed, was relaxing in her old room; and Dana toweled off in the bathroom while Gabe looked into the steamy mirror, wiping the last trace of shaving cream from his face.

She stood in the bathtub, the fluffy brown terry sheet held against her while she rubbed at her hair with a corner of it.

"When are you going to find time to help Jack with his book?" she asked. "You hardly have time to breathe now."

"An all-new computerized Warrenton *Register* will make life easier for all of us."

Dana frowned at his reflection in the medicine cabinet mirror. "What do you mean?"

Gabe wiped off his razor and dropped it into a drawer. "I talked to Ben Wagner's son Todd this morning," he said, splashing on a spicy after-shave. "He's a carpenter and he's worked up some plans for remodeling the office. We're supposed to meet him Tuesday morning to talk about it."

She felt an instant, powerful stab of suspicion, followed by an even more powerful jolt of fear. He was going to carry through with all the renovations they had once talked about. But where would the money come from?

Gabe's hands on her bare waist lifted her out of the tub, and she pulled on the towel clutched to her as he tried to tug it free.

"I'll dry your back," he said, his pointed look noting her sudden shyness. "What's the matter?"

"Nothing." She relinquished the towel and turned her back to him, wondering what was the matter with her. She had once offered to pay for the very changes he was now planning to put into effect. What perverse little demon inside her made her resent the fact that he might be taking her up on it?

Gabe rubbed her shoulders and back vigorously, his touch gentling as it ran over her bottom and down her legs.

He tossed the towel aside and, holding the back of her to him with a strong arm around her waist, planted a kiss over her shoulder on the mound of her still damp breast. He smelled of toothpaste and spice, and she turned in his arms, wrapping hers around his waist, splaying her fingers against the warm flesh of his broad back.

She wouldn't believe that he had married her for the money to bring his precious weekly into the computer age. He had promised he loved her for herself. The best way she knew to fight her suspicions, to cling to his promise, was to lose herself in his arms.

She moved invitingly against his chest, noting abstractedly the quiver of his muscles, his indrawn breath.

She looked into his eyes, found passion kindling in them, and asked on a whisper, "Is there time?"

Without a moment's hesitation, Gabe swept her into his arms. "There's always time," he whispered huskily and carried her to the bedroom.

AFTER DINNER they went to Sheila's for coffee and more conversation. It seemed, now that the family was united again, each seemed reluctant to let the others go. Watching her father all evening, Dana saw him hang on Jack's descriptions of his weeks in Afghanistan and knew that it was more than his journalist's interest. It was genuine fascination with his son.

Jack, too, seemed unable to believe that his father was here now, that he had traveled to Paris to bring him home. Several times during the evening he said, "And I looked up from my crème de cacao at this little café on the rue de la Paix and who did I see? Dad!" Not "my father" in a tight, strained tone, or "Barton Freeman," as he used to refer to the man while he and Dana were growing up, but a completely accepting "Dad!"

Her own relationship with her father was still an unfinished story, however; and she watched him greedily, wishing she had her brother's gift for following his instincts and usually being right. She seemed to have the uncanny ability to analyze things from every angle and somehow still make the wrong move.

With a possessive arm around Dana, Gabe joined in the spirited conversation, flinging friendly insults at Jack and taking them back with like enthusiasm.

"I can't believe you married my sister!" Jack said when Sheila's clock struck midnight and the conversation began to wind down. "I suppose you compromised her and felt you had to do the honorable thing."

Gabe laughed. "Nope. She kept threatening me with your towering rage should you come home and find I'd harmed her."

"Well," Jack said on a chuckle, "I'm glad I don't have to go up against you. I'd have hated to hurt you."

Gabe nodded dryly. "Merciful for all of us. So are you going to return the favor?"

"And marry your sister? You bet." Jack stopped Sheila, who was clearing cups and plates, and pulled her into his lap. She landed with a little shriek of laughter. "I've got to get to New York with my story, but I'll be home in a week. Can you guys stand up for us?" He named a date and turned to Barton. "Think you can make it, Dad? And bring Janine?"

Dana saw her father swallow as though the invitation were a little bit of a surprise. "Of course. We'd be honored."

"Sure we can," Gabe said. "But I don't know if I can stand being this close to you. I mean friend and landlord was all right, but now we're going to be brothers-in-law and partners."

"Partners?" Dana asked. She looked around the room in surprise and thought it strange that no one else appeared to consider that news.

Sheila nodded with a broad smile. "Jack's buying into the paper. We're all going to be a corporation."

She smiled awkwardly. "Oh."

"Oh?" Jack repeated with exasperation. "That's my pragmatic sister. She becomes vice-president of a major corporation, one that will soon be listed on the New York Stock Exchange, and she says 'Oh.' Really, sweetheart. You've got to lighten up."

"A listing on the stock exchange might be a little premature, Jack," Gabe said, laughing. Then he looked at Dana, his expression sobering. "Sorry to have it sprung on you like that, but Jack and I talked about it before he went to Afghanistan. Now that he's home, he's sure that's what he wants to do."

Hurt feelings at not having been told were replaced almost immediately by a bright smile as Dana realized that Gabe's new partner was very likely his source of capital to cover the renovation of the Warrenton *Register*.

"That's wonderful," she assured her husband. "I'm pleased, of course."

They discussed business for another hour, Freeman making suggestions for equipment based on the word-processing setup used by his newspapers.

"But be sure to decide on something that's Dana-compatible," he said with an indulgent glance at his daughter. Then he turned to his son-in-law to explain. "For a young woman, she had an awful lot of trouble learning to cope with the computer age."

Dana's head shot up to look at her father with wide, startled eyes. The *Daily News* had switched typesetting procedures shortly after she had joined the staff, and her slow and painful adapting had been a city room joke. Even the old-timers had learned to cope with the patience-testing electronic hardware before she had. But how had he known that?

"And you cast aspersions on *my* equipment?" Gabe asked Dana, the picture of affronted dignity.

"Your equipment came over with Lewis and Clark!" Dana silenced him heartlessly, then turned back to her father. "How did you know I had so much trouble with it?"

"Spies," he replied easily.

"Wise man," Gabe complimented, rising to his feet and bringing his wife with him. "You got to watch her every minute. We've got to hit the road, Sheila. I have to stop at the *Register* on the way home."

"But it's one o'clock in the morning," she pointed out, distributing coats.

"I know. But Jack's arrival interrupted the makeup of an ad I have to show a proof of in the morning. Won't take me long."

Jack and Sheila, arm in arm on the doorstep, waved their guests off as Dana waved back, sandwiched in the front of the rented car between her father and her husband.

They dropped Gabe at the office, and he insisted that Dana go home with Freeman.

"But how'll you get home?" she asked in concern.

"It's only three blocks, cupcake, remember?" He leaned back into the car to kiss her. "I'll walk."

"But—"

"You're hovering," he accused with gentle amusement.

She grinned sheepishly. She was. That was what love did to one.

"Sorry. Don't be long," she said, then added softly, "I'll wait up."

"Good girl."

"And Gabe?" Freeman's voice stopped him as he started away. He stooped to look into the car again.

"I'll take care of that little matter we discussed first thing in the morning."

Gabe smiled. "Right. Thanks. Good night."

AT HOME, Dana double-checked the room her father was using to be sure he had everything he needed.

"You're hovering again," Freeman said and smiled, hanging up his suit jacket. "But I must admit I like it." He turned away from the closet and went to the foot of the bed, where she had placed an extra blanket.

"Even though it's June," she said, fiddling with folding and unfolding the length of plaid wool, "it's still chilly here in the evenings. I know you'd like to leave early, so I'll have breakfast ready at—"

"Dana." Freeman took both her hands in his, effectively silencing her. "Tell me what you're thinking. Tell me to go to hell or tell me... tell me I'm forgiven. But don't waltz around me."

She smiled. "Nobody waltzes anymore."

"Janine and I do," he corrected. "Like one pair of feet. As though one foot was just waiting for the other."

Her smile broadened because she understood now how that was. "You're forgiven," she said, squeezing his hands. "And I love you."

No longer cautious, Dana raised her arms to circle her father's neck, then laughed at the bear hug he immediately gave her, first crushing the breath out of her, then holding her as though she might break. She was overcome with an indescribable, bittersweet sense of belonging.

"I do love you, Dad," she said, her hands on his arms as she looked up into his face. "I used to think some failing in me wouldn't let you love me. And I couldn't help but hold that against you."

Pain crossed his beaming face. "And I'll pay for that every day for the rest of my life. But let me try to make it up to you, Dana. God!" He crushed her to him again, then finally released her with reluctance.

"How *did* you know about my battles with the computer?" she asked.

"I did have spies," he admitted shamelessly. "I met with all the department heads regularly, of course; that's just good business. But Bill Spalding, your city editor, always stayed a little longer to catch me up on what was happening with you personally, as far as he knew." Freeman shrugged away the man's complicity. "He had a son he was always at war with. He understood my problem."

Pain, mingled with frustration, filled Dana's eyes. "I would have loved to tell you about it myself," she said.

Freeman shook his head, his eyes telling her he shared her pain. "No, you wouldn't have. You'd have walked away from me. Do you know how many times you've walked away from me in your life? So many times that I got to the point where I couldn't have taken it once more. When you accepted the job and said you'd only take it on condition that I never spoke to you there, I knew I'd have to find another way to keep track of you. And I did."

Shame, regret welled in her. "I'm sorry," she whispered.

"So am I," he said, cupping her face in his hands, his eyes filled with emotion. "But let's stop regretting and just start being father and daughter, all right? You can come to my wedding, and when you and Gabe have your first child, you'll invite us to the christening. We'll write letters and call more often than we should, and someday, when I retire, I'll look for property on the Oregon coast."

"If you'd like to be near us, I suppose you'll have to," Dana replied, laughing. "Your son-in-law plans to go to his final reward while making prints in the Warrenton *Register*'s darkroom."

"With the new equipment and the job printing he'll be able to take on, Gabe's going to be a force to be reckoned with in a few years. And with your fearless brother on his team, they'll be dynamite."

Dana laughed again. "It's a good thing Jack decided to join the team when he did. I think Gabe's equipment has needed a financial shot in the arm for years."

"From what I understand of their arrangement," Freeman explained, lifting his suitcase onto the bed to pull out his pajamas, "Jack's to be just a working partner, without a cash investment."

Carrying his shaving kit to the dresser, Freeman failed to notice his daughter's sudden pallor, the instant loss of sparkle in her eyes. She stared vacantly as her earlier suspicions re-formed in her mind.

"You all right?" Freeman asked, walking back to her.

"Sure. Have you got everything you need?" she asked with forced brightness.

"More than I need. Thank you," he said, snapping his case closed and replacing it on the floor. "You'd better get to bed. You look tired. Tomorrow you have to start gearing up toward another deadline."

"Right." Dana hugged him good night and hurried out of the room.

She sat in the dark in the middle of the big bed she shared with Gabe and tried to rid her mind of the implications of her father's news. But they wouldn't stop nagging her. They clung to her consciousness with claws that tore at her composure.

She doubted that any loan agency would grant the Warrenton *Register* the kind of money Gabe and Jack's plans would require, considering the state of the local economy and the *Register*'s current financial condition. If Gabe wasn't planning to use Jack's money, he must be planning to use his bride's. And though she had once offered him that option, he had denied her suggestion so vehemently that she had firmly believed he would never use her money, even as a last resort.

She was powerless to control the hurt and suspicion that filled her. Finally crawling under the blankets, Dana curled into a tight ball. Her father had gone to bed and the house was silent, except for the contented purr coming from Sidney, who lay at her feet.

Dana tensed as the front door opened and closed quietly and Gabe ran lightly up the stairs. Turning her face into the pillow, she tried to breathe slowly and evenly in an imitation of sleep. She felt Gabe lean over her, felt his gentle hand in her hair, then his lips on her cheek.

He moved away, and she relaxed as the quiet sounds of his undressing came from across the room. Then he was beside her, gently securing an arm around her waist and burying his face in her hair.

Dana stared wide-eyed into the darkness for hours.

Chapter Eleven

Todd Wagner had wonderful plans for the Warrenton *Register*. What was now a useless backyard would become a well-lit, comfortably fitted answer to every small newspaper's dream, a modern press room. A small space beside it would be a mailing room, complete with baling machine.

The present rustic back room would be divided into a large photographic darkroom and camera room, another room for phototypesetters—no more Just-o-Writer to fight with—and an area with light tables for pasteup. The front office would be left for public contact, with spaces allocated for classified and display advertising and editorial desks, one labeled "Dana." The lunchroom boasted its own bathroom—no more running across to the all-night restaurant. Finally, there was a small conference room.

Gabe and Dana looked at each other over the plans at Pop's Restaurant.

"What do you think?" Gabe asked.

Todd's plans were exciting, creative and astute; it was as though he had gone beyond the rough sketches Gabe made on newsprint and read the thoughts right out of the publisher's mind. They were perfect.

"They're wonderful!" she said brightly, taking a hasty sip of coffee. "I'd say go right ahead with them as soon as possible."

Gabe observed her over the rim of his coffee cup, then placed the cup carefully in its saucer. "Why don't you like them?" he asked gently.

She looked up at him defensively, her eyes so dark the pupils were lost. "I said I like them."

"But you lied."

Dana studied her watch with a brisk movement of her wrist. "Look, I'd better get moving on the typing."

Gabe caught her hand as she reached for her purse. "There's plenty of time. I want to talk about this."

She was half standing, and still holding her wrist, Gabe gestured with his free hand for her to sit when she did not immediately comply. "Stay put!" he said more firmly. "You're going to sit there and tell me what's bothering you."

"At the moment," she snapped back, "*you're* bothering me."

He frowned. "I can see that. And it started Thursday night and has been building all weekend."

Her heart pounding, anger and anxiety all confused inside her, Dana sat and stared at her knotted hands, glancing up only once to give him a dark glare.

"You never sleep with your face in the pillow," Gabe pointed out calmly, "and you pretended to be asleep after telling me you were going to wait up. For the past four days you've made every effort to be wherever it is that I'm not, and every time I touch you you stiffen up like a cadaver—and you're about as warm. What is it?"

Dana stared at him angrily and he stared back.

"I understand that Jack is investing effort and ideas

but not money into the Warrenton *Register*," she said finally, feeling her own blood pulse as she spoke.

Gabe frowned in confusion, as though that had been the last thing he expected her to say. "That's right, for a smaller share. He'd like a little freedom to pursue a few ideas of his own, and I don't need his money."

She let the silence hang for a moment; then she asked heavily, "Because you've got mine?"

The silence stood between them again, but this time it was deafening. She saw understanding dawn in his eyes and, right behind it, a flashing anger that both pleased and frightened her.

"I see," he said with alarming quiet, his eyes darkening to slate. "You're on to me at last. What was it that gave me away? The dollar signs in my eyes?"

Dana's glare sharpened. "How dare you joke!"

"My behavior is in keeping with our relationship, Dana," he said, dropping the darkly humorous tone. He leaned toward her, his eyes darkening even more. "If you mistrust me that easily, then everything between us is a joke."

"I don't mistrust you that easily," she repeated his word scornfully. "I distrust you because it's all so familiar!"

"Of course it is," he agreed. "Because you've wallowed in it for a whole year. You know why you can't shake the suspicion? You've opted for the pain. You won't let yourself love me and trust me because I can make you forget Scott ever happened to you."

He was on his feet, anger a glowing aura around his casually clad body. "Well, I, personally, am not into pain," he said, slapping a bill down on the table. "So I suggest you spare us both and take your precious money back to San Francisco."

Words stuck in Dana's throat and he looked at her as he slipped out of the booth. "Nothing to say?" he demanded coldly.

"It's Tuesday," she said stiffly. "And we lost a lot of time with Todd this morning. We're way behind."

"I did it without you before," he reminded her coldly. "I can do it again. And the way things are, I'd prefer to."

Dana leapt up and snatched his arm as he turned to leave. "Gabe," she said conciliatorily, the very thought of leaving him a terrifying prospect. Her eyes pleaded. "Where *is* the money for the renovation coming from?"

He looked at her for a long moment, then he gently but firmly removed her hand from his arm. "Goodbye, Dana," he said, and turned away.

DANA DROVE aimlessly for hours. In all she had endured of loneliness and pain throughout her childhood, then during her marriage to Scott, the future had never looked this bleak. For a few brief months Gabe had given her something without which she would never be complete again. And she would hurt all the more for having tasted love and lost it.

She slammed the steering wheel with the palm of her hand. Calling Gabe every name she could think of, she turned back toward the *Register* office, knowing the only alternative was to finish out the day. Only an absolute pig would leave Gabe alone the day before deadline.

Darlene, hard at work typing, looked up in surprise as Dana walked into the office.

"Feeling better?" she asked in concern.

When Dana looked back at her blankly, Darlene supplied, "Gabe said you'd gone home sick."

Dana snorted. "Well, I've had a miraculous recovery."

"Ohhhhh," Darlene said, stretching the word as though something was suddenly clear to her. "Had your first fight, huh? Don't worry about it. My parents have been doing it for years."

When Dana fixed her with a glower, Darlene turned back to her work with a hastily spoken "sorry."

It was almost dinnertime, and Darlene had already gone home, when the office door opened. Dana flung her head up, her eyes angry at the interruption. Seeing Jack, she forced a smile.

"Hi. You're supposed to be home writing your story."

He waved a manila envelope in the air. "I did it. I want Gabe to look it over."

"He's in the darkroom," Dana snarled.

Jack sat on the edge of her desk. "First fight, huh?"

Dana growled, tossing down the blue pencil with which she'd been correcting Darlene's almost flawless galleys. "How'd you like to go back to Afghanistan," she asked, shaking a small fist at him, "without benefit of an airplane?"

"Tsk, tsk," he clucked, shaking his head at her. "And you used to be such an even-tempered young woman. Being in love isn't supposed to make you mean."

"I'm not mean, I'm just... I don't know. Tired, I guess." She looked at him crossly. "Why can't *I* check your story, anyway? I'm in the business, too, you know."

"I know," he said, grinning. "But the chief's a real pro, you know what I mean?"

She did and he was right. But it burned her pride clear through.

"Shall I announce you," she asked. "Or can you find your way back by yourself?"

Jack shook his head in a "touchy, touchy" gesture and went into the back room.

Dana had locked the front office and run across the street to bring back a sandwich by the time Jack reappeared.

"Lord!" he said emphatically, looking back in the direction from which he had just come. "He's got the same thing you've got."

"He hated your story and your pictures?" Dana guessed.

"No. He liked them. It's me he doesn't seem overly fond of."

"It's probably because your investment in our little merger is only your sterling talent," Dana said, tearing the galley as she scored through an error. She tossed the pencil down angrily.

"What?" Jack asked after the briefest pause.

Covering her face with her hands, Dana shook her head. "Never mind," she finally said, offering Jack a smile that was only half sincere and very sad. "Go on home. Forget I said anything."

But Jack sat on the corner of her desk and frowned down at her. "Do I detect a problem you need to share?"

"No."

"You and Gabe did have a fight."

"It's none of your business."

"My sister and my best friend are none of my business?"

"Sheila is your business," Dana said briskly, trying to get to her feet. Jack planted a foot on the arm of her chair, effectively blocking her exit from behind the desk.

"She's shopping for a wedding dress," he said, studying his sister's face closely. "What's happened between you two since Thursday night? You looked like disgustingly typical newlyweds."

Dana's bottom lip quivered, and Jack pushed her back into her chair. "He won't tell me about the renovation," she blurted, drawing a deep breath to halt tears.

Jack shook his head in obvious confusion. "I was there when he first showed you the plans. And isn't that what the two of you did with Todd this morning?"

"I mean..." She shot her brother a reluctant glance. "I mean... the financing."

"There is no—" Jack began, then stopped midsentence as he finally understood the source of their altercation. He looked at her with a disgust almost as complete as Gabe's had been. "So, that's it. The money paranoia again."

"Jack, we're talking tens of thousands of dollars here!" Dana pointed out aggressively. "With the financial shape this paper's in, no bank would give it to him, and he's not getting it from you."

"I offered," Jack said coolly. "He turned me down."

"Then where," she demanded, "is it coming from?"

"This may surprise you, sweetie," Jack said, folding his arms and fixing her with a judicious look, "considering your personal preoccupation with our money, but there are other people besides us who have it; people who have worked and saved for it; people who don't need or want other people's money."

Dana's eyes, dark with misery, widened. "Gabe?"

"He was the L.A. *Times*' highest-paid correspondent for more than a decade," he explained with a distinct edge to the patient sound of his voice. "He made a few wise investments, and when he moved here, he sold a custom-designed house on Puget Sound and one in Malibu. He's not quite in our moneyed class, I suppose, but he can well afford the renovations, I'm sure. And he earned every dime. I'm ashamed of you that after knowing him you could have ever thought what you did."

Afraid to believe that Jack was right, not simply because it meant that she had been wrong but because it dangled the hope that Gabe really did love her, Dana asked helplessly, "Well, if he's had the money all along, why did he wait so long to do something about the old equipment and—"

"Because, twit," Jack said, getting to his feet, "he was doing fine until Sorensen backed out with his grocery ad, thanks to you. Gabe wanted to know how involved the community was with this little rag and how much they needed it—that takes time. Well, it's proven itself. People read it! He's doubled its circulation, and the only reason he hasn't tripled the advertising is that the area's so depressed. But with electronic typesetters and printing equipment that we can use for job printing as well as putting out the paper, we can generate all sorts of peripheral income that'll help us along till things pick up. With the right management we can give that nearby daily a run for their money and maybe even the *Oregonian*."

Jack was thinking big, Dana knew, but then he believed in Gabe. If only she had.

"And the amenities he's proposing are because you and Sheila will also be at the office all the time. He's trying to upgrade your working conditions and you accuse him of marrying you for your money." Jack shook his head and tucked his envelope under his arm. "It's time to come out of the past, kiddo. Gabe Cameron is not Scott MacKenzie, and if you confuse the two, you deserve to live your life alone. See ya."

IT WAS ALMOST NINE when Gabe emerged from the darkroom and then it was to bark that he was going to get something to eat. He was back in half an hour wearing an expression Dana didn't dare challenge. She went back to work proofreading his editorial, in which he came down harder than ever in favor of the Work Corps.

Gabe and Dana worked in silence except for the few orders he flung at her. In the small hours of the morning they drove home without speaking; and as they walked into the living room, he tossed his jacket on the chair. "You can have the bed," he snapped. "I'll sleep on the sofa."

"I'll make some coffee while you're showering," she said in a cold, emotionless voice, unable to find a chink in his armor through which to approach him with an apology.

"I'm not thirsty," he told her, heading for the stairs.

"You gobbled down your dinner. Can I fix you—"

"No." And he was gone.

Dana flipped on the lights in the kitchen and filled the coffeepot anyway. She just saved the can of fragrant ground coffee from falling as Sidney leapt onto the counter to rub against her.

"Hi, Sidney." Now good friends with the feline, Dana took him in her arms and stroked his rich, black fur, feeling his purr vibrate all the way through her.

Their unorthodox meeting had been forgotten by both of them, and Dana now searched the butcher's for tidbits for him, and in return, he slept at her feet.

She looked into his amber eyes, slitted in contentment, and suddenly remembered Gabe's words when he was trying to encourage her to see her father. "Don't make decisions in the dark," he'd said, comparing her fear of meeting her father again with the terror she'd felt when first meeting Sidney in the basement. Gabe was responsible for so many changes in her life, for so much good that had come out of darkness.

Dana put the cat down decisively and drew a deep breath. She was going to apologize to Gabe if she had to sit on him to make him listen!

When she topped the stairs she turned to the bathroom and heard the sound of water running in the shower. She knocked loudly on the bathroom door. No answer. Of course, if he was washing his hair, she reasoned, he wouldn't be able to hear her. She tried the door and it gave. Taking one small step inside, she called his name.

"Gabe!" She waited; no answer.

Taking another step inside, she called a little louder, "Gabe!" No answer.

She saw his form outlined through the plastic shower curtain and was sure now that he was simply ignoring her. She poked the curtain at his shoulder level. "Gabe!" she shouted.

"What!" he demanded impatiently.

"I want to talk to you."

"I'm taking a shower!"

"When you're finished!" she called back, summoning patience.

"When I'm finished I'm going to bed!" was his terse reply.

"All right, Cameron," she muttered, slipping out of her shoes. She yanked the curtain aside and stepped fully dressed into the tub behind him.

He looked at her over his shoulder, a look he usually reserved for ink-cleaner salesmen. "I'm busy," he said, soaping his shoulder.

"I noticed that," she returned dryly, taking the soap from him to run it in wide circles along his back. "If I'm to fit this little talk in between your shower and your going to bed, this is my only alternative." She soaped his firm, muscular backside, noticing his muscles tauten, then ran the soap along his thighs, down to the backs of his knees. She straightened and said calmly, "Turn around and rinse the soap off and I'll do your chest."

"No," he said, putting his hand back for the soap. "I'll do it myself. Get out of my shower."

Exasperated now, she grabbed hold of his arm for balance and stepped carefully around him. Fixing him with a scolding look, she shook a finger at him, preparing to lecture him. Unfortunately, she had stepped directly under the shower spray and the hot water directly on top of her head shocked her into silence, though her mouth remained open and her scolding finger raised.

For a long moment they looked at each other, he fighting to retain his glower and she, her hair in a drenched and blinding sheet over her face, recognizing that her dignity was lost.

They began to laugh simultaneously and he pulled her to him, reaching behind her to turn off the water. Still laughing, Gabe began to peel the clothes from her, laughter bubbling afresh every time he looked up at her face. Her light laughter mingled with his deep booming sounds until she stepped out of her panties and they both stood naked in the warm, steamy room.

Gabe put a hand to the tiles behind her head, the fresh smell of his clean body filling her nostrils. "What was so important that you had to jump into my shower to tell me?"

"I'm sorry," she said simply. She looked away from him to her hands. "I have this paranoia thing about... about money. And... I mean... you're really too good to be true, you know. When you started talking about the renovation, the old fears came back to haunt me. Then when you said Jack was going to be your partner, I thought you were getting the money from him. When my father told me you weren't, I didn't know what to think!"

At his challenging look, she admitted meekly, "I know. I jumped to a faulty conclusion, and I'm sorry. Jack set me straight this afternoon."

"What really hurt my feelings," Gabe said, his expression still condemning, "was that you confused me with Scott."

"No, I didn't!" she shouted at him; then, when he looked at her skeptically, she repeated forcefully but in a quieter tone, "I didn't confuse you with anybody. How could I? I think I'm just afraid to believe that something this good has happened to me. I'm waiting for somebody to tell me there's been a terrible mistake and you and your love were really intended for... for Linda Evans."

Gabe laughed, his eyes still grave. "She's older than I."

"Maybe," Dana agreed. "But she's built like someone who'd fit in your arms."

He laughed again, the gravity finally leaving his expression as he enfolded her in his arms. "You fit just fine. In fact, I've almost died of wanting you the past few nights."

Gabe reached out of the tub to snatch a towel from the rack and wrap her in it.

"I swear to you," he said, "that I love you and that's why I married you; that I don't want your money or your brother's. All I want is you—and I want you always."

"And I love you," she said, her eyes wide and earnest. "And I'm so sorry I doubted you."

"That," he said softly, his mouth closing in on hers, "is just what I wanted to hear."

He kissed her as though drawing life from her, and Dana allowed herself to be devoured, herself drinking from his questing mouth with a thirst that made her tremble. His large hands ran along the towel, rubbing motions over her back and bottom pressing her into his body, thrilling her with the evidence of his passion for her.

He yanked the towel from her and asked, his hands framing her glowing face, "Have you ever made love in a bathtub?"

Her eyes sparkled at him. "Are we about to?"

"Otherwise we'd have to run for the bed," he said with a soft laugh. "And that's so uncool."

"Then that's definitely out." She smiled at him a little uncertainly. "What is the social etiquette for making love in the bathtub?"

"Simple. We place the towel on the bottom of the tub for the lady's comfort." He did as he explained, then helped her sit and held her hands as she reclined, smiling. He knelt astride her, his grin broadening. "You pretend you're Deborah Kerr and I'm Burt Lancaster and that the towel is sand and that there's water lapping at our ankles. Pacific Ocean water."

Delighted with his playfulness, drunk with her love for him, Dana raised her hands up to his neck to draw him down. "Okay, I've got it. Let's play the scene."

Pillowing her head in his cupped hands, Gabe entered her swiftly, easily. She strained against him greedily, exploding in the forcefulness of his lovemaking. Like a thrill seeker on a roller coaster ride, she rode the crest, then swooped down, up and down and up again to perch one lengthened moment in delicious, delirious agony, before plummeting down again.

Breathless, gasping, she lay on the towel, her heavy eyelids opening to see Gabe's smiling face. She looked around, almost surprised to find herself in the bathtub.

"Now we can make it to the bed," Gabe said, trying to pull her up.

She resisted. "No. I want to stay here and do it again."

"We'll do it again in bed."

"I want to do it again here," she insisted, laughing, trying to pull him down again.

"Dana!" He tickled her ribs to make her let go and she screamed, a foot kicking out in protest, striking the shower knob. Warm water struck Gabe's back full force and as he swore and ducked aside, it drenched Dana, who screamed, then collapsed again in helpless laughter.

"See what you've done, you little monster!" Gabe scolded, still laughing.

Convulsed, Dana allowed herself to be pulled to her feet. "You said to imagine water lapping at our ankles!"

Chapter Twelve

Wednesday morning brought the usual last-minute crises, but Gabe and Dana faced them with a light-heartedness that had been absent from their work the past few days. Gabe rushed in and out to get doughnuts for their morning coffee, to cover a special commissioners' meeting, to take a last-minute photo of a cargo ship that had run into the dock.

Every time he passed her, Dana was kissed, caressed, pinched or otherwise made to feel his presence. There was no time to talk, but everything that had to be said pulsed between them. After the previous night there was new music between them—their relationship had deepened, and Dana felt the first tentative steps toward their growth as a couple.

Instead of lunch, when deadline was finally met, they went home to make love until Darlene finally called late in the afternoon to find out why the papers hadn't been picked up from the *Daily Astorian*.

And the glow didn't pall until the following day. Gabe left for the office late, recommending that Dana spend the day at home. That suggestion was accompanied by a lascivious wink that made her laugh and thrilled her to the center of her being.

With the considerable amount of activity that had taken place the night before and the limited amount of time they had for sleep, she would have been entitled to sleep late and have a leisurely breakfast. But she woke feeling so charged, so full of a vibrating energy that she couldn't lie still longer than it took Gabe to leave for work. Then she was up and dressed and ready to clean every room in the house from top to bottom.

After a quick breakfast of toast and coffee, she did the few dishes and straightened the kitchen, singing and dancing as she worked. Sidney, perched on a stool beside the cupboard, watched her movements around the room like a spectator at a tennis match, the amber eyes in his bewhiskered black face unrevealing. But Dana suspected by the erectness of his posture and his slight withdrawal toward the back of the stool every time she pirouetted by him that he was offended by her loss of dignity.

However, a thorough tickling under his chin reestablished her reliability, and he eased down onto the stool to purr, front paws tucked under his chest.

By lunchtime she had worked her way through the whole house. She was standing in the middle of the living room, wondering what to do next, when the telephone rang. At the sound of Gabe's voice Dana's heart began to behave erratically, and she marveled at the joy she felt at finally knowing, without a doubt, that she was loved for herself and not for the Freeman money.

"Hi!" he said, a gentle growling quality in his voice that she remembered from the middle of the night. "What are you doing for lunch?"

"Nothing," she replied. "What did you have in mind?"

"If you want to eat, come on down to the office and

I'll take you to the Buccaneer.'' He paused, then added in a suggestive undertone. "If you'd like to just while away the hour, I'll be right home.''

Her laugh bubbled up and she heard his low, growling response. "Can't we do both?" she asked.

"Sure," he agreed readily. "In what order?"

"No, you don't," she teased. "I'll come down and we'll eat first. Otherwise, knowing you, we'd never get to it. What time?"

"Half an hour?"

"I'll be there."

"Would you drive the van down?" he asked. "I walked this morning, but Todd called from Portland. He'll be back late tonight and asked me to pick up his load of two-by-fours this afternoon so he can get to work first thing in the morning."

"Okay. Anything else?"

"I love you so much I could die of it," he said, his voice urgent, heavy.

"Oh, Gabe. I've been dancing around the house all morning. Sidney thinks I'm crazy. I love you, too!"

There was a pause; then he asked reluctantly, "You're sure you're hungry?"

"Yes!" she said with a laugh. "But I'm also hungry for you. So don't begrudge a poor chef's salad twenty minutes of my time."

He, too, laughed. "All right. See you at one."

Dana bathed quickly, wound her hair up into a fancy knot and changed into a slim cotton wraparound dress in neon shades of yellow and blue. Completing her outfit wih raffia bag and shoes, she gave Sidney a parting pat and ran out to the van.

It was a beautiful early-summer day. The sky was bright blue without a sign of cloud and the air was still and warm. A robin hopped across the highway out of her path, and she noted that all the blossoms on the trees lining Main Street were gone and bright green leaves caught the sun and shimmered in the stillness. The street was quiet and Dana pulled up directly in front of the office.

As the motor died and the old van shuddered to a halt, the glove compartment fell open and the usual stack of papers Gabe stuffed into it fell out onto the mat. Wondering if Gabe's money would ever run to purchasing a new van with a glove compartment that remained closed, Dana reached down to retrieve the papers. As she put the odds and ends of notes and receipts into an orderly pile, her eyes were caught by the name of her father's corporation. Frowning, she pulled out the slip of paper on which the name was printed and found it to be a check. A cold fist of feeling settled in her chest; the amount for which the check had been written impressed even Dana.

She consciously fought the suspicions that rose to her mind. She countered the thoughts of a loan or an outright gift from her father to Gabe with the vivid memories of the long night she'd spent in his arms, his promise that money had nothing to do with his love for her, and his reassurances of love that morning and, just now, on the telephone.

But all the years of self-seeking friends, ambitious suitors and a grasping husband fought the memories down, and she had to face the threat squarely.

With her eyes on the spring-green trees and the quiet main street that had become more dear to her than any home she'd ever known, Dana realized that her brief idyll was over.

The wrenching pain she had spent the past year and a

half fighting down now rose to blanket her so that
every inch of her skin and every pulse of her soul ached
with it. She screamed aloud in the confines of the van
and finally the sound of her own anguish made her
livid with rage.

How dare he! After all he had said to her and
all...all he had done. To deceive her like that—to use
her! As though taking money from her father didn't
prove as clearly as taking her own money would have
that he had married her for the sole purpose of doing
just that.

Snatching her purse off the passenger seat, Dana decided that Gabe was about to get a scoop on some news
he wouldn't be able to print. As she prepared to step
out of the van she spotted Sorensen coming down the
street, face flushed, mouth working in low but colorful
obscenities. He carried a rolled-up newspaper in one
hand, and she didn't have to wonder where he was going.

As Dana rounded the van and stepped onto the side-
walk, the grocer burst through the front door of the
Warrenton *Register*. She stormed in after him, and as
she closed the door behind her, he stood across the
office in front of Gabe's desk roaring profane threats.

Gabe, leaning back in his chair in a relaxed pose,
looked from the man towering over his desk to his
wife. "Why don't you wait for me in the van, Dana?"
he suggested.

"No," she replied equably. She was never going to
wait for him anywhere again, but before she told him
what he could do with his renovations and said goodbye, she had another bully to settle with.

Gabe didn't know it, of course, but she could deal

with Sorensen now. In the excitement of Jack's home-coming, the talk about his marriage to Sheila, her father's visit and all the other stories on which she'd been hard at work, she'd completely forgotten to tell Gabe what she had learned the day she and Sheila had searched out Sorensen's country cottage. And suddenly she saw a way to use what she had learned.

She ignored Gabe and sat on the corner of his desk, deliberately placing herself between him and Sorensen.

"I've heard dirty words before." She looked up at the florid face of the man towering over her. "I am impressed, though. You do make them sound dirtier than anyone else I know. What's the problem today?"

Sorensen looked at Gabe over her head. "We'll talk outside."

"Dana—" Gabe began.

"No, we'll talk right here, Mr. Sorensen," Dana said sweetly, smiling into his purple face. "Why don't you sit down and we'll all try to be civilized. No? Well, we'll see." She had hooked a chair with her foot and gave it a kick that slid it behind the big man. "I have to be here for this conversation. I know a little more about this story than my husband does." Dana looked over her shoulder at Gabe. He studied the battle flares in her eyes with a warning glare in his own.

"Oh?" he asked mildly.

"Yes." She turned back to Sorensen. "We've got your number. Did the development company you've been dealing with lower their bid for your land when they heard a Work Corps facility might be going in across from it instead of the condominium?"

Sorensen's face turned an even deeper shade of purple. "Tomorrow you will not have one advertiser in this town!" he snarled. "I hold private loans on sixty percent of Main Street, and if they want to stay in business they'll know which side to take!"

"I imagine Mrs. Phillips will know which side to take also," Dana said quietly. It gave her great pleasure that he reacted as though he felt seriously threatened. Had she felt less suicidal herself, his look of horror would have made her laugh.

"What," he asked, bluffing, "does that mean?"

Dana took Gabe's camera from the spot on the corner of the desk where it always rested, ready, and ran her fingers absently over the leather cover. "It means," she said, looking up at him, her eyes sharpening, "that she would not be pleased to know about what happens out on the airport road, Box 277."

For a full moment he simply stared at her. Then he fell into the chair she had kicked behind him earlier, his eyes still riveted to her face, anger and shock mingled in them.

She shook her shoulder in a mock shudder, lowering her eyes lest she betray her delight in besting him at last. "Not to mention what the mayor himself would think of it. Unless, of course, you were planning to leave your lovely wife and your wealthy mother-in-law for Mrs. Crowell?"

The big man swallowed, fear and greed apparent in his face. Dana glanced back at Gabe, to find him once again relaxed in his chair, a hand at his mouth as though he shielded a grin.

Sorensen seemed to collect himself and stood over Dana. Gabe rose behind her, and she felt a little like a valley between two erupting mountains. The men glared at each other over her head; then Sorensen looked down at her.

"If you breathe a word..." he began to threaten.

She dangled the camera in front of her by its strap. "I don't have to," she said significantly. "There are a set of prints in our safety deposit box, and a set in the hands of our attorney, should any injury come to a member of the Warrenton *Register* staff or to the premises itself...."

He faced her for a long moment, a war going on in his eyes.

"You're bluffing!" he said finally, if a little weakly.

"Am I?" she challenged, and at just the right moment, when she saw in his eyes that he thought she might be, she stood up. "She wears a lovely black peignoir," she said, lowering her voice and running her hands in a V down her front. "Very décolleté," she added. Then she took the boutonniere from his lapel, passed it under his nose several times as she had seen the woman do, then tucked it back into the buttonhole. "And she has a pet name for you that would make a great headline."

Hate, fear, fury and disbelief were all reflected on his face. Then, though he tried to hide it, there followed a look of defeat. He turned around and left the office, the door closing behind him with a final slam.

For a moment Dana and Gabe simply sat there, she with her back to him, perched on the corner of his desk, he standing behind her. She could feel his eyes staring at the back of her head.

Finally he came around to look down at her. "Where in the hell," he asked, "did you find out all that?"

"The day I went to the courthouse. You were right. All his and Mrs. Sorensen's community property is in her mother's name. But I checked the records in his name, just to see. And I found property at Box 277 on the airport road." She sighed heavily, the adrenaline that had primed her to fight Sorensen seeming to leave her in a rush. She now felt tired and drained. "Sheila and I went to check it out and found him leaving the cottage, with Mrs. Crowell waving him off in her negligee."

"And you got pictures?" Gabe asked incredulously.

Despite everything, she had to smile at that. "No. There wasn't time even if I had thought of it. I was bluffing. But we did see her put a flower in his lapel. Apparently that lent sufficient credibility to my bluff. And everybody's got a pet name they probably wouldn't want to see in print."

"Well," Gabe said dryly, "if he doesn't sue us for extortion, I'd say he is no longer a problem."

Dana got slowly to her feet to face Gabe. She didn't seem able to dredge up the fury she had felt in the van. What predominated now was an overwhelming sense of sadness and disappointment.

"We've solved the problem of Sorensen," she said heavily. "Now all that remains to be settled is the problem of us."

Gabe folded his arms across his chest, his gaze narrowing on her. "Yes. I knew something was wrong when you walked in the door. What has become a problem for us since we spoke on the phone not even an hour ago?"

She drew a steadying breath, angling her chin. "Specifically, it's a problem for you. It won't be a problem for me—" *Ha!* she thought grimly "—because I've been through this once before. It hurts like hell but you get over it. You, however, will have to find an alternative source of funds for your renovation project. I'm calling my father to have him stop payment on this check immediately."

Almost surprised to find that she still held it in her hand, Dana balled it up in her fist and swallowed a sob before throwing it in his face. She took a mere second to note the anger flaring in his eyes before turning on her heel to walk briskly out to the van.

That she could still walk and breathe, that her heart could still beat when broken, amazed her, but she couldn't concentrate on her body right now. Fitting the key in the lock of the van door was a monumental project considering the way her hand trembled, the way she really wanted to put her fist through the window.

The hand that closed over hers while it struggled with the key didn't help. She stared at it rather than look up at Gabe.

"Get your hand off me," she demanded quietly as an older couple walked by and smiled.

"Dana—" Gabe began dangerously.

"Get your hand *off* me!" she repeated, a trifle louder this time.

"Dana, if you don't let go of that damned door handle and listen to me," Gabe demanded, "I'm going to apply this hand where it'll do the most good!"

She gave him a withering glance. "I'm terrified. Now buzz off and—"

"I'm going to ask you once more," he said, his voice carefully controlled, the hand on her tightening further as hers struggled beneath it. "Come into the office and let me explain."

"You needn't explain," she said, smiling as several of the downtown merchants she had come to know walked past them, presumably on their way to Pop's for lunch. "I understand. All that temptation was too much, even for you. Well, I won't—Ah!"

The door handle almost tore off in her hand as Gabe

yanked her away from the van. He pointed to the office, his eyes blazing. "Get in there," he ordered darkly, "before we become material for our own headline!"

The order was shouted and all the passersby stopped to observe. Dana glared at Gabe, her face reddening, her eyes spewing fire.

"I can shout just as loud as you can!" she screamed at him. "And I won't go in there because I want nothing—"

That was as far as she got before he spun her around, circled her waist with a brawny arm and, lifting her feet clear of the ground, carried her through the knot of grinning, interested spectators and into the office. Despite her kicking feet and clawing hands, Gabe walked across the room with her to his desk and dumped her roughly in the chair.

"Damn you!" she screamed at him, tears of anger and frustration and pain streaming down her face. "You lied to me! You made me love you! And now that I can't live without you, I find out you're just like everybody else!"

Gabe sat on the edge of the desk facing her. He snatched up the telephone receiver and held it out to her. He looked as miserable as she felt but his pain was glazed with an anger that seemed even more powerful than hers.

"Call your father," he said, his voice a quiet roar. "And tell him to stop payment on the check."

"You do it!" she said, weeping and trying to stand up. "I'm getting out of here!"

"No, you're not," he corrected, a yank on her arm landing her back in the chair. "You're staying right where you are. Here. I'll even help you." One long finger stabbed out her father's number at the *Daily News*; then he forced the instrument into her hand.

When a cultured, professional voice answered with the name of the newspaper, she held the receiver to her ear.

"Barton Freeman's office, please," she forced herself to say, wiping tears from her face with the back of her hand. All right. She would do it his way. Whatever it took to get her out of here.

"May I tell him who's calling?"

"His daughter."

The deep, familiar voice was on the line instantly.

"Hi, sweetheart. What's up?"

"Dad." Dana swallowed, making a desperate effort to compose herself. "I want you to...to stop payment on the check."

"What check?" he asked, then added on a note of concern, "Dana, what's wrong? What's happened?"

"The check you wrote to Gabe!" she said forcefully. She glanced at her husband who glared back at her. Looking away, she said, "I want you to stop payment on it."

"You mean he's changed his mind about selling the stock?"

There was a long moment of silence. "The stock?" Dana repeated.

"Yes," her father said. "His stock in Freeman Publishing. Dana, what's going on?"

Dana felt the phone slip from her fingers as she stared up at Gabe, openmouthed.

"Stock?" she said again as color flooded her face, ringing invaded her ears, and a debilitating tremor began in her fingers.

The receiver clattered to the floor and Gabe reached

across her to grab the cord and reel the instrument in like a fighting fish.

"Bart?" Gabe asked.

Dana was unable to focus her attention on the exchange that went on between her husband and the man on the other end of the line.

Stock, she was thinking. "He made a few wise investments," Jack had said. Stock in Freeman Publishing? The check covered the liquidation of his stock in her father's corporation.

"Here," Gabe was saying, forcing the phone back into her hands. "Your father wants to talk to you."

"You listen to me, Dana Cameron," Barton Freeman said firmly as she took the receiver from Gabe. "Jack and your husband both invested money in Freeman Publishing when they came home from Vietnam. Jack wasn't speaking to me but he knew a good investment when he saw one. I've managed to earn them twenty times their investments. Gabe wanted to sell back his stock and use the proceeds to modernize the Warrenton *Register*. I did it. That was the check."

"There was nothing on the stub," she said lamely.

"I ran it through another account to speed it up for him. Dana—" Freeman's voice was grave. "—you owe him an apology. And if he doesn't accept it, I wouldn't blame him."

Dana didn't know what to say to that. A quick glance at her husband's face told her that the likelihood of that happening was strong.

"Thank you, Daddy," she whispered as emotion clogged her throat.

"'Bye, sweetheart," her father replied, then added with a note of sympathy, "I love you."

"I love you, too. 'Bye."

As she hung up the phone and concentrated on holding the shreds of her life together, Dana was comforted by that exchange. She'd found a relationship with her father she'd have never thought possible before moving to Warrenton. But had she forfeited her marriage?

Looking up at Gabe, she found it impossible to tell what he was thinking. The anger in his face had been replaced by a watchful quiet that was almost more unsettling because of its indeterminate direction. If living with Gabe had taught her anything, she decided, squaring her shoulders, it was that there was love in her, and she'd be damned if she'd lose her reason for it without a fight.

"I suppose you're angry," she guessed, wincing as she heard her own absurd words.

Except for the movement of a pulse in his cheek, Gabe didn't react. "Smart girl," he said.

"I'm sorry. I thought I was over the suspicions and the fears, but I wasn't." She shook her head, trying to will herself to make sense so that he would understand the demons that drove her. "That check," she went on, having to pause as her throat constricted, "was all my fears materialized. I saw that large figure and my father's signature, and all I could think of was that it was...happening again. Only this time it wasn't the embarrassment that hurt. It hurt because...because I love you so much!"

"But you don't trust me," he accused, unmoved by her penitence.

Dana sighed in anguish. "I guess it looks that way to you, but it isn't so. It's just that...the check was so incriminating. Anyway..." She glanced at him with a defensive expression when she saw no softening in him. "Considering that you know how I feel about it, couldn't you have told me where the money was coming from?"

He looked at her steadily for a moment; then, his expression still unchanged, he replied, "I've been handling my own financial affairs for a long time. It didn't occur to me."

She could have reminded him that now that he was married that sort of decision might be of interest to his wife also, but decided that from a psychological standpoint, it would have been ill-timed.

Determined to make one final effort to get through to him, Dana stood up and looped her arms around his neck, looking into his eyes. She saw the barest reaction flicker in them.

"Gabe," she said earnestly, "you told me that lovers never lose, remember?"

He studied her for a moment before nodding, his arms still folded across his chest. "Yes."

"You didn't qualify that. You didn't say smart lovers, or brave lovers, or lovers who never make mistakes. You just said lovers. That's us, Gabe. You and me. I'm so sorry I hurt you and I swear to you that I'll do everything in my power to be loving and trusting and smarter than I've been in the past. Please..." She was desperate enough to use her eyes and her body, leaning gently into the inside of his thigh as she stared pleadingly at him. "Couldn't we start again?"

His eyes roved her face and she thought for one glorious moment that she had won. Then he said quietly, "No."

The whole world died in her with a tortured, audible moan. The stiffening left her knees, but Gabe's hands clamped on her arms.

"No?" she whispered.

"No," he said. "You can't start again when something was never over to begin with." He looped his arms around her waist and gave her a smile that felt like sunshine on her face. "We both move on with what we've learned: you, that you can trust me; and I, that I don't live alone anymore and I have to be more open about what I'm doing."

It took her a full minute of staring at his smile to absorb what he had said. "We move on," she asked cautiously, "together?"

He pulled her into his embrace, holding her so hard she couldn't breathe.

"Do you really think I could live without you?" he demanded roughly, his warm lips at her ear. "That I would ever knowingly do anything to drive you away from me? You've become the center of my existence, cupcake. I want us to grow old together putting out weekly editions of the Warrenton *Register* and several limited editions of Gabe and Dana Cameron."

Laughter rose in her, and it felt so good after this long hour of pain. "I suppose you'd like to skip lunch and go to work on those limited editions right now?"

"I knew you'd see it my way. Wait right here."

Gabe went to lock the front door, then came back to scoop her off the floor and carry her into the darkroom. He deposited her on the now familiar stool. Her wraparound dress was easily dispensed with while she undid the buttons of his shirt. He paused to pull it off; then she shuddered as her slip and panty hose made a seductive path down her legs. She sat up to allow their removal; then after a moment's rustling in the darkness, Gabe's tall, taut body was between her knees and he was pulling her up against him, her teeth nipping into his shoulder as his hands traced a delicious path up and down her hips and legs.

"You've been trying to make love to me on this stool for weeks," she said a little doubtfully. "Are you sure this is going to work?"

He chuckled deeply against her breast. "Have you ever known anything tried between us that didn't? Lovers never lose, remember? And they don't fall off stools while making love, either."

"Easy for you to say," she teased as he eased her body back against his strong hands. "I'm the one on the stool."

"You don't think I'd let anything happen to you, do you?" he asked. "Anything that wasn't in your best interest?"

He wouldn't, of course. And he proved it.

Chapter Thirteen

"Are you ready?" Gabe asked gently. He sat behind the steering wheel of their new station wagon while Jack and Sheila pulled luggage out of the back, laughing and joking as the stack of suitcases in the driveway continued to grow.

Dana, seated beside her husband, had yet to unfasten her seat belt. She was staring at the broad expanse of lawn, a little brown now that it was late fall in San Francisco, and the large Georgian mansion that her father had purchased when she was just a little girl. There were many ugly memories connected with this house for her, and for the first time in the months that she'd been married to Gabe, Dana felt uncertain, insecure.

She turned to look at him, reading in his eyes that he suspected what was on her mind.

"I'm having a crisis," she admitted candidly.

"Do you want to stay at a hotel?" he asked, slipping his hand under the wavy sheet of her hair to rub the taut muscles of her neck. "We can probably come up with some plausible excuse."

Closing her eyes, she leaned back into his ministrations. "Of course not." She sighed heavily. "We couldn't do that."

At Barton and Janine's wedding, to which Gabe and
Dana and Jack and Sheila had flown and returned
home in one day because of the *Register*'s schedule,
Janine had extended an invitation to spend the Thanks-
giving weekend with them.

It had seemed so far into the future at the time that
Dana had felt comfortable in accepting. In the interim
she had consoled herself with the fact that it could be
another quick trip like the last one, when they didn't
even have time to go to the house before flying home.
But this time Darlene had insisted that Friday and
Saturday were quiet days anyway, and since there was
no school, she would be happy to keep the office open,
answer the phone, and do some of the preparatory typing.

Jack and Sheila had seized the opportunity for a four-
day stay since they hadn't had time for a honeymoon.

"And neither have we," Gabe had reminded Dana.

Now, she realized, tugging at her seat belt, she actually had to go into that cold formal house. Somehow,
everything that meant loneliness and failure and pain
for her still seemed tied up with that house.

"I'll make you a bet," Gabe proposed, giving her a
soft smile, "that going into the house will not be the
same as you remembered it; you're different and I'll
bet the house is different, too."

"I don't know, Gabe...." she said doubtfully.

"That darkroom is still dark," he pointed out, tugging at her hair as he removed his hand. "But you're
no longer afraid of it."

"What do you get if you win this bet?" she challenged.

He grinned. "An hour on the stool in the darkroom."

"And what do I get if I win?"

His grin widened. "An hour on the stool in the dark-room."

"Okay!" Jack said, yanking Dana's door open and pulling her out. "The Freemans unloaded *all* this luggage." He emphasized the word "all," a broad sweep of his hand showing a stack of bags that did seem excessive for a four-day stay. "Now the Camerons, who did so little to help, can carry it up to the house."

"That's Sheila's luggage," Gabe said, slamming his door. He walked to the luggage and pointed to the lavender cases that comprised a good three-quarters of the stack. "I'm not carrying Sheila's luggage. She's your problem now, buddy."

Jack frowned down at the cluttered driveway. "Some of this has to be Dana's."

"Not mine," Dana denied quickly. "All my clothes have been ruined at the *Register*."

"Oh, Lord, here we go!" Gabe looked heavenward in supplication. "I haven't a thing to wear. Everything I own has ink on it." He parodied Dana's small but husky voice so perfectly that she had to hold her laughter back through sheer willpower.

"It's true." She glowered at him, barely controlling the tick in her lower lip.

"Well, then, I wonder who that other woman is whose clothes have completely taken up my closet so that I have to keep my things in my office?"

"The only reason your clothes are in your office," Dana said, swatting Gabe's shoulder, "is because when your shoes are in our closet we can't close the door. Turn-of-the-century design was not meant to accommodate shoes of that size."

Gabe feigned hurt feelings. "That was nasty, Dana."

"Straighten up, you two," Sheila whispered, pointing to the front door of the house. "Somebody's coming."

There was a small procession of three white-coated men, apparently the senior Freemans' household help, coming toward them.

"They've come for you at last, buddy." Gabe clapped Jack on the shoulder. "We'll take care of Sheila for you until you're rehabilitated."

Jack glared at his friend, then demanded of his sister, "Whose idea was it to bring him along?"

"I thought you invited him." Dana shrugged innocently.

Then Barton and Janine were running down the walk toward them, and their teasing banter was lost in hugs and handshakes.

"Come on." With an arm around each woman, Janine led them toward the house. "I just made a pitcher of margaritas, and Ignacio should have dinner ready in an hour or so. Are you exhausted?"

Sheila carried the conversation with Janine while Dana braced herself for entry into the house. She wished she had Gabe's firm arm to hold on to, but he was trailing behind the household help, along with Jack and her father, his arms loaded down with luggage.

They stopped in the hallway with its sparkling hanging chandelier and the elegantly curved stairway. Sheila, unacquainted with such opulence, stopped in her tracks.

Dana was also staring, remembering red velvet drapes at the floor-to-ceiling windows on the landing and dark, Oriental carpeting on the stairs. But there were no drapes, unless the filmy nylon panels that showed off the darkening sky could be considered such, and the walls had been painted a stark white and the woodwork a warm, soft apricot that was also the color of the thick carpeting that ran down the stairs. At the bottom of the stairway was a fat white pot of tall branches still bearing their red, gold and orange leaves.

"Don't be alarmed." Still holding both girls by the shoulders, Janine hugged the openmouthed Sheila to her. "This house scared me to death at first, too. You've just got to decide for yourself that even though it's big, it's still just a house. And it can say to you whatever you want it to say. Right now—" she turned to smile at Dana "—it's speaking to me of margaritas."

"I could certainly use one," Dana admitted.

It was easy to see, she reflected a moment later as Janine led them into the enormous living room, which Dana remembered so well as dark and cold, that the house spoke to her father's new wife in ways it had never communicated with her mother.

Apricot was everywhere here, combined with whites and a soft blue. There was linen on wicker, bright polished cotton with enormous flowers that reflected the color scheme, flowers in china bowls, and all the wide windows sported the same gauzy panels that let in light instead of closing it out.

Unable to speak, Dana stopped in the middle of the room and looked at Janine. Suddenly seeming at a loss herself, Janine gestured Dana to move into the room.

"Welcome home," she said.

Sheila had gone forward to investigate the view, and Dana, fighting the constriction of her throat said heavily, "Home was never like this."

"I know." Janine's voice was sympathetic, her eyes warm. She pushed Dana onto the bright, overstuffed sofa and reached to the glass coffee table and the pitcher of margaritas. "But it is now. Barton—your father—wants so much to put his family back together. I'm so pleased that you've come."

"It was nice of you to ask us. Thank you," she said as she accepted the frosty, salt-rimmed glass. "After waiting so long for Dad, I'd have thought you'd want to hoard him to yourself."

Janine's smile was warm and fond. "He defies hoarding. That mind moves in so many directions at once, but after you get past his abrupt, businesslike manner, he's all warm and caring." Her eyes filled, and Dana thought for a panicky moment that she would cry. "And that was locked up inside him—choked—for so long. That's a terrible thing to do to another human being." Janine took a hasty sip of her drink.

"You look wonderful," Dana said briskly, seeking to divert the conversation. In this beautifully light and airy room, she refused to discuss her mother. "I'd only seen you a few times before the wedding, but I remember you in wool suits and silk blouses and looking as though you could run the corporation with or without Dad."

She laughed, a youthful, almost giggly sound. "I practically did when he was out of town. After all those years of corporate life, I owned nothing that could be worn to stay at home in." She swept a hand down the silky, bottle-green dress that skimmed her youthful figure flatteringly. "So I had to buy a few things, get my hair done." What had always been a sensible chignon was now a softly waving cut that fell just below her chin in flattering, face-framing movement. Dana realized that in estimating her age, she had probably given Janine ten years more than she deserved because of the utilitarian way she had always dressed.

"Anyway, I don't go to the office anymore, but I'm

getting more and more involved in acquisitions and investments. It's very exciting for me. Sheila, come and have a drink."

As Janine poured for Sheila, the men reappeared, Jack admitting in horror that most of the luggage really was Sheila's.

They discussed the new typesetting system the *Register* had acquired, on which Darlene had proved an instant whiz. Janine excused herself to check on dinner and soon afterward her laughter could be heard coming from the kitchen.

Freeman cocked his ear at the sound and smiled. Dana, catching his eye as conversation went on around them, winked. It *was* good to hear laughter in this house.

Dinner was long, conversation carrying on hours after dessert had been cleared away. They retired to the living room to talk longer still, and it was after midnight when they began meandering toward the stairs that led to the bedrooms.

Feeling Gabe's guiding hand at her back as she followed her father and Janine, Dana's pulse began to accelerate. This would be the ultimate test.

They parted at the top of the stairs, Jack and Sheila moving toward his old room and Barton and Janine stopping at the master bedroom. Reluctantly, Dana led Gabe along the corridor in the opposite direction to the first door on her left. She hesitated.

"Remember the darkroom," her husband, the clairvoyant, said.

She gave him a grim smile in the darkness of the hallway and pushed the door open. The coolness of a freshly aired room met them as she groped for the light switch.

When she flipped on the light, Dana felt as though she had walked into a bouquet of flowers. The room was bright with primary colors in the small print of the wallpaper, the pattern on the bedspread and in solid-colored accent pieces all around the room. Everything had been changed. And though Dana had no idea why she deserved it from this woman who was practically a stranger, the transformation had been made with love.

Perhaps, as Gabe had once told her, once you set love free it's there for everyone. And Janine, who had had to hold her love close for so long, could now be bountiful with it.

On the wall beside the bed were all the awards and mementos Dana had hidden in the bottom of the dresser and left there when she moved out to marry Scott. With her father never there to admire them and her mother simply not caring that she had earned them, there had seemed little point in displaying them.

Now they hung, framed, as an overt boast that someone cared. She felt lighthearted suddenly, free of the last shadows of her childhood.

Gabe wrapped his arms around her from behind and read over her head, "Second place, Saint Francis School for Girls Invitational Swim Meet; honorable mention, California state essay contest, Girls' State participant, 1974." He leaned closer and laughed at a photograph. "Is that you and Jack?"

She, too, laughed. They had been four and six when the housekeeper had taken their picture as they set off for Sunday school. Jack, in a white suit and the same grin he still wore today, was squinting into the camera, his arm around Dana, who wore a ruffled dress, anklets with lace and patent leather shoes. She was smiling, but it was obvious that the expression was forced.

Gabe hugged her a little harder. "You were scrawny," he said.

Laughter bubbled up inside her and she turned in his arms to smile at him, this smile very genuine.

"I prefer to think of it as petite. Perhaps you're wishing you had married some plump, voluptuous—"

Gabe swung her up in his arms and placed her on the bed, then walked around it to flip off the light.

"Nope," he said, landing beside her in the dark. "I have a thing for scrawny."

"Petite."

"Whatever. As long as it describes you. Come here, Dana Cameron. I've been dying to give you a hickey all evening long."

She laughed helplessly as he nibbled at her neck. "Don't you dare! I haven't got one turtleneck with me!"

"I know," he said absently, working his way along her shoulder. "They were all ruined at the *Register* office."

"That's right. And if you don't take me shopping Friday, I won't have anything to wear home."

"That could be interesting. How come," he asked impatiently as he pulled off her sweater and found himself confronted by the buttons of a blouse, "if you have so little to wear, you wear it all at once?"

She giggled. "It's called the layered look."

"Well, it's a hell of a lot of trouble," he grumbled good-naturedly as he rolled onto his back and pulled her astride his waist. He reached up to go to work on the buttons.

"So how do you feel about coming home?" he asked, his voice still light but with an underlying current of gravity.

"I think I feel fine," she assured him, holding her wrist out to have her cuff unbuttoned. "Anyway, this is Dad and Janine's home. It's a wonderful place now, and I'll never have qualms about walking into this house again, but you were right when you said I had changed. My home is on Main Street in Warrenton in a blue Victorian house. I belong there now. The past is over. Janine has made a beautiful place for us to visit—a beautiful world for my father to live in. And I'm glad we're here, because you were right about something else. Now that I love you I've got love enough for everyone, and I want my father to know that."

The blouse slid off her shoulders and she leaned down to allow Gabe to reach around her back, taking advantage of the moment to kiss him deeply as he unfastened her bra.

He unbuttoned and unzipped her slacks, then laid her back beside him to pull them off.

Rid of his own clothes, he joined her again and pulled the blankets over their heads, enclosing them in a warm cocoon of darkness.

"Do you have any idea how much I love you?" Gabe asked, nipping at her ear while his fingers traced a tantalizing line along her spine.

"Yes," she replied, planting kisses on his sinewy shoulder. "I think I do. But you know how thick I am. You'll have to keep telling me."

"You know what they say in advertising. A picture is worth a thousand words."

She leaned into his body, relishing its warmth and its strength. "Show me."

You're invited to accept 4 books and a surprise gift Free!

Acceptance Card

Mail to: **Harlequin Reader Service®**

In the U.S.
2504 West Southern Ave.
Tempe, AZ 85282

In Canada
P.O. Box 2800, Postal Station A
5170 Yonge Street
Willowdale, Ontario M2N 6J3

YES! Please send me 4 free Harlequin American Romance® novels and my free surprise gift. Then send me 4 brand new novels as they come off the presses. Bill me at the low price of $2.25 each —an 11% saving off the retail price. There are no shipping, handling or other hidden costs. There is no minimum number of books I must purchase. I can always return a shipment and cancel at any time. Even if I never buy another book from Harlequin, the 4 free novels and the surprise gift are mine to keep forever.

154 BPA-BPGE

Name	(PLEASE PRINT)	
Address		Apt. No.
City	State/Prov.	Zip/Postal Code

This offer is limited to one order per household and not valid to present subscribers. Price is subject to change.   ACAR-SUB-1

Readers rave about
Harlequin American Romance!

"The stories are great from beginning to end."
—*M.W., Tampa, Florida*

"...excellent new series...I am greatly
impressed."
—*M.B., El Dorado, Arkansas*

"I am delighted with them...can't put them
down."
—*P.D.V., Mattituck, New York*

"Thank you for the excitement, love and
adventure your books add to my life. They
are definitely the best on the market."
—*J.W., Campbellsville, Kentucky*

Names available on request.

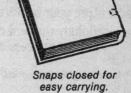